THIS DAY
CHANGES
EVERYTHING

ALSO BY EDWARD UNDERHILL

Always the Almost

THIS DAY CHANGES EVERYTHING

A Novel

EDWARD UNDERHILL

WEDNESDAY BOOKS
NEW YORK

First published in the United States by Wednesday Books,
an imprint of St. Martin's Publishing Group

www.wednesdaybooks.com

Library of Congress Cataloging-in-Publication Data

Names: Underhill, Edward, author.
Title: This day changes everything : a novel / Edward Underhill.
Description: First. | New York : Wednesday Books, 2024. |
    Audience: Ages 13–18.
Identifiers: LCCN 2023027603 | ISBN 9781250835222 (hardcover) |
    ISBN 9781250835239 (ebook)
Subjects: CYAC: LGBTQ+ people—Fiction. | Interpersonal
    relations—Fiction. | New York (NY)—Fiction. | LCGFT: Romance
    fiction. | Novels.
Classification: LCC PZ7.1.U483 Th 2024 | DDC [E]—dc23
LC record available at https://lccn.loc.gov/2023027603

Our books may be purchased in bulk for promotional, educational,
or business use. Please contact your local bookseller or the
Macmillan Corporate and Premium Sales Department
at 1-800-221-7945, extension 5442, or by email at
MacmillanSpecialMarkets@macmillan.com.

First Edition: 2024

10 9 8 7 6 5 4 3 2 1

For the trans and queer "Logistical Headaches."
May you all find your epic love stories,
and a crew to cover for you.

THIS DAY CHANGES EVERYTHING

ONE

ABBY

THERE'S A SCENE in my favorite book, *The Hundred Romances of Clara Jane,* where the main character (Clara Jane) takes an elevator to the top of the Empire State Building in New York City, and just before the doors open, she realizes she's about to be free, because she is really, truly, madly in love with the guy who's waiting on the other side.

See, the whole setup for this book is that Clara Jane keeps living the same day over and over, but each time, she falls in love with a different guy. At the end of the day, she takes the elevator up to the top of the Empire State Building to meet whichever guy she's fallen for this time, but on the ride up, she realizes he's not really her true love. He's the wrong guy. And as soon as she realizes that, the day starts over. She never makes it to the top.

But at the end of the book, she takes the elevator up and realizes that this guy (his name is Chris—kind of a boring name, if you ask me) *is* her true love. The elevator doors finally open, she sees Chris, and they kiss at the top of the Empire State Building, breaking the time loop.

It's not a great book. I mean, the dreamboat guy's name is *Chris*. And Clara Jane doesn't really have a hundred romances. She has eight. I guess the author thought *The Hundred Romances of Clara Jane* sounded better than, like, *The Eight Romances of Clara Jane*.

Which it does. A lot of people have probably had eight romances. People who aren't me, anyway.

I read a theory on Tumblr suggesting that Clara Jane could have been living the same day over and over before the book even starts, so she actually *has* had a hundred romances, and we just don't see them all. But I've read this book twenty-four (and a half) times, and I think it's perfectly obvious that Clara Jane hasn't relived the same day over and over before the book starts, and the first romance in the book is, in fact, her first one.

Although, just to be safe, I sent the author an email asking for clarification, care of her publisher. She never replied.

Anyway, *The Hundred Romances of Clara Jane* may not be a Great Book, but I love it. Even though it's cheesy.

Because the truth is . . . *I'm* cheesy. I believe in fate. And true love. And kissing your true love at the top of the Empire State Building.

I guess what I mean is—I believe in the Universe. That sometimes you end up in the right place at the right time, or with the right person, and (sometimes) magical things really can happen.

I hope I'm right about that. Because I'm leaving a lot to the Universe on this trip, and I could really use the help.

I might be kind of cheesy, but I don't think I'm completely out of my mind. I mean, the Universe has already made some magic happen. Right now, our entire marching band from Westvale, Missouri—all ninety-six of us, plus our band director, assistant band directors, chaperones, instruments, flags, and uniforms—is heading to New York City for the biggest marching event in the country: the Macy's Thanksgiving Day Parade.

Hundreds of bands sent in audition tapes, hoping for one of a dozen slots, according to our band director, Mr. Sussman. And

Macy's picked *us* to be one of those bands. We were "unique, polished, fun, and quirky." That's what the rep from Macy's told us when he showed up in our band room eighteen months ago, armed with a confetti cannon and a giant banner that said *You're Going to the Macy's Thanksgiving Day Parade!*

The rest of that day was a blur of screaming and laughing and crying and ducking into the band room between classes to make sure that big, bright banner was still there, strung up over the percussion lockers. It was pretty freaking magical, especially since all I'd ever wanted was to play clarinet in the marching band at my older brother's football games, instead of joining the debate team, like my mom suggested.

Not that I would have made the debate team in a million years anyway. I can memorize and perform a whole halftime show no problem, but the minute I have to talk in front of a lot of people, I want to sink into the floor.

Our band spent the next eighteen months putting together a performance and raising money to get ourselves all the way from our boring sorta-suburb of Kansas City to New York. We practiced in the mornings, in the evenings, on weekends. In the band room, on the football field, in the high school parking lot on a giant green tarp with the Macy's Parade logo on it, held down by traffic cones borrowed from the driver's ed teacher. (Our school had the tarp specially made, just to practice with. It's exactly the size of the big green rectangle on Thirty-Fourth Street, so we could plan every formation, every step, to perfectly fit.)

We marched across that tarp hundreds, maybe thousands, of times, all on top of the usual football games we had to play. On top of last spring's concert band schedule. On top of marching in the Kansas City Fourth of July Parade and playing in the park before the local Westvale fireworks show. On top of two state championships.

And whenever we weren't practicing, we were fundraising. Car washes. Bake sales. I literally celebrated my sixteenth birthday at a pancake breakfast (not as fun as it sounds when *you're* the one serving the pancakes).

But now—finally finally *finally*—it's here. In two days, on Thanksgiving morning, we'll be marching down Sixth Avenue in our purple-and-white uniforms, with white feather plumes in our shakos, surrounded by giant balloons and decked-out floats filled with Broadway stars. We'll perform a medley of jazzed-up Christmas carols while our color guard waves red-and-green flags in front of all those cameras. Millions of people will watch us live on national TV.

And, I mean, that's magic. One day I'm scooping ice cream at Sundae Fun Day to add something to my college fund, and the next, I'm scooping ice cream at Sundae Fun Day while everybody who comes in tells me congratulations. Going from being a nobody to getting a bigger cheer during halftime than the football team gets during the whole game is . . . well, it's magic. There's *no way* that's not some Universe-intervention magic.

So, the way I see it, if the Universe can do *that*—if the Universe can get our band from Missouri to Macy's—then maybe it can help me tell Kat Wu I'm madly in love with her.

Kat Wu, who plays flute, wears her shoulder-length black hair in perfectly messy updos, and sews her own vintage-inspired dresses because she wants to go to fashion school.

Kat Wu, the only other person I know who has read *The Hundred Romances of Clara Jane* and loves it as much as I do.

Kat Wu, who is currently sitting next to me, eighteen hours into this endless bus ride to New York, because she's my best friend.

Kat and I have been telling each other everything—and I mean *everything*—for years, ever since we met in middle school band. I was the first person she told about her dreams of going to fashion school. I know she still sleeps with the stuffed pig she's had since she was little. And Kat knows I cried at my first sleepaway camp because I was that baby who was homesick. She knows pineapple makes my tongue itch. She even knows exactly how many *Clara Jane* fanfics I've read (a number I will never tell another soul, ever).

But there's one giant, looming thing I haven't told her: I've had a crush on her for months, ever since the traditional end-of-the-school-year marching band pool party at Westvale Park. The night ended with a bonfire, and everybody spread out towels and sat around playing cards or goofing off. Kat and I lay on our backs, talking through the events in a *Clara Jane* fanfic we'd both read. And somehow, partway through discussing whether Clara Jane working in a coffee shop was more compelling than Clara Jane working at a magazine, and whether the original character created to be the love interest of Clara Jane's best friend, Olivia, was compelling at all, and whether fanfics should even *have* original characters . . .

Our fingers ended up twined together.

My stomach turned to butterflies. I kept waiting for her to let go, but she didn't. Not until Mrs. Lewis told us it was time to go home.

When I got home, I googled *how to tell if you're gay*.

I know it's ridiculous to google it, but I didn't know what else to do. I'm not sure how much it helped anyway. I mean, half the stuff I read made it sound like I'd have to actually kiss a girl to really know if I'm gay. And I have definitely *not* kissed a girl.

I've *thought* about kissing Kat. A lot. Mostly at the top of the Empire State Building.

Part of the problem might be that I haven't kissed a boy, either. I haven't kissed anyone. I did have a crush on this guy in band last year. He was a senior and nothing was ever going to happen between us, but he played trumpet and he had blond hair that made him look like a surfer, and I found Clara Jane's boring dreamboat Chris a lot more interesting once I started picturing him as Blake Orlowski.

So . . . maybe I'm not gay. Or maybe I only had a crush on Blake Orlowski because almost every girl in school did. I'm kind of suggestible.

The only girl who didn't seem to care about Blake Orlowski at all was Kat.

Which gives me a little bit of hope. Because whether or not I'm gay according to Google, I *definitely* want to kiss Kat Wu. And now that I'm on my way to New York City, with boring Westvale fading behind me, I'm hoping—really hoping—I might finally get my chance.

From now on, at least for this trip, I'm going to take risks. I'm going to throw myself out there and let the Universe catch me. I'm going to be fearless Abby Akerman. Done with Google. Done with my own personal time loop, where every day I wish I could tell Kat how I feel . . . and then don't. Done with being confused and indecisive and *stuck*.

Fearless Abby Akerman has a plan. A plan that Clara Jane is going to help me with.

Kat and I both have dog-eared, sun-faded paperback copies of *The Hundred Romances of Clara Jane*. Kat found them at a discount bookstore in Kansas City and got them because the Empire State Building is on the cover, and Kat has wanted to visit New York City for years. She thought it would be fun if we both read this book at the same time. Then, obviously, we got obsessed with it, and the rest is history.

But two months ago, I found a mint-condition, hardcover copy *signed by the author* at the same discount bookstore. I have no idea how it got there, but it felt like a sign from the Universe. So I bought it, and I spent weeks finding and underlining my favorite lines. I spent weeks carefully selecting the pages with the most romantic scenes, and writing romantic notes to Kat in the margins.

How when I looked into her eyes, I felt just like Clara Jane did in this scene.

How I wanted to lean my forehead against hers, just like Clara Jane in that scene.

How I'd close my eyes at night, and picture Kat's smile, and feel that smile *spreading through my entire being, to the ends of my fingers,* just like Clara Jane does on page 84.

It felt a little sacrilegious, at first, writing on the pages of a book. I've checked books out from the library where people wrote in them, and it always made me mad. Who does that?

But this wasn't a library book that a hundred other people would read. This was a gift for Kat. This was my version of a love letter, written in the pages of our favorite book.

And anyway, I did it all in pencil, just to be safe.

Now the trip is finally here, and I have the mint-condition, signed-by-the-author-and-carefully-annotated-by-me copy of *The Hundred Romances of Clara Jane* in my backpack, and if the Universe can help me find the right moment . . . I will give it to Kat. I will tell Kat I love her.

And then, I hope, I will kiss a girl.

I scroll to the next page of the *THRoCJ* fanfic I'm currently reading on my phone and glance over at Kat, who's still sketching out new dress designs in a notebook, sitting cross-legged on the seat next to me with her earbuds in.

I wouldn't even need three guesses to know what she's listening to: *Pixelated Dreams,* the last album of Damaged Pixie Dream Boi, this weird, indie, alternative group and Kat's favorite band. They're originally from Kansas City, and Kat's even more obsessed with them than she is with *Clara Jane.* Their music sounds like video game bloops mixed with death metal if you put it in a blender with a lot of angsty complaining, but Kat loves it. Which is kind of funny, given that her other favorite genre is musicals. She's been listening to this album nonstop ever since the band broke up over the summer. Supposedly two of the guys in the band were dating, and when they broke up, that broke up the band.

Which is more evidence that gives me some hope. Exhibit A: Kat held my hand at the pool party. Exhibit B: she didn't care about

Blake Orlowski at all. Exhibit C: her favorite band is *gay*. Maybe that's even why she likes them.

I haven't asked her this, of course. If I asked, she'd want to know why I was asking, and then I'd be stuck. I'm not very good at lying, and I couldn't just say, *Well, I'm trying to figure out if you're gay for no reason at all.*

Besides, in Westvale, Missouri, being gay isn't something you shout from the rooftops. Nobody talks about it—like somehow, if we pretend the whole concept doesn't exist . . . it won't. I've never even heard a teacher say the word *gay*. And I don't think it's because they're all raging homophobes or anything. It's just that at this point, talking about it means someone will get upset and complain, and then there might be legislation. Or . . . more legislation than there already is.

Maybe it would be a little different if we lived in Kansas City, or even across the border in Kansas. But in my suburb, on the Missouri side, being gay is something you erase from your search history and never even write in your journal. Or at least . . . I wouldn't, if I had a journal.

Which is why I think it's possible—even though Kat and I don't normally hide things from each other—that we both might be hiding this. That maybe there's a reason we never talked about the night we held hands. And if I haven't told Kat I might be gay, maybe she hasn't told me she is.

It's possible.

But in New York City, you can shout anything you want from the rooftops. You can be anybody. It's the kind of place where Magical Interventions of the Universe happen all the time. I've never been there before, obviously, but I have that feeling. After all, the author of *The Hundred Romances of Clara Jane* lives in New York City, and she set the book there. She must know what she's talking about.

Plus, Kat is obsessed with New York. And not just because our band gets to play in the Macy's Parade. New York City is the fashion capital of the country; it's exactly where Kat wants to go to fashion school. She even wants me to go with her. Not to fashion school—just to New York, for college. I have no idea what I'd want to study. My two favorite things are marching band and reading, and I don't really know how to turn either of those things into a major. Unless I want to be a band director, and I definitely don't. For one thing, I'm too short. Nobody in the back of the band would be able to see me. I'd need stilts.

But that's not the point. The point is: New York City is objectively romantic.

Kat is obsessed with New York City.

We're both obsessed with a romantic book set in New York City.

And that's why this trip is It: the time to confess my feelings to Kat, if I'm ever going to.

Next to me, Kat brushes a stray wisp of black hair behind her ear and pulls a tube of ChapStick out of her pocket. "Where are we now?" she asks, squinting past me to the bus window.

I quickly stare out the window instead of at my best friend. "Um . . . I saw a sign a little while ago that said *Welcome to New Jersey.*"

"New state!" Kat balances her sketchbook on her knees and holds up her phone. "Freeway picture time."

That makes me laugh. As soon as we were out of Missouri, Kat decided we should take selfies at least once in every new state, with the scenery going by out the window. Except the scenery has been freeways, bare trees, and flat brown fields, and all the pictures have looked the same. "Seriously?"

"Yeah, look!" Kat waves a hand at the window. "There are buildings now. Totally more exciting. Anyway, we have to complete the set."

"Of kind of pointless pictures?"

Kat gives me a very offended look. "Of beautiful American vistas to commemorate our journey."

I grin. "Fine." I do my best to strike a pose, like I'm presenting the squat gray buildings flashing past, and Kat snaps a picture on her phone.

"Perfection." She turns the phone around so I can see. I'm completely backlit in the photo. With my curvy shape, and the hood of my sweatshirt pulled over my mass of curly hair, I kind of look like a gnome-shaped black hole.

Which makes me laugh. "You should post it on your Tumblr."

Kat snorts. "Maybe I can turn it into a meme."

Kat has a Tumblr where she posts whatever sewing project she's working on and "fashion inspo." So far, the fashion inspo has been images Kat collects from around the internet, everything from shimmering evening gowns to European architecture. And a lot of pictures of New York. I know she can't wait to add pictures of the city that she takes herself. She'll finally be in the middle of all that fashion inspo, instead of lurking around the edges of it, everything filtered through a Google search or a Pinterest board.

Everything Kat posts on Tumblr gets hundreds of reblogs, which just goes to show that she has good taste. I can't imagine sharing anything with that many people, but I made a Tumblr anyway, so I could follow Kat. And look up *Clara Jane* fan posts.

Lately, I've also been looking up queer stuff, scrolling hashtags by myself late at night, in the hopes of feeling a little less like an Only. The Only Maybe-Gay Girl In Westvale. The Only Person Looking For Herself On Tumblr.

The Only Person Reading That One Gay *THRoCJ* Fanfic . . . over and over and over again. (The one where Chris is Christina, and Clara Jane breaks the time loop when she realizes she's in love with a woman.)

So I use my Tumblr to look up flags (there are so many flags). And what queer people wear. And whether if I'm gay I should cut my hair short.

All I've figured out so far is that apparently queer girls wear a lot of plaid flannel shirts—just like me. I have no idea if this means I'm gay, or if it's just a coincidence.

And I don't want to think about it right now, so I turn around to lean over the back of my bus seat. "Hey, Jared, what's your phone say?"

Jared Nguyen looks up from whatever game he's playing. He's been obsessively tracking our location this whole bus ride. "Hang on." He switches to a map. "Looks like Union City, New Jersey. I think."

"Where's that?"

"Um." Jared looks confused. "New Jersey."

"Yeah, I got that. I mean, is that close to New York?"

Jared squints back at his phone. "Hang on, I'm too zoomed in—"

"Hey, look!" Morgan Ellis, across the aisle from us in her usual seat next to Amira Aboud, suddenly jabs her finger at her window. "Guys, that's New York! That's totally New York!"

"Where?" Kat pops up from her seat, sending her sketchbook to the floor.

"Hang on, hang on . . ." Jared scrolls madly on his phone.

But nobody's waiting for him. Around us, the whole bus wakes up, people pointing, voices rising. Morgan is pulling out her phone to film the view. Amira is trying to see around Morgan. Even Lacey Thompson, who slept through three whole rest stops, is blinking and twisting around in her seat.

But I can't see anything. The bus window next to Morgan is too far away and too tinted, and outside my window are the same houses and trees and low buildings we've been driving past for a while now.

"I got it, I got it!" Jared triumphantly waves his phone in the air. "That's New York! That has to be New York!"

The bus turns, following the loop of the freeway around in a half circle, and for a minute, everything around us is a wall of trees. Then the trees fall away, and across the lanes of concrete and the traffic roaring past my window is an expanse of blue water, and past that, a jagged skyline of endless skyscrapers, going right down to the water's edge.

New York City. Real, actual New York City. I've never seen it before, in real life, but there's no mistaking that that is *definitely* New York City.

The whole bus erupts, everyone shouting and cheering. Kat lets out a whoop and grabs me in a sideways hug. We're almost there. We're *finally* almost there.

Which suddenly feels like a huge relief. I've been doing okay so far, but now it's like the eighteen hours we've spent on this bus catch up with me all at once. My butt is numb. My back is sore. It really does not smell great in here.

The bus turns away from the view, following the loop of the road down a gentle slope.

"Uh-oh," says Jared.

Kat's arm leaves my shoulder as she turns to look at him. "What?"

But it's already obvious. We're heading down into a tunnel. And we're slowing to a stop.

"The map says this is the Lincoln Tunnel," Jared informs us. "And it's a straight line of red in the traffic data. My phone says it'll take . . . Hang on. I lost signal . . ."

"We're going under the water," Mrs. Gunnerson says helpfully, from her spot up near the driver. She's one of our chaperones, and the mother of Zach Gunnerson, who is the most annoying human alive and, luckily, not on our bus. He's on the bus behind us. "The Lincoln Tunnel goes under the water into New York City. Isn't that cool?"

Well, it would be cooler if the tunnel wasn't full of brake lights. Apparently everyone wants to go the same direction we're going.

"Maybe it's Thanksgiving traffic," Jared says.

Morgan groans. "It's *Tuesday*."

Kat sinks back down in her seat. "You want to listen?" She holds out one of her earbuds.

I take it and sit down next to her. All the fanfic has drained my phone's battery anyway. Kat turns to a blank page in her sketchbook, draws the outline of a dress, and hands the pencil to me. It's a game we invented on the bus ride to the championships last year: we pass the pencil back and forth, each of us adding one design element, like a flower, or a ruffle, or a big bow, until we run out of room. The first few dresses we made looked pretty reasonable, but now it's almost like a contest to see who can be the last one to cram something on. The dresses from our last band trip were pretty ridiculous.

Approximately five lifetimes later (or six dresses—we've gotten pretty good at cramming), we finally escape the tunnel. The last of the late-afternoon sun brightens the bus, and I stop halfway through adding what's supposed to be a lace collar, because just like that, we're *here*.

Skyscrapers shoot up all around us, so high they block the sun, and I can't see the tops even with my face pressed against the window. The city streets around us are crowded with cars and trucks and yellow taxicabs, and the sidewalks are crowded with people, all bundled up in coats and scarves. I've seen homecoming crowds on the football bleachers in Westvale, and that's a lot of people. I also went to a Royals game in Kansas City once, and that was even more people.

But those were events. New York City has huge crowds of people just *walking around*. Where are they all going?

"Oh my god." Kat grabs my arm. "Abby, look."

Outside our window is a tall, rectangular sign, sticking out from the side of a building. Black, white, green . . . it's a sign for *Wicked*. Underneath the sign are much more unassuming letters, spelling out GERSHWIN.

"It's the Gershwin Theatre!" Kat turns to me with a huge grin. "We're gonna see a Broadway show."

I can't help but grin back. "I know."

"We're gonna see *Wicked*. You and me!"

A shiver runs up my back. According to our itinerary, we're going to see the matinee show, tomorrow at two o'clock. If I'm being totally honest, I'm not sure I'm as into *Wicked* as Kat is. She can sing every song from memory. Musicals just aren't quite my thing. I like songs where you can't tell exactly what they're about. Where they aren't really telling a story, but the words are still beautiful. Then it's easier to imagine your own story to go with them.

But still. A real Broadway show. With Kat.

I let myself wonder, for a minute, if maybe I'll be holding Kat's hand tomorrow, in that Broadway theater. If maybe, by then, I'll have given her The Book.

The bus turns down another street, which isn't quite so crowded. We crawl past more taxis and a food cart that says HALAL and finally creak to a stop.

Mrs. Gunnerson stands up. "All right, everyone, please make sure you grab all your belongings and let's be polite getting off the bus."

I shoot to my feet so fast that Kat's earbud yanks right out of my ear. "Oh, crap. Sorry . . ." But Kat isn't looking at me. She's fumbling with the cord, shoving it away in her backpack with her sketchbook.

Nobody pays attention to Mrs. Gunnerson. We're all too desperate to get off the bus. Jackets hit me in the face. Backpacks bump off each other. Everyone's shouting and pointing and cheering.

I turn sideways and suck in my breath as I inch down the aisle behind Kat. My legs are so stiff that I almost fall over when we finally step onto the sidewalk, just behind Morgan and Amira. The air is crisp and cold and not exactly *fresh*—honestly, it smells kind of like gasoline—but it's still a whole lot better than bus air.

It's a good thing this street doesn't seem to be nearly as busy as the last one, because two big charter buses and a truck full of instruments take up a lot of space, and now that we're all getting off the buses, we're taking up an awful lot of the sidewalk, too.

In front of us is a big black awning that says GRAND FELIX HOTEL in white letters with lots of flourishes. Under the awning are gold-trimmed sliding doors, which Mr. Sussman is currently heading toward, gently nudging people out of his way. "I gotta get us checked in, guys. Listen to your chaperones. Excuse me, Nick."

The bus drivers open the cargo doors in the sides of the buses and the whole sidewalk devolves into chaos as everyone dives for their suitcases. Mrs. Gunnerson is yelling and waving her arms, but everyone ignores her. So much for listening to our chaperones. We're too excited to get our stuff and get inside the hotel.

"Oh, I see our bags!" Kat dives into the mess and emerges hauling two matching purple duffel bags behind her. We bought them together, for that first sleepaway camp, the summer before high school. (Yes, I cried because I was homesick at age fourteen. Whatever.) Kat's mom made us rainbow pom-poms out of yarn to tie to the bag handles, because she was worried some other kid would walk off with our luggage. Kat's pom-pom fell off ages ago, but mine is still knotted to the handle of my bag. It's sort of ragged now, but I haven't been able to part with it.

And anyway, now it might . . . Mean Something. Maybe after this trip, I'll have to keep it because it'll say something about who I am. Or maybe I'll want to throw it away for the same reason.

"Come on, Abs!" Kat is already lugging her bag toward the gold-trimmed sliding doors.

I pick up my bag and follow her. We made it to New York. I take a deep breath.

All right, Universe. Here we go.

TWO

LEO

HOW DOES THE Universe hate me? Let me count the ways.

One: I just spent twelve hours on a bus, utterly convinced I was seconds away from barfing into my backpack.

Two: I am now in New York City, the bustling hubbub of hell.

Three: I'm going to be on live television in two days.

And now, the bonus round: another marching band just pushed through the hotel lobby doors like a many-headed amoeba.

It's definitely a marching band, because they've all got matching varsity jackets just like we do, stuffed suitcases and backpacks just like we do, and wide-eyed wonderment plastered all over their faces just like . . . well, like most of us do.

"He's making the Face," says Gina.

Evan looks down at me. "Yeah. You're making the Face."

I roll my eyes. I've apparently been making the Face for the whole trip so far, but this late in the day, after three hours of sleep and several close vomit calls, I'm done caring. I know I'm supposed to be Happy To Be Here, Grateful For The Opportunity, but twelve hours stuck in a cramped bus seat trying not to hurl isn't going to put any-body in a good mood.

Gina jerks a thumb toward the other marching band. "He has seen more people partaking of the Enjoyment."

"He too could partake of the Enjoyment," Evan says somberly, "but alas, he would prefer to make the Face."

They're trying to make me laugh, but I am too far into my grumpy rut. "Yeah, I get it, guys. I'm the worst."

I mean it to be sour—but it comes out *really* sour.

And it wipes the grin off Evan's face. "Come on, man, we're try-ing to help."

Now I feel guilty. Evan must be worried if he pulled out *man*. He doesn't love Dude Language and neither do I, but he also knows that calling me *man* always makes me feel, well, more like a man. Or a boy. A guy. Whatever.

And that means he thinks I'm not feeling like a guy right now, because I'm stressing about my extended family and being on TV.

I'm annoyed that he's right.

He usually is. Evan Cartwright knows a lot of things about me, even though we've only been friends since we met as terrified fresh-men in high school band camp two years ago. I ended up next to him courtesy of the alphabet, because my last name is Brewer. I was a lanky weirdo who hated my first name (but didn't know why) and hadn't come up with a better one yet, so I glared at everybody, hoping nobody would ask what my name was.

The only person who *didn't* ask my name was Evan. Even then he was a good head taller than everybody else, which should have made him intimidating, except that he's . . . well . . . Evan. He sat down next to me on the football field during roll call on the first morning, noted that my giant T-shirt said I MARCH TO MY OWN DRUMS, and proceeded to cheerfully call me "Drums" for the rest of the summer.

He still does, sometimes. But mostly he uses my real name now—the one I finally figured out last year.

I sigh and make myself shrug. "Look, I know you're trying to help, I just . . . I'll get into it eventually."

I don't really believe myself, and judging by the way Evan's eyebrows disappear up into his messy blond hair, he doesn't believe me either. If he'd consider a haircut every once in a while, he'd look more like Captain America than a marching band nerd. I tried to point this out to him once and he just gave me a puzzled look and said big muscles are useful for carrying sousaphones.

Which is the same thing he tells Coach Barton, every time Coach Barton tries to steal him for the football team. Coach Barton should know better. We all hate the football team. It's a requirement of being in marching band.

Anyway, Evan has never been one to notice his own chiseled jaw, or how many of the cheerleaders talk to him before games.

All he says now is "Well, we're not on TV tomorrow. You've got a whole day to sightsee and loosen up."

Gina gives me the side-eye. "Yeah, or implode."

I give her my best glare, but honestly, I feel like I might implode. Just the mention of TV has me ready to hurl all over again. The text that's been sitting on my phone for over ten minutes, still un–replied to and currently burning a hole in my pocket, is not helping:

MOM

Everybody's so excited to see you!!!!!!

My mom's overuse of exclamation points borders on criminal.

No, my family is not going to magically appear in New York City in two days. That's way too expensive. They're all going to watch me on their TV from the great suburb of Springfield, North Carolina.

My parents are hosting family Thanksgiving this year, which they have never done before. Usually we trek out to Grandma and

Grandpa Brewer's house near Fayetteville, but this year, with me in the parade, Dad told Grandma and Grandpa that he and my mom would be staying home to cheer me on. Honestly, I think he was excited to have an excuse not to go. Every Thanksgiving, Grandpa Brewer "still can't believe" my dad would rather be an engineer than take over the Brewer family car dealership, Grandma Brewer "forgets" my mom is a vegetarian, my uncle says something vaguely racist, and then my aunt fights with him about it while my dad awkwardly tries to keep the peace. I honestly don't know why we keep going. My parents never seem to enjoy themselves.

Unfortunately, when Dad said he and Mom would be celebrating at home, Grandma and Grandpa interpreted this as "hosting Thanksgiving" and announced they'd be happy to bring the Jell-O salad. And because my dad is my dad, he couldn't manage to say no in the moment, which meant that within an hour, my aunt and uncle, their spouses, and my cousins had all confirmed they'd be coming, too. My aunt even said she'd give my older sister, Casey, a ride from NC State in Raleigh.

And then, because Mom was furious about all this, she called her brother up in Baltimore and insisted he take his family over to Nonna Cesari's assisted-living facility, turn on the parade there, and help Nonna set up Skype so they could all call in and be part of the festivities, too.

Maybe some people dream of being outed to their entire extended family during the Macy's Thanksgiving Day Parade on national live TV, but I am not one of them.

As far as my extended family is concerned, my name is something a lot girlier than Leo, I have short hair because I'm a *tomboy,* and I play percussion and not, like, flute because *girls can do what they want, this is the twenty-first century.*

In other words, as far as my extended family is concerned, I am not a trans boy.

Next to me, Evan shrugs. He's watching the other marching band staring around at the high ceiling, the sleek black fountain in the middle of the polished lobby floor, and, inevitably, us. "You know," he says, "I still think you're short enough that the cameras will totally miss you. You'll just be a gold feather going by." He marches his index finger past my face, humming a Sousa march.

"I'm only short next to you," I grumble. I'm almost five nine, taller than plenty of people (which sometimes helps with passing, honestly), but Evan is six three.

Gina looks miffed. "Actual short person is offended."

"I'm also on the outside of the line, in case you forgot," I say to Evan. "I'm going to walk right past the cameras. And there's still the news segment, remember?"

Evan sighs. "Leo—"

"It's going to air *twice*."

Gina also sighs. "We know."

She and Evan fall into silence. Neither of them wants to talk about the news segment because none of us knows what to do about it.

Evan might be right—my family might barely see me marching past the cameras in New York during the parade. But the parade is only part of the problem. The *rest* of the problem is all the local news coverage. Springfield has been having a field day with this. Finally— real, actual news. A whole lot more interesting than another report on the raccoon problem in Hiller Park. (They're stealing from picnics in broad daylight, *what could possibly be next*?)

Local News Channel 4 has been filming a segment ever since we found out we're going to Macy's. They filmed our practices. They filmed our fundraisers. They filmed me practicing drum cadences with the rest of the drumline—not in uniforms that hide all sorts of bodies, uniforms that are practically genderless, but in T-shirts and shorts. With my chest flat thanks to my binder and my legs unshaved.

And when you're a pale white guy with dark hair, unshaved legs are *noticeable*.

Channel 4 even interviewed me and Evan. It was the shortest

interview on the planet, and they were interviewing so many people that I just went along with it, because everyone else did. *What do you play?* Drums. *Are you excited about the parade?* Yeah. *Have you ever been to New York City before?* Are you kidding?

But I told them my name was Leo. Because they asked. Even worse, Evan definitely pulled an Evan and referred to me as *my man Leopold* while draping a long arm around my shoulders and complimenting our drumline.

And I forgot to think about what they'd be doing with all this footage . . . until last week, when I found out that Channel 4 was going to air their segment on the local news, right before the Macy's Parade started. And again after.

You know, in case my extended family didn't get the message that I was trans the first time.

My parents freaked out as soon as they found out about it. I thought, for a brief moment, that this might finally force their hand. Welp, the jig is up, might as well tell Grandma now.

Nope. They wanted my permission to shrug it off. Claim *Leo* is a fun new nickname, and Evan was calling me *Leopold* as a joke. Which he was, kind of, since my name is just *Leo,* not *Leopold.* It's just not *that* kind of joke.

My parents wanted my permission to call me a tomboy yet again, like they've been doing for months. Honestly, if I gave them the chance, they could probably even come up with an excuse for the leg hair. *Forgot to shave! Too busy practicing! Such dedication!* A little weird, sure, but they'd try it.

Except I didn't give them permission. We got in a giant shouting match instead.

Next to me, Evan waves a hand. "What's with this band?"

He's clearly trying to change the subject, and I'm tired of thinking about all this, so I'll let him have it. I follow his gaze across the lobby, where several girls in purple-and-white varsity jackets are whispering to one another and staring right at us.

"It's you," I say, faking a yawn. "They've seen Evan the Heart-throb."

Evan and Gina both groan. Evan because he hates it when I call him a heartthrob, and Gina because boy-crazy girls are Gina's nemeses. Gina Ramos is five foot two, would kill to play trombone in a metal band, and is currently wearing a T-shirt that says *Black Girl Magic* in white letters made with carefully applied bleach. (She made it herself.) Gina would prefer to meet more girl-crazy girls.

Not an easy feat in Springfield. Our town might sell itself as a suburb of Greensboro—and, sure, some people definitely commute to Greensboro—but it also has one pizza place and no Starbucks. There's literally nothing to do. Maybe that's why our marching band got so good. What else are we all going to do on Saturday mornings?

I expect Ms. Rinaldi also had something to do with it. Ever since she took over as band director for Springfield High almost ten years ago, our band has started winning competitions and pissing off the bigger city bands that were used to taking home those titles.

Speaking of Ms. Rinaldi . . .

I look over at the check-in counter. It feels like she went to check us in hours ago. I know we're seventy-five people—not counting various parents volunteering as chaperones—but seriously, how long is this going to take?

Ms. Rinaldi is still at the counter, but she's currently laughing it up with a balding guy in a purple-and-white jacket that says *Westvale* on the back.

Oh, *terrific*. Ms. Rinaldi has met the other band's director. Based on how long Ms. Rinaldi can spend talking to other band directors at competitions, we'll be here all night.

I just want a hotel room so I can go to bed. Who cares what time it is. I'm wiped.

I settle for glaring at the marching band across the lobby from us, and my eyes catch on a girl at the edge of the group, near the sliding doors.

I don't know why I notice her. It's not like she particularly stands out. She's white, kind of short, with long, curly brown hair. Honestly, the only thing unusual about her is the bright purple duffel bag she's holding, which has a rainbow pom-pom tied to it.

I find myself wondering if it Means Something.

Short Girl also seems to be the only person over there who isn't talking or laughing or staring at us. She's staring at the ceiling instead.

So, obviously, I look up, too. Just to see what she's staring at.

It's a huge chandelier, all black pipes and exposed lightbulbs, like it's trying to be some kind of upcycled warehouse-industrial chic. Definitely trying too hard.

But above the chandelier is the ceiling, painted deep black with stars stenciled on it in gold foil. The chandelier light makes them shimmer.

It's actually kind of beautiful.

I tip my eyes back down. Short Girl is now looking at me. Not Evan. Me.

Shit.

She thinks I'm weird. She's trying to figure out what gender I am. She's about to get that vaguely confused, middle-distance look I get *all the fucking time.* This is going to turn into a preview of what my whole extended family will look like on Thursday, when they see me on TV. I wonder how awkward it would be if I inched behind Evan right now . . .

Short Girl smiles at me.

And I smile back. Automatically, my mouth stretching before my brain catches up.

Short Girl looks away, turning to an Asian American girl who has the same purple bag, minus the pom-pom. Probably her friend, I guess. I look away, too, down at my faded sneakers, so I'm not staring at her.

"Brewer! Clyde! Ramos! Simmons!"

Gina elbows me. Mrs. Waggoner is coming toward us, dyed blond hair perfectly styled and makeup perfectly neat, even after a ten-hour bus ride (which . . . how?). Mrs. Waggoner is the mom of Lindsay Waggoner, our senior drum major. Lindsay will be leading us for the cameras on Thursday and loving every minute of it, just like Mrs. Waggoner seems to love every minute of being lead chaperone. She ran almost all the informational meetings before this trip. I'm getting the impression she likes telling people what to do.

Evan grimaces at me. I make myself shrug. We tried. We filled out the roommate request form together. We even got the Nilsson twins—Ben and Jason, who both play trombone with Gina—to join in so we could fill a whole room.

And Springfield High said *lol nope*.

I mean, they didn't really say that. They said a much longer and more polite thing about how "we as an institution value and support each student's expression of individuality" but also, "due to concerns from parents, we have a strict policy to separate students according to gender." Nice and vague.

Might as well have slapped me in the face.

Because the thing is, school hasn't been terrible, up to now. I basically just hang out with people from band, and none of them give a flying fuck that I'm trans. Ms. Rinaldi has always called me the right name, always used the right pronouns. So have my other teachers, after a few flubs. Yeah, there's only one single-stall, gender-neutral bathroom in the whole school and it's the only bathroom I feel comfortable using, but at least it's there.

Low bar, but it's a smallish town pretending to be a suburb in North Carolina. I was prepared for worse.

Then along came this trip. And yeah, I guess I knew trying to room with Evan and Ben and Jason would be a long shot, but what really got to me was the school using the word *gender*. As if everything I've been saying since I officially came out—about how gender isn't the same as sex and there aren't just two of those, either—only mattered to my school until I became a Logistical Headache.

And then, suddenly, gender and sex meant exactly the same thing. And there were only two. Because *parents were concerned*.

My mom tried to tell me the school had valid reasons, even if they worded them badly. They had to pack four students into each room in order to afford the trip. Four students to each room means people sharing beds. And teenagers sharing beds makes grown-ups anxious.

I don't feel like she has much of a leg to stand on when she and Dad are still in Camp It's-Cool-You're-Trans-But-Please-Not-In-Front-Of-Your-Relatives.

Plus, you know, the whole idea of grouping us by "two genders" because of bed sharing just assumes everybody's straight. Nice to know Gina's also getting erased.

As soon as I told Evan and Gina what happened—which was at lunch on the day I got the Email from the school—Gina shouted "THE FUCK" loud enough for the entire cafeteria to hear, and then stormed straight to the admin office to fill out the form to be my roommate instead.

"Us queers gotta stick together," she told me, and then roped in Rebekah Clyde and Zuri Simmons to fill out our room. Rebekah is straight (as far as I know), but Zuri is bi. She's not really out, but she and Gina kissed once, sophomore year, and immediately decided that they both liked girls, just not each other. They're still friends, though. Zuri plays trumpet, and Rebekah plays trombone with Gina. So the three of them are a bit chaotic—just like drummers. At least we all have that in common.

Mrs. Waggoner marches up to the four of us, a cheery smile plastered on her face, holding a stack of folders and a clipboard. "Hello, girls," she says.

Gina looks ready to rip her head off. "Girls and boy."

Mrs. Waggoner's smile slips. "Right." But she doesn't say anything else—just hands out four folders and four key cards, checks us off her list, and marches on to her next victims.

If looks could kill, Evan and Gina would have murdered Mrs. Waggoner several times over. Even Rebekah and Zuri look pissed.

That helps, a little, even though I'm not sure Mrs. Waggoner said *girls* on purpose. Maybe it slipped out. A side effect of suddenly being presented with the gender binary at every turn—everyone shuffled into their groups, all those *M* or *F* boxes neatly checked, all of it decided by somebody else.

It seems so random when you think about it. Like, who cares? Really?

Except everyone does, including me. I don't want to be in the box everyone else decided I'm in, but I want to be in a box. Even if I also want to burn all the boxes down at the same time.

How's that for complicated?

But hey, at least I have an actual hotel key now. I'm one step closer to that bed.

We wait around until Evan gets his key, and then all five of us—me, Gina, Evan, Zuri, and Rebekah—lug our duffel bags and backpacks to the elevator. It's the fanciest elevator I've ever seen. There's a TV screen inside, with some chipper guy with really white teeth pointing at a map and telling us the weather forecast.

It's weirdly mesmerizing. Or maybe we're just sleep-deprived. We stare at it for several seconds after the elevator doors close, before Rebekah remembers to hit the button for the eleventh floor.

The lobby might be impressive, but the eleventh floor of the Grand Felix Hotel looks pretty much like any other hotel—aggressively inoffensive. Neutral carpets. Neutral art. Signs pointing out the directions of different rooms, in that font that I swear every hotel on the planet uses. I guess the Grand Felix buys its signs from the same supplier as the hotels in Charlotte, Charleston, and Atlanta—all places we've gone for band competitions.

Zuri is currently reading the font. "Our room's this way." She jerks her head, box braids slipping over her shoulder.

"Oh." Evan's face falls, and he shoots me an anxious look. "I'm this way." He points in the opposite direction.

Did they seriously divide "boys" and "girls" on either side of the elevators?

Gina juts out her jaw, the way she always does before she's about to explode, and normally, I'd be here for her swearing up a storm about *cisheteronormativity*, but right now, I don't want to be a Logistical Headache. And Gina swearing up a storm, even if it's on my behalf, is still acknowledging that's what I am.

"Well, hey," I say, "at least we're all on the same floor."

It's a pretty terrible attempt at cheerfulness, but Gina and Evan seem to catch my drift. Gina sighs and Evan shrugs, and then we're all distracted by the second elevator opening. It's Ben and Jason Nilsson, along with Nate Clyde, Rebekah's older brother.

"Hey, guys." Nate gives us all an easygoing grin. He plays mellophone and is pretty chill, which led us to nickname him Mellowphone. It's not a good joke, but we all thought it was hilarious at midnight on the bus back from Atlanta last spring.

Evan hesitates, looking at me one more time, and then he turns and follows Nate, Ben, and Jason down the hall.

And I turn and follow the girls. Nate's a nice guy and everything, but I still feel like he's taking my spot in that room.

The hallway might be bland, but the hotel room itself is pretty sleek, if kind of small. One wall is a giant floor-to-ceiling window. Another has a big flat-screen TV. The beds have dark leather headboards, fluffy white comforters, and about ten pillows apiece.

Zuri whistles. "This is *nice*."

"Y'all, look at this bathroom." Rebekah flips on the lights, revealing walls of mirrors, shiny chrome faucets, and stacks of folded white towels. "Leo, you want to shower first?"

It's a nice offer, and obviously an attempt to make me feel like less of a Logistical Headache. "It's cool, I just want to sleep. You guys can go ahead."

Rebekah shrugs and heads into the bathroom. Zuri follows her, muttering, "My teeth feel *scummy*."

Gina takes the opportunity to fling her backpack onto the bed closest to the big window. "I say we call this one."

"Sure." I drop my bags and wander to the window. From this far up, the people on the street below look Lego-sized.

Gina comes over to stand next to me. We both stare down at the street. After a minute, she says quietly, "You okay?"

I give my best noncommittal shrug. "Yeah."

It's not really true, but not totally untrue, either. I feel how I've been feeling for months, anytime I've thought about this trip. Like I don't want to be here. Guilty that I don't want to be here. Mad at myself that I *can't* just be here—away from Springfield in big, exciting New York City. It should be the perfect chance to forget about the anxiety eating away at me.

I'm perfectly aware that New York is big and exciting and I should partake of the Enjoyment, as Evan and Gina said.

But I can't seem to make myself do it. And that makes me feel even more like a failure.

At this point, I'm kind of my own Logistical Headache.

"You wanna punch a pillow?" Gina jerks her thumb over her shoulder at the massive collection on the bed. "We have options."

That makes me grin, a little. I really appreciate Evan—a lot—but somehow, with Gina, I always feel like I have more space to vent. Or punch pillows. Maybe it's because she's queer, too. She gets that, sometimes, the last thing I want is a sympathetic look. Sometimes I'd rather be pissed, and she's happy to be pissed with me.

But right now, I just feel tired. "I'm good."

"Okay. Well . . . standing offer." She sighs. "I better call my mom. The daily check-in." She pulls her black curls into a ponytail and shoots me a grin—Gina's parents almost didn't let her go on this trip, because New York is a lot farther away than Atlanta, or any-where else we've been so far. They only agreed after she promised to call them every day.

"Yeah," I say. "Go for it."

Gina bumps her shoulder against mine and then pulls out her phone and leaves the hotel room. I hear her muffled voice out in the hall, talking in Spanish.

I flop down on the bed closest to the window. Finally, a chance to sleep.

Except now, of course, I'm wide awake. Listening to the sound of the sink running in the bathroom, and Rebekah and Zuri talking around their toothbrushes, and the sounds of traffic—plus the occa-sional siren—floating up from the street eleven stories below. From my spot on the bed, I can barely make out a sliver of darkening sky in a gap between two buildings.

What's wrong with me? I'm in a swanky hotel room in the mid-dle of Manhattan. I should be Happy To Be Here, Grateful For The Opportunity.

Instead, this is all just a reminder of how much the next two days are going to suck.

Thanks, Universe. Fuck you, too.

THREE

ABBY

NEW YORK CITY in the morning is so busy and fast, it's like a shot of caffeine just walking down the sidewalk.

I also have actual caffeine, though, in the form of a paper cup of coffee I'm passing back and forth with Kat. We got it from the buffet at Planet Hollywood, where we had breakfast. Planet Hollywood was better than our dinner experience last night—mediocre pizza and pop at folding tables in a hotel conference room—but it still wasn't exactly what I was picturing from a Manhattan restaurant. The restaurants in *The Hundred Romances of Clara Jane* are full of candles and white tablecloths and people with jobs like "magazine editor."

I guess looking at costumes from Star Wars while eating waffles was kind of cool. But it didn't seem very . . . New York. Since, you know, Hollywood is in California.

I take another sip of coffee. It tastes terrible, although that might be because I never drink coffee. Maybe the gritty and bitter taste is something you get used to.

Kat doesn't usually drink coffee, either, but as soon as she saw it at the breakfast buffet . . . "We have to get some," she said. "We can't risk missing a *moment* of today."

The way she leaned on the word *moment* sent shivers down my back. I agreed instantly.

Besides, neither of us got a lot of sleep last night. We were too excited. We lay next to each other in the big, luxurious hotel bed, in the room we're sharing with Morgan Ellis and Amira Aboud, looking up all the places we were going to visit on our phones. Even after Kat finally fell asleep, I stayed awake for another hour, listening to the noise wafting up from the street. The hum of traffic, the occasional siren, someone laughing. Things were still open and people were still going places. The city was still *alive*.

When my parents had dropped me off in the high school parking lot at ten o'clock on Monday night, everything in Westvale was closed. The high school parking lot was the only place anything was happening—a line of cars idling with their headlights on while we all got our bags loaded onto the buses.

"This is kind of weird," I said to Kat. We were hauling our bags toward the lead bus.

She glanced back at me. "Why?"

"It's so dark, and everybody else is going to bed." My breath puffed in a cloud in front of my face. "I feel like we're in another dimension or something."

Kat grinned. "Liminal space."

"What's that?"

"Like . . . a space that's between. Not where you've been and not where you're going." Pinpricks of headlights danced in her dark eyes. "The time between *what is* and *what's next*. Damaged Pixie Dream Boi has a song about it, remember? I've totally played it for you . . ." And she started singing it, which didn't really help, because I didn't remember it. Not without the accompanying bleep-bloops.

I glance at Kat now, watching her hold up her phone, a big smile on her face, to take a picture of an enormous digital billboard—an androgynous model twirling in a long, sleek coat. Her fashion inspo, twenty feet tall on the side of a building across the street.

I wrap my fingers tighter around the coffee cup. It's nice to have something warm in my hands, because every street in Manhattan is a wind tunnel. I was prepared for cold. We get plenty of it in Westvale. But I'm still glad I put on a flannel *and* a sweatshirt under my band jacket.

I did not tie my hair back, though, which I now regret. Even worse, I somehow managed to leave all my hair ties in the hotel room. We had to get up early today, to fit in breakfast before embarking on our grand sightseeing tour of New York City. A sightseeing tour during which—whenever the Universe gives me the right moment—I will give Kat the copy of *The Hundred Romances of Clara Jane,* complete with my confessions of love.

That's why I forgot about hair ties. I was too busy thinking about which flannel/sweatshirt combo I wanted to wear on the day I hand Kat The Book. And then I spent too much time checking on The Book in my backpack. I didn't even think to take my clarinet out of my backpack, which is definitely adding several extra pounds I'm now stuck carrying around all day. And The Book is not light, either. It's a hardcover, way heavier than the little paperback copy of *THRoCJ* I'm used to reading.

I bat my hair out of my face as another wind gust hits us dead-on. Why did I think it mattered what I wore, anyway? If it stays this windy, I'm never going to take off my jacket.

Kat and I were literally looking at maps on our phones all night, so I know that Manhattan is surrounded by water. But it's still weird to walk for twenty minutes (passing the coffee back and forth with Kat, taking pictures of everything we see) and suddenly reach the ocean.

Okay, *technically,* as Jared Nguyen points out, it's the Hudson River. But it connects to the ocean. It's salty. It counts.

I have never seen the ocean before. I've seen *rivers*—there's one that runs right through Kansas City—but as for large bodies of water, the biggest I've ever seen is the thoroughly midsized lake we went boating on when I was ten.

But here, directly in front of us, is more water than I have ever seen in my life, and behind us, everyone in New York carries on like this is normal.

A big sign nearby says PIER 83. (Does this mean New York City has at least eighty-three piers? Because that is a lot of piers.) Directly in front of us, sitting right at the water's edge, is a building with a picture of the Statue of Liberty above its doors. Underneath the picture, in big red letters: CIRCLE LINE. And underneath that, in smaller white letters on a green awning: AMERICA'S FAVORITE BOAT RIDE.

A few people are strolling along the waterfront, but we're definitely the biggest crowd here. Which makes sense, because we have this particular boat tour to ourselves. A ride just for us, out onto the Hudson, past the Statue of Liberty, and back.

It sounds so romantic that my heart flutters every time I think about it.

The boat waiting next to the pier is low, wide, and oval-shaped, kind of like a giant, floating almond—if almonds were two stories tall and had a whole crew in matching white windbreakers manning them. After a head count, we all file onto the boat, and without saying anything to each other, Kat and I immediately head for the stairs that lead to the upper level, with Morgan and Amira right behind us. We're going right by the Statue of Liberty—I definitely want the best view possible.

From up here, the air smells sharp and salty. The sky is almost the same color as the water: flat, slate gray. I can see all the way across the Hudson to the trees and buildings on the opposite shore. Is that New Jersey?

"Roomie selfie!" Morgan waves at me and Kat and Amira. We crowd around her, the railing against our backs, while she snaps several pictures. Morgan's on practically every social media site there is, and I'm sure this picture will immediately go up on all of them. She'll probably make a TikTok once we get to the Statue of Liberty.

The deck underneath us rattles, the boat's engines firing up. Everybody cheers.

I suddenly feel like the coffee is knotting my insides together. This is it—*what's next* has turned into *what is*. The big day is here.

I just have to wait for the Moment. Wait for the sign from the Universe.

I really hope I don't miss it.

"Abs, you okay?"

I jerk. Kat is watching me, looking slightly worried. "Yeah! I'm good." I try to smile. "The coffee's making me jittery."

"Oh. Okay . . ." Kat looks like she doesn't believe me. Which isn't surprising. I've been terrible at lying since pretty much forever. I once made the mistake of trying to plan a surprise birthday party for Kat, and she guessed what I was up to after, like, three days. It turns out when your best friend asks you if you're planning a party, laughing hysterically and exiting the room at top speed does not actually make you look innocent.

Before Kat can say anything else, though, there's a deafening blast from the boat's horn. We both jump. Everybody around us cheers again.

"Welcome to New York City, Westvale High School Marching Band!" a disembodied voice thunders over the boat's PA system. "Are you ready to see the Statue of Liberty?"

The answer is a lot more cheering. Kat shoots me a grin and then cups her hands around her mouth and whoops.

But my stomach drops straight to my knees. What was I thinking? This is a boat tour. Of *course* there's a tour guide. He's going to be hyping us up, pointing out every single landmark, droning on about the history of everything.

This isn't going to be a romantic boat ride at all.

The boat leaves the harbor and slowly motors into the river, giving us a perfect view of the Manhattan skyline, skyscrapers rising into the low, gray clouds.

Kat sucks in a breath. "Could you take a picture for Tumblr?" she asks. "Just really quick?"

"Oh. Sure." I pull out my phone and push my anxious thoughts aside, slipping back into being Kat's friend. It's not hard; I've been doing it for months. Pretending nothing's different, pretending *I'm* not different. "Um . . . stand there? No, a little more that way. That's good."

I'm usually Kat's photographer whenever she finishes sewing a new dress and wants to model it for her Tumblr, so it's an easy role to slip back into. Snapping picture after picture of Kat in different poses. She's wearing black jeans tucked into brown boots, a thick, cozy cable-knit sweater, and her band jacket—none of which is really that stylish, but somehow, she sells it. Or maybe it's just that everything looks more stylish when there are skyscrapers rising into the clouds behind you.

It's turned colder and windier by the time we're done, the boat chugging farther out into the Hudson. I pull up my sweatshirt hood (which at least helps contain my hair) while we choose the best pictures for Kat to upload later, looking up every time the tour guide points out a famous landmark. The Chrysler Building. The Empire State Building.

Kat grabs my arm. "That's it!"

My heart leaps. The Empire State Building is so recognizable, but it's different to see it in real life. It's tall and grand but also somehow ordinary—just existing, in among all those other buildings, like it does every day.

"God, I wish we could see it at night, all lit up." Kat leans her elbows on the railing. "You know, like it is when Clara Jane realizes Chris is her actual true love."

"Yeah." I nod, trying not to think about *THRoCJ,* or The Book in my backpack . . .

Wait a minute.

The Empire State Building. And Kat just mentioned true love. Maybe *this* is the Moment. Maybe this is the Universe giving me a sign. Or at least a hint.

My heart pounds until I can practically hear it, drumming in my ears. I take a deep breath. Do I talk first? Pull out The Book first?

Maybe talk first.

Definitely talk first.

"Um, Kat? There's something I wanted to—"

And that's as far as I get before Jared Nguyen barfs spectacularly over the railing.

A chorus of groans and grossed-out noises erupts, so loud it even drowns out the tour guide on the PA. Then Mrs. Gunnerson is elbowing her way through the crowd to Jared, who looks positively green.

Morgan, of course, is documenting the whole thing for TikTok.

Mrs. Gunnerson might be a tiny woman with short blond hair like Tinker Bell, but she apparently has the strength of an elephant, because she heaves Jared through the crowd like it's easy, heading for the stairs down to the lower deck, muttering something about *what do you expect* and *kids staring at their phones.*

She might have a point. I definitely feel kind of woozy after staring at Kat's phone, choosing pictures for her Tumblr. But I also feel bad for Jared. He takes his fact spouting and location tracking very seriously. Plus, he's about to be Morgan's latest viral TikTok. Everyone at school will know about this by the time we get home. That's rough.

"Were you about to say something?"

I blink. Kat's looking at me, eyebrows raised.

But everything's wrong now. The tour guide is droning on, and people are leaning over the railing, pointing, like they're looking for Jared's vomit in the ocean (ew). The Empire State Building is fading behind us.

The Moment passed. Or maybe it wasn't the Moment to begin with. Maybe I got it wrong.

I try to shrug casually. "I forget."

Kat grins. "Another moment ruined by Jared."

I somehow manage to grin back. It's fine. That didn't have to be the Moment. We have a whole day of New York City ahead of us—that's plenty of moments.

We slowly leave Manhattan behind, and the tour guide talks about Governors Island, and then Ellis Island, and finally, we catch sight of the thing we're really here for: the Statue of Liberty. I've seen it in pictures and movies and on TV, but here, in person, it's *way* bigger than I thought it would be. The statue dwarfs the island it's standing on. Even the pedestal is taller than the trees around it.

Morgan immediately wants Amira to film her for TikTok, Kat asks for another Tumblr picture and then pulls me to the railing for selfies, and the next ten minutes turn into enthusiastic chaos as our whole band talks and points and takes pictures, holding up phones and craning to get the best view of the statue.

Eventually, the boat turns around in a lazy circle and starts back toward the pier. Most people follow the view of the Statue of Liberty to the other side of the boat, but Kat and I stay with our elbows on the railing, watching the skyscrapers of Manhattan get closer again instead.

We're alone. And the tour guide is quiet, at least for now.

I have a second chance.

I slip my backpack off my shoulder, ready to tug the zipper open. Ready to pull out The Book. "So, um, about that thing I was going to say earlier ..."

She looks up. The wind has blown a few wisps of black hair loose from her messy bun, sending them into her eyes. She's so close, so perfect ...

And I freeze. I completely clam up. The tour guide picks back up, droning on about the sea life of the Hudson. Zach Gunnerson starts trying to climb the boat's flagpole to make a group of color guard girls laugh, while several chaperones try to get him off the flagpole, which is what's actually making the color guard girls laugh . . .

And my brain turns into one giant blank space.

This can't be the Moment, because I don't know what to say. And Andy Brentner is cheering and Morgan is filming, while Mrs. Gunnerson shouts at Zach that he's embarrassing her, and nothing about this feels magical at all.

Kat pokes my arm. "Abby? You zoning out?"

I shoulder my backpack again, forcing my brain to work. "Let's look at those pictures with the statue. Which one do you want to post?"

Kat looks at me for a moment longer, and then she pulls out her phone, launching into her thoughts about the pros and cons of each shot.

I let out my breath. Back into friend mode.

FOUR

LEO

SO FAR I have learned:

Rockefeller Center has naked statues, a giant-ass Christmas tree, and an ice-skating rink.

Fifth Avenue is full of yellow taxicabs and people carrying shopping bags that say things like MICHAEL KORS and TIFFANY & CO.

And Central Park has a freaking castle in it for no discernible reason.

It didn't take long for me to be really glad I'd chugged a cup of coffee at breakfast, in a hotel conference room that could only be described as Beige. I'm pretty terrible with mornings; whenever we have early band practice, Evan has to pull out his sousaphone and blast a low E-flat in my face to wake me up. It's like having my own personal foghorn.

But all our instruments are packed away in some back room of the hotel, so I had to settle for awful-tasting coffee. At least it kept me from actually falling asleep, since it turns out listening to a tour guide shout about the Rockefellers commissioning statues—with every third word out of his mouth snatched away by the wind—was about as interesting as watching paint dry. Fifth Avenue was even worse; I didn't see how looking at fancy stores was interesting in the slightest, even if a lot of them *did* have cutesy Christmas displays in the windows. Or, you know, an entire façade of Christmas lights twisted into the shapes of trees, several stories high, dripping with glittery icicles. It was impressive, and some people seemed to enjoy it, but the more stores we passed, the more annoyed Gina got, and even Evan started to look uncomfortable.

This trip was a lot of money for all three of us, but I think it felt like more money to Evan and Gina. Gina's parents run a corner store, and Evan's mom teaches first grade. (His dad up and left when Evan was four.)

My dad is an engineer, and my mom is a nurse. They were definitely relieved when Casey got a scholarship from NC State, but they never seem that stressed about money otherwise. It's not like we're taking fancy vacations all over the place, but when my mom's old Honda crapped out last year, she didn't seem to worry that much about needing a new car. Or a new-to-her car. I don't think my parents have ever actually bought *new* cars. Grandpa Brewer thinks they should, and they should buy them from the Brewer car dealership. Family loyalty. Free advertising. Yet another awkward subject Dad tries to avoid at every family gathering.

But walking down Fifth Avenue—in addition to slapping you in the face with Christmas—kind of makes you feel like everyone in New York is rich. Macy's gave us a grant to kick-start our fundraising for this trip, but now I'm wondering why they can't just pay all the travel expenses of every marching band they want in the parade.

Central Park, on the other hand, just looks like a giant park. Lots of trees. Random huge rocks. And yeah, also a giant castle, but at least everyone walking around the park looks pretty normal. People with dogs, people with strollers, even a few people Rollerblading.

The view from the castle is pretty cool. It's on a hill, so we're looking out over large swaths of open space, the green grass slowly turning brown. From up here, I can see skyscrapers poking up above the tops of the bare trees. But from the ground, except for the occasional siren, I wouldn't even know the city was there.

"Man, we'd sound so awesome in that amphitheater," Evan says.

The amphitheater is in the distance, on the other side of what's either a very small lake or a very big pond.

"I think we'd sound the same as we do in the band shell," I say. Practically the only thing Springfield has going for it is a halfway decent public park with a band shell. The high school puts on a musical there at the end of every school year, and about half our marching band usually ends up playing for it. It's hot and sweaty and you get mauled by mosquitoes, but other than that, it's actually pretty fun.

Evan looks at me like this is the most ridiculous thing I've ever said. "Uh, *no*. That amphitheater is way bigger than the band shell. We would sound *way* more epic."

"What does size have to do with anything?"

Gina groans. "Do you even *hear* yourselves?"

Evan ignores her. "Okay, now I want to do a performance where there's one marching band in the amphitheater and one marching band up here on the castle and they do call-and-response. The echoes would be amazing! You could record it with, like, a drone flying overhead so you get the full effect . . ."

Gina and I look each other. We fully expect Evan to go to a big university with a top marching band—like Ohio State or the University of Tennessee—probably on a merit scholarship, and then become a band director. He already hosts a party to watch the Drum Corps International World Championships every year. It's basically like the Olympics for marching bands. The formations are mind-blowing.

Like, defying-the-laws-of-physics, how-did-anyone-even-figure-that-out mind-blowing.

A level of mind-blowing that Evan spends the week after analyzing. Drawing on graph paper like he's making his own drill book. Eagerly talking about new ideas he's gotten.

This is why he's going to be a band director.

But I push that thought out of my head. I've started getting information packets from colleges—either in my parents' mailbox or via the pile on the guidance counselor's desk at school. It's already too much. Mostly because I don't know what I'm going to do if Evan and I go to different schools. I'm so ready to get out of Springfield, but I also have no idea where I want to go. And no idea how I'll survive anywhere without Evan. Or Gina.

My phone buzzes in my pocket. I pull it out. On the screen is a text message.

CASEY

LEO

From my older sister.

CASEY

WTF

Oh, boy.

CASEY

Mom says you guys got in a huge fight on Monday

My sister always texts like this—like everything is really intense and she can't put more than ten words in a single text before starting a new one. Casey's text messages read like stream-of-consciousness shouting.

CASEY

I thought you were gonna work this out

With them

What happened

Groan.

I love my sister. A lot. She's the first person I came out to, and there was a reason for that. I knew she would be okay. I knew she wouldn't ask any questions. And I was right. She took it in and moved on.

Mom and Dad asked questions. They didn't get upset. They said they loved me.

But they also said, *Isn't it possible you'll change your mind?*

And *Couldn't you wait to transition until you're eighteen?*

I don't think they meant to hurt my feelings. But it was still a lot different than Casey saying, "Yeah, okay."

The only problem is that Casey has never, ever given a flying fuck what our parents think about anything she does. Which is great. For her.

But she doesn't get why I *do*.

I probably shouldn't. Sometimes I wish I didn't. But it's different when you're the youngest. It's different when your older sibling goes off to college and you're suddenly the only kid in the house with your parents and no extra buffer.

It's different when you have to respond to a different name every time you visit your grandma. When you have to remember that name ever even belonged to you.

Anyway, hormones aren't like piercings where you can run off and lie about your age and get them in secret. I mean, I guess I could *try,* but that would be an amazingly bad idea for about five million different reasons.

I better head this off before Casey really gets going.

ME

Fight wasn't that bad. Just the usual.

CASEY

Is this about the ex family again

I know she means the extended family, although it's really tempting to reply that the way Mom and Dad talk, it's like they think it *will* be the Ex Family after Thanksgiving Outageddon.

My thumbs hover over the keyboard. The last thing I want to do right now is talk to Casey about Mom shouting that just because the extended family calls me a different name and uses different pronouns doesn't mean they don't still love me. Or Dad shouting that *this sort of thing* is a lot for people to take in, and some people in the family aren't ready for it yet.

And I really don't want to talk about what happened after the fight. The last dress rehearsal our band had on the football field, in front of the whole town. The dress rehearsal that should have been a simple run-through of the show we'd practiced thousands of times, while everybody packing the bleachers cheered.

Except, *of course*, there was that Channel 4 news van, parked right next to the bleachers. Filming last-minute footage to slip into their segment.

That was more than I could take. Every formation, every single rhythm I was supposed to play—in that moment, it all went straight out of my head. I fell out of step—everyone else on *left*-right-*left*-right and me on *right*-left-*right*-left—and then I turned the wrong way, crashing into Sandy Dixon and his snare, and after that it was dominoes. Because everybody in marching band is super focused on walking really fast, in step with everyone else, and playing the right notes, all of which you've memorized, while aiming your instrument the right way. There's no time to focus on anything else. No time to look out for some fool who made the most basic mistake and caused a pileup halfway through the dress rehearsal for the biggest moment in any of our lives.

"Leo." Gina lightly slaps my arm. "Come on."

I look up. We're starting to move again, leaving the castle and heading back down the paved path.

I shove my phone back in my pocket. Maybe if I ignore her, Casey will leave me alone. You never know. Pigs could fly.

It works . . . for long enough that I can at least sort of appreciate the much bigger lake we're currently walking past. I try to turn my brain off, and just listen to Evan and Gina argue about whether this lake is, in fact, bigger than the entirety of Hiller Park in Springfield. (Gina: Yes. Evan: No, it only *looks* bigger because everything is big in New York.)

The lake fades behind us, and we're walking along the edge of an enormous open grassy space when, of course . . .

Buzz buzz.

Crap. I should've put my phone on airplane mode, like I usually do—because my phone is from the Bronze Age and its battery barely holds a charge. I didn't do it today because . . . Well, I'm on a big trip. In a big city. I felt like I should be *reachable*.

Maybe I was hoping—faintly—that Mom and Dad would call. Or text. Suddenly say the fight was all their fault and they're telling everyone the truth after all.

Instead, I just get Casey. And I can't make myself ignore her. I pull out my phone again.

CASEY

Just tell the ex family yourself.

Who cares.

And here it is: the flip side of Casey firmly believing that me coming out as trans wasn't a big deal. If it wasn't a big deal for her, why would it be a big deal for anyone else?

No, that's not fair. She gets that some people might have a hard time with it. She just doesn't understand why I should care if they do. Why I can't blow it off the same way she did when Grandma Brewer pitched a fit after Casey got her nose pierced.

She doesn't understand how to me, coming out is something I don't *want* to be a big deal, but at the same time, it is. How it isn't just about whatever the Ex Family might say in response.

It's about what it does to me and Mom and Dad, if we don't tell them. And what it might do to Mom and Dad if I *did* tell everyone, without them.

ME

Mom and Dad want to tell their families themselves.

CASEY

They keep saying that so you won't tell anyone yourself.

Nonna still thinks Mom can actually cook ffs

They're never going to tell the ex family.

My stomach knots. For a second, I hate Casey for saying this. Actually hate her.

Then . . . No, I don't hate her.

I hate that I'm worried she's right. I hate that I've been wondering the same thing. Maybe Mom and Dad are just stringing me along, promising they'll tell Grandma and Grandpa and Nonna and everyone else. Promising there will be a magical Right Moment.

Some Right Moment when telling everyone won't be A Big Deal.

When it won't be A Lot To Take In.

When it'll be the sort of thing everyone shrugs about, because I can room with Evan, because I can walk into the men's bathroom without my heart rate going through the roof, because I won't make anyone uncomfortable by just existing in a space that (I guess) is somehow theirs.

If that's the Right Moment my parents are waiting for . . .

Well, it'll probably never come. I wish it would. I wish I could even say I *hope* it will. I guess, on my better days, I do. Hope.

But mostly I feel like I'm waiting to turn eighteen. Like my parents are waiting for me to turn eighteen. At least then I can go to college and they can't be blamed for my decisions anymore.

And until then, they'll just keep asking the same things of me: please don't take it personally, please try to understand it from everyone else's point of view, yada yada.

So maybe Casey's right. Maybe Mom and Dad don't really intend to tell anyone in our extended family that I'm trans.

But even if that's true, the idea of telling the whole Ex Family myself . . .

Well, I must be the world's biggest hypocrite, because honestly, I'm not sure I wouldn't rather keep pretending.

"Leo! Hey!"

It's Evan, shouting at me from several yards ahead. I got too distracted by those texts—I didn't even realize I was falling behind. The rest of the band is already out of the park, milling around next to an enormous stone pillar with three shining gold horses on the top, along with a shining gold woman who looks like she's standing in a seashell. There are more statues of people around the base of the pillar.

New York City really likes its statues.

I stuff my phone back in my pocket. Forget this. I'm supposed to be *on this trip,* not fielding intense texts from my sister.

By the time I catch up, everybody's splitting into the small groups we were assigned to before we left the hotel this morning.

Each group has its own chaperone to keep tabs on us at our various stops throughout the day. And it's going to be a long day. Not only do we have a whole lot of scheduled tourism, we've also got a practice run-through on Thirty-Fourth Street in front of Macy's, with the cameras and everything . . . at three in the morning. Required for all bands participating in the parade.

What self-respecting high school marching band needs sleep before performing live on national television? We're hardcore. We'll sleep when we're dead.

I wonder if anybody lives near Macy's. I wonder how much they hate the night before Thanksgiving.

At least I'm in a small group with Evan, once again thanks to the alphabet. Our small group is honestly not that small—there must be close to twenty of us, which is clearly too many for our chaperone, Mr. Corbin, who's been dabbing at his forehead with a handkerchief all morning. His daughter, Hallie, plays sax and is pretty nice. Mr. Corbin is also pretty nice—or at least, he's breezed right past my name every time he's checked me off his list so far, like there's nothing weird or unusual about any of this.

Maybe I shouldn't be surprised. Like I said, I really haven't had any problems at school until this trip. But after the email from the school, saying I couldn't room with Evan because *parents had concerns* . . .

Well, I have no idea who those parents are. And this trip is big, so we have more parents volunteering as chaperones than we've had for our more regional trips. Feels like any one of them could be *concerned*.

Maybe Mr. Corbin is just too distracted to give me any trouble. He looks kind of overwhelmed now, paging through a big three-ring binder, his glasses slipping down his nose, while Actual New Yorkers shoot us dirty looks, annoyed that our presence on the sidewalk means they have to walk ten more steps to get around us.

Are New Yorkers perpetually in a hurry?

"All right, everybody," Mr. Corbin says. "We'll be getting to our next destination by taking the subway." (Evan waggles his eyebrows at me. Fair reaction. Springfield has zero public transportation.) "We have MetroCards for you, and these have all the fare you'll need for the day already loaded on them. Don't lose them." He hands out the bendy yellow rectangles of plastic. "If you lose them, you'll have to pay for a replacement yourself."

Evan grimaces. Not that he needs to be worried. I'm not sure Evan has ever lost anything in his life.

"Please stay close by," Mr. Corbin continues. "The subway system is crowded and large. Now, all of the chaperones know where we're going"—he doesn't look confident about this at all—"but I'm going to tell you how we're getting there, just to be extra safe . . ."

My phone starts buzzing. The long, drawn-out buzz that means someone's calling me. Three guesses who that could be.

Yep. It's Casey. But she's not just calling—she's FaceTiming me.

I shouldn't answer. I really shouldn't answer.

"We're taking a tour of abandoned subway stations," Mr. Corbin drones, "starting from Chambers Street. So to get there, we'll be taking the A train . . ."

My sister knows I'm on this trip. She knows I'm busy.

". . . from Fulton Street, we'll take the J uptown one stop . . ."

But I jog a few steps away from my group, because I can't ever say no, and answer the FaceTime. "Hi, Casey."

"Leo." My sister is sitting on her bed in her dorm room, in front of a Taylor Swift poster, wearing an oversized sweatshirt and oversized glasses. She inherited our dad's terrible eyesight. "You're going to be on TV *tomorrow*."

"Uh, yeah, I know. Thanks, Casey." I edge into the shade of the giant pillar, glancing over my shoulder. Mr. Corbin is still talking. "I'm kind of in the middle of things here."

Casey sighs. "Fine, I just . . . I'm worried about you. About what's going to happen tomorrow."

That makes me annoyed. "You're going to *be there* tomorrow, Casey."

Now she frowns at me. "Yeah, I know. Which means I'm going to have to witness the family meltdown."

Oh, woe is you. "So why are you bugging *me* about this?"

"Because it's *your* identity. You have a right to tell people."

I glance over my shoulder again. Evan's looking back at me, waving. Our group is starting to move. All the groups are starting to move, crossing the street, heading for a Starbucks on the opposite corner and the subway station entrance next to it. I wave back at him—*be there in a minute.*

"Look, Casey, I get what you're saying, but have you met Grandma? Telling her would be a nightmare."

"You're just scared of rejection."

Is she joking? "Yes, that's *exactly* what I'm scared of."

She flushes a little. Maybe she knows that was a sort of brainless thing to say. "Sorry. I just mean . . . Come on, we both know Dad needs to *tell* Grandpa he's never going to take over the dealership, but he never does. Mom and Dad will keep letting this go on for as long as you let them. They love you, but they're totally useless. They're those people who vote and think *that's it, I saved my country.*"

Casey's taken part in several protests since starting at NC State. Her big issue right now is voting rights, and I'm both really intimidated by and intensely proud of her, but it does mean she's started putting political metaphors into every conversation.

I know what she means, though.

She means Mom read a Trans Issues ebook and thinks that's enough. She means Dad called the school and now hopes he'll never have to engage with anyone about this ever again.

And she means that all of that means something, and it still doesn't mean enough.

I rub my eyes. My head is starting to hurt. "Casey, I gotta go."

My sister sighs. "Yeah, yeah. Look, I love you, okay? But it's your

life. Maybe take some action for once. You know, unlike Mom and
Dad."

I can't decide whether I want to yell at Casey that she's being a
jerk, or cry because I'm afraid she's right. I settle for glaring at her. "I
have to go." And I end the call.

Of course, all the things I should have said immediately pop into
my brain. *I'm not the only one who could take some action. Maybe
don't put all the responsibility on me. Maybe don't act like I'm a coward
if I don't want to give all our relatives the chance to be shitty to my face.*

No time to think about that now. I turn around and . . . *oh, crap.*
My whole group is gone—my whole marching band. Straight-up
disappeared from the sidewalk. They must have gone down into the
subway station.

My phone vibrates in my hand.

EVAN

Hurry up, we're heading for the train

Shit.

I run for the crosswalk. Wait for a gap in traffic and then dash for
the subway entrance and bolt down the stairs. I'm going so fast that
my sneakers slip and I almost go flying headfirst; I catch myself on
the railing just in time.

Calling the station crowded is an understatement. It's mobbed.
People *everywhere,* and none of them walking as fast as I want them
to be. I duck and weave to get to the turnstiles where people are swip-
ing their MetroCards through a reader. Okay. Looks simple enough.

I fumble the yellow MetroCard out of my pocket, swipe it, and
push against the turnstile.

The turnstile doesn't budge. All I get is a message on the tiny
screen next to the card reader: SWIPE AGAIN.

Oh, now is *not* the time, turnstile.

I swipe again. Now the message says TOO FAST.

Are you kidding me?

Swipe. SWIPE AGAIN AT THIS TURNSTILE.

I JUST DID THAT.

Fourth time is the charm. The turnstile lets me through, and I run. What did Mr. Corbin say? The A train. That was it . . . I'm pretty sure that was it . . .

My phone buzzes again.

EVAN

Where are you

We're getting on the train

Should I tell Mr. Corbin to wait??

So Mr. Corbin hasn't even noticed I'm gone? Well, that's great. I've gone from being a Logistical Headache to being invisible.

But I don't take the time to reply to Evan. I just run, trying to read the signs over my head at the same time. Everything is a maze of UPTOWN and DOWNTOWN and BRONX and BROOKLYN. There are still people everywhere, and everyone seems to be trying to go a different direction . . .

Aha. Finally! A sign with a white *A* printed in the middle of a blue circle.

I run in the direction the arrow points. Down another set of stairs. And there, waiting at a concrete platform, is a train. A big, boxy subway train with dull silver sides and a blue circle with a white *A* in its windows.

The doors are open. A tinny voice filters out from the nearest train car. *"Stand clear of the closing doors, please."*

Someone pushes past me—a blur of purple and white, diving for the train.

I dive, too . . . *and I make it.*

The train doors whoosh closed with an off-key *ding-dong,* and I let out a sigh of relief so big that my knees wobble. I made it. Thank fuck.

My phone buzzes. Evan again. Great, he can tell me what car they're all in. Maybe I can switch cars at the next stop and catch up before Mr. Corbin notices I'm gone. Or worse, Mrs. Waggoner.

EVAN

YOU'RE ON THE WRONG TRAIN

I stare at the text. How would he know if I was on the wrong train? Is he here, in this train car? I glance around, like he's somehow small enough to hide somewhere.

But why would he tell me I'm on the wrong train if . . .

"Oh, shit," says the girl next to me. She's wearing a purple-and-white varsity jacket. Her long, curly brown hair is a wild mess. And she's staring through the rectangular windows in the train's doors like the world is ending.

I follow her gaze. There, across the platform, is another train with a blue circle and a white *A* in its windows.

And staring back at me through those windows is Evan, looking horrified.

"Oh, shit," I say.

FIVE

ABBY

THIS IS WHAT happened:

The boat pulled back into Pier 83 with The Book still in my backpack.

We walked to Port Authority—which is both a bus terminal and a subway station, and not at all romantic because it smells like pee—and took a train to Central Park.

Central Park was beautiful, full of couples strolling arm in arm, and families chasing little kids across the grass, and people walking their dogs.

And I stepped in dog poop approximately ten feet into the park. Kat and Morgan and Amira thought it was funny, but I wanted to cry. It felt like the Universe was laughing at me. I couldn't give Kat The Book with dog poop all over my shoe. I spent the whole time trying to wipe my shoe off on the grass.

When we finally left the park to head to the subway station, I thought things were looking up. There was a food cart right near the subway entrance—and it had napkins!

So I yelled to Kat that I'd be right there, and I grabbed a handful of napkins, and I cleaned off my shoe—as best you can when you're trying very hard not to get your hands anywhere near dog poop. I don't think the food cart guy was very happy with how many napkins I used, but I apologized, and I did mean it, even if then I had to turn and run for the subway station.

I didn't think I took that long, but when I got down into the station, I didn't see Kat or Morgan or anyone else anywhere. And then I realized I'd dropped my MetroCard, and I had to run back up the stairs to look for it. (I found it, luckily, on the sidewalk near the food cart guy, who glowered at me and snatched the napkin box away, like I might try to take more.)

By the time I finally got through the turnstile and ran down the tunnel to the platform, the train was *right there* and the doors were about to close, so I took this flying leap . . .

And for a perfect moment, I thought the Universe really was looking out for me. I made it onto the train. This day was about to get back on track—pun absolutely intended.

But no. This is the wrong train.

Which I realized the second the doors closed, when Kat texted me—because she'd been leaning out of the open doors on the other train, looking for me, and she saw me get on this train.

Shit.

And now, here I am, in the last car of the wrong train. Which means I get to spend seven agonizingly long seconds watching the train across the platform, the train I'm supposed to be on, slide away in the opposite direction.

Taking Kat—and my chance to salvage this disaster of a day—with it.

"Shit!" says the person next to me.

That's the second *shit* they've said since we got on this train, so I actually look at them, and realize . . . this person looks familiar. And is wearing a black-and-gold varsity jacket that also looks familiar.

Oh. It's that person from the other marching band I saw in the hotel lobby yesterday. Or at least, I assumed they were in another marching band.

I also assumed they were a guy. They're dressed like a guy—gray beanie over short dark hair, burgundy hoodie under their band jacket, jeans and scuffed-up Adidas sneakers.

Then again, who says any of those things have to be guys' clothes? I've spent enough time browsing queer looks on Tumblr. I should know better than to assume anything by now, shouldn't I?

Beanie notices me staring and frowns. "I saw you in the hotel."

The train whisks us into the darkness of the tunnel. Subway trains, I'm learning, are *loud*. I swear I can hear my bones rattling.

"I'm not supposed to be on this train," I say.

It's not exactly a polite, introductory thing to say, but it's what comes out. I've got a few things on my mind.

Beanie keeps frowning. "Me neither."

"Um, so are you supposed to be with your band—?"

"On the other train."

"Yeah. Me, too."

We stare at each other.

"Well . . ." I take an awkwardly large gulp of air, trying to slow down my breathing. "We just get off at the next stop, right? Turn around?"

"Right." Beanie nods, still frowning. Is that just their face? "Get off at the next stop, change directions, go back. We'll probably only lose a couple minutes."

I nod, too. This is fine. A minor hiccup. "So how far is the next stop?"

"I don't know."

We both look around the train car, like we might find the answer here somewhere. The car isn't very crowded. Most of the orange plastic seats are empty, which isn't what I expected, since the station itself was so busy. Maybe everyone else was heading for different trains, or going the opposite way. An older Black man is reading a newspaper in one corner. A younger white guy in a suit is scrolling through his phone, one hand wrapped around the vertical pole that runs from the floor to the ceiling.

Wait a minute. *Phone.*

I pull mine out. What's wrong with me? I should text Kat; I should've texted Kat as soon as she texted me.

ME

On wrong train but I think I can get off at next stop and turn around.

Three little dots pop up on the screen. Kat's typing.

KAT

What should I do??

I could tell a chaperone???

"You have signal?"

I jerk and look up. Beanie has their phone out and is scowling at it.

"Yeah," I say. "You don't?"

Beanie just grunts and scowls harder. I look at their phone, too. It looks kind of basic. And old.

And I don't have time to pay attention to that now, because I don't want Kat to tell a chaperone. Not yet. Like Beanie said, we'll probably only lose a couple of minutes, so there's a chance no one will notice, right? There's a chance I can catch up and slip right back in with the group before the abandoned subway tour.

I type out a message to Kat, hit send . . .

Message Failed to Send

What? "No, no, come on . . ." But the single bar I had is gone. Now my phone says *No Service.*

"Maybe we're too far underground," Beanie says.

"Or maybe your phone just sucks." It comes out sharp and mean, and makes no sense, since my phone doesn't have signal anymore either. I feel bad immediately. "Sorry. I'm having kind of a terrible day."

Beanie just says, "Yeah."

And keeps frowning. Maybe I'm not alone in having a terrible day. We're both on the wrong train, after all.

I hesitate. I don't know Beanie, and I'm in a big city, and every single info meeting before this trip had some variation of *be aware of your surroundings, don't talk to strangers* . . . But Beanie doesn't seem all that threatening, despite the frown.

So I say, "I'm Abby."

Beanie glances at me and chews their lip, still frowning. "Leo."

Okay. So. Leo is usually a boy's name, right?

Maybe?

All the queer people I see on Tumblr post their pronouns on their profiles, or on their selfies. I've been thinking about putting my pronouns on my social media sites—but I keep chickening out, because I don't know what I would say if Kat asked me about it.

So maybe I should ask Leo's pronouns. Or would that be rude?

"She, her, hers." I blurt it out. "I mean, those are my pronouns. You could tell me yours. If you want. You don't have to."

Leo's frown disappears, replaced by something that looks a whole lot like complete surprise.

Oh, no. I've made a huge error. Leo is a straight cis guy who has never heard anyone say their pronouns and doesn't even know what *cis* means because straight cis guys do not browse queer Tumblr late at night. I thought Leo was my age–ish, but who knows, maybe Leo's a really tall freshman who doesn't have a single molecule of facial hair yet and now thinks I'm the weirdest person ever.

Leo says, like each word is being yanked out, "He, him."

It takes me a second to even process this, and then my face turns warm. "Um, great, sorry. I didn't mean to put you on the spot . . . I didn't know if I should ask, or if I should say mine, or . . ."

Leo's eyebrows are going up.

Stop talking, Abby. "Sorry. Nice to meet you."

Sort of shockingly, the corner of his mouth turns up. Just a little. "Nice to meet you, too."

"I'm cis," I say, because I can't seem to stop.

Leo looks like he's either going to laugh or barf, and I can't totally tell which. "Okay, Abby. I'm trans. And nobody says they're cis."

My face is now fully on fire. "Well . . . maybe they should." Time to change the subject, before Leo asks me why I'm such an awkward human. I look back down at my phone, but it still has zero bars. "You have any signal yet?"

Leo glances at his phone. "Nope."

"I didn't used to have problems like this. I mean, I've never been on a subway train before, but I swear I had good signal until my parents switched to this cheapo carrier." I look out the window into the dark subway tunnel. *I'm still talking too much.* "Feels like the next stop should be soon, right?"

Leo moves away from me, and for a second, I think maybe he's had enough of me being weird, but then he jerks his head. He's pointing at a map on the wall.

Oh.

We both lean toward the map. It's a maze of different colored lines, labeled with letters and numbers. How does anyone navigate this? Why are some trains labeled with numbers instead of letters? Why is there a G train and a J train but no H or I trains? You'd think the A, B, and C trains would all neatly be the same color, but no, the B train is on an orange line for some reason. This makes no sense.

My eyes catch on one thing that *does* make sense: a big green rectangle that has to be Central Park. "There!"

My finger shoots forward at the same time as Leo's and our hands run right into each other.

We both pull back. *Ouch.* I think he mashed my finger.

"Sorry," he mutters.

I pretend I don't notice. "Columbus Circle is right there, next to Central Park."

"Yeah." He traces a narrow finger along a blue line. His fingernails are really short. I wonder if he bites them. "Here's the A train . . ."

Something crinkles loudly behind us. "You kids okay?"

It's the man with the newspaper. He's peering at us over it, his reading glasses pulled down on his nose.

Leo's frown is back. *Don't talk to strangers* goes through my mind again, but we need the help. "Do you know what the next stop on this train is?"

"One Hundred and Twenty-Fifth Street," Newspaper Man says.

Wait . . . "But Columbus Circle is Fifty-Ninth Street, right?"

He gives me a sympathetic look. "Sorry, kids. You hopped the uptown A right as it goes express." He goes back to his paper.

Leo and I look at each other. Express? So this train is running from Fifty-Ninth Street to 125th Street without stopping?

My brain won't do the math. I turn back to the map, following the blue line of the A train up, all along the edge of Central Park . . .

My stomach sinks. "That's really far."

"There are other stops, though." Leo points. "Look."

"But those stops say C. That must be another train."

"Local line," Newspaper Man says from behind the Arts section. "This is the express."

Leo turns around and shoots him a glare, like this is somehow Newspaper Man's fault. Luckily, Newspaper Man doesn't seem to notice.

Leo groans. "Shit."

I'm also really tempted to curse. Or curl up in a ball on the floor and cry, even though the floor of this train looks disgusting.

Why did I have to get on the one train that goes express past five billion stops? (There's one now, in fact, flashing past outside the window.) If I'd just paid a little more attention, I would have seen the other A train when I ran down the stairs. If I'd just taken a second to *look* . . .

Leo stalks back to our original spot near the doors, shoulders hunched up under his jacket. I don't know what else to do, so I follow him. But he doesn't say anything to me. Just stands with his back against the doors, looking grumpy.

When I can't stand the (relative) silence anymore, I say, "So, where were you supposed to be going?"

"Um . . ." Leo's frown deepens, but now it looks more like a thinking frown. "Chambers Street. We're taking a tour of subway stations or something."

For a moment, a little hint of excitement finds its way back in. "Oh, so are we! Maybe we're taking the same tour!"

This makes Leo look grumpier.

And makes me feel defensive. "What? A tour of abandoned subway stations sounds cool to me. Like . . . haunting, and magical."

Leo snorts.

Well, that's rude. What's wrong with finding deserted subway stations haunting and magical?

I wait for Leo to apologize, but he doesn't. He just glowers into the middle distance like he's forgotten I exist. And here I thought meeting other queer people might be fun.

But I'm not going to make him talk if he doesn't want to, so I sit down on the orange plastic seat closest to the doors and pull out my phone. Except I still don't have any bars; the only thing I can really do with my phone is look at the pictures I took of Kat earlier . . . and that isn't going to make me feel any better.

So I open my backpack and pull out the hardcover copy of *The Hundred Romances of Clara Jane*. I gently turn the pages to one of my favorite scenes—one I heavily annotated for Kat—and start reading. Maybe for the next few minutes, I can lose myself in the story.

Remember writing all these notes and underlining all these passages and assure myself that there's still time to fix everything that's gone wrong. It's not even noon. There's plenty of day left.

Several pages later, the train finally starts to slow down. The guy scrolling on his phone stops scrolling and wanders over to the nearest set of doors. And we come rumbling into a station, big green columns and white tile walls shooting by.

Leo pushes himself away from the doors, the frown gone from his face. "I think this is it."

I fumble with my backpack, trying to tug the zipper back open, but it's stuck.

The brakes squeal, and the train grinds to a halt so abruptly that Leo loses his balance and unceremoniously falls over right on top of me. He knocks me sideways. The Book goes flying out of my hands.

And my beautiful, signed, carefully annotated hardcover copy of *The Hundred Romances of Clara Jane* thunks on the sticky subway floor like a brick and slides away under the row of seats across from us.

"Get off me!" I push Leo away and give my backpack zipper a ferocious yank. It gives way. *Yes.*

The train doors whoosh open. I launch to my feet, ready to dive across the car to grab The Book . . .

. . . but Leo grabs my arm and pulls me onto the platform.

I'm so surprised that for a second, I let him drag me through the jostling crowd of people trying to get onto the train.

And then—

"Hey!" I yank myself free and turn back for the train. But I'm short, and nobody's paying attention to me, and I can't get through anybody. "Excuse me! Sorry! I just need to—"

Ding-dong.

The doors close. The train creaks forward, slowly gaining speed, until it's shooting away into the tunnel, taking with it all my underlines, all my notes, all the hearts I drew in the corners of the pages.

Oh, god.

"Abby." Leo tugs my jacket sleeve. "Come on."

I shake him off. I am suddenly, overwhelmingly, completely furious. "What the *fuck*?"

He stares at me in slack surprise.

"You made me leave my book on the train!" I'm shouting, my voice bouncing off tile and cement and echoing in the station, but I don't care. "What the fuck is wrong with you?"

Leo's scowl comes back with a vengeance. "I didn't make you do anything. I was trying to get us both off the train since you weren't paying attention!"

Of all the . . . "I was paying attention. I dropped my book, and it was *important,* and I would have been able to grab it and still get off the train if you hadn't been such an *ass* and pulled me away!"

He blinks at me. "*I'm* an ass? Well, excuse me for trying to make sure we didn't miss our stop."

"I wasn't going to miss the stop."

"You were going after a freaking *book*!"

I have never wanted to punch somebody in the face more than I do right now. "It was an important book, and it was a gift for an important person, and now I've lost it, and it's *your* fault."

I turn and stalk toward the stairs. I half expect everyone on the platform to be staring at us, but nobody is. They're all scrolling on their phones or reading their books like nothing happened. I'm not sure if that makes me feel better or worse.

I'm also not sure if I'm stalking off in the right direction. Am I actually supposed to be going up these stairs? Where are the signs?

Footsteps pound up the stairs behind me and Leo says, "Downtown train is on the other platform."

I purposefully don't look at him and don't ask him how he knows this. Great, we're going the right way. I still feel angrier than I have in my entire life.

We climb the stairs from the uptown side, walk about twenty

steps across the station, and go down more stairs to the opposite plat-form. It all feels very embarrassing.

But at least now the signs above my head all say DOWNTOWN. That's promising, right?

The downtown platform is more crowded than the uptown one. I'm hoping this means I can lose Leo—but he keeps up with me. Curse tall people, cruising through crowds while I just bounce off everyone. I finally give up in front of a big map in the middle of the platform, because we should probably look at it anyway.

And I should check my phone. *Yes.* I have signal again. I resend the message to Kat. I hope she hasn't already told someone what hap-pened.

The way Leo is punching away at his phone makes me think he must have signal, too. He turns to the map in front of us. "We're both going to Chambers Street, right?"

I glower at him. "Yeah. I'm pretty sure that's what they said."

"You're pretty sure?"

Now I full-on glare. "I had shit to deal with, okay? Literally. On my shoe."

For a moment, he just stares at me. And then he snorts—and quickly turns it into an unconvincing cough.

The desire to punch him comes right back. Which is fine. At least it's distracting me from *oh god I lost The Book, I lost this whole day, I lost all the weeks I spent writing those notes . . .*

I fold my arms, like somehow that will hold in my panic. "What's your big excuse for getting on the wrong train?"

That wipes the smirk off his face. "My sister FaceTimed me," he mutters, and turns back to the map. "Looks like Chambers Street is a stop on the A train, so we can just take one train the whole way."

The platform underneath us rumbles. Light glimmers in the tunnel, and a subway train comes roaring into the station, brakes shrieking. We push forward, swept along with everyone else on the platform, and cram ourselves onto the train. There aren't any free seats this time, so we end up wedged in the middle of the car, holding on to a pole, so close together that my face is practically in Leo's armpit.

As if this needed to get worse.

The doors close with an out-of-tune *ding-dong* and the train jerks forward.

Finally. We're on the right train, going the right direction.

The opposite direction that The Book is going. The Book is moving farther and farther away by the second, and probably getting kicked and stepped on and covered in dirt.

All my rage at Leo crumples in on itself. My eyes fill up until everything around me turns to a blur.

I feel sad and silly and embarrassed. There's no salvaging this day now. It's ruined, whether Kat tells a chaperone where I am or not. And maybe it was a ridiculous fantasy anyway, everything with The Book, but it still meant something, and I thought it could happen. I believed the Universe could make it happen.

"Um," Leo says. "Are you okay?"

God, I wish he would go away. This is the last thing I need—crying in front of someone I just met who has completely dashed all my hopes for a perfect, romantic day in New York.

All I manage to say is "I really liked that book."

The train slows down, gentler this time. We pull into another station lined with white tiles. Do all the stations just look like massive underground bathrooms?

Wait a minute. Why are we stopping? Aren't we supposed to zoom past all of these stations on an express track for the next ten minutes?

"*This is One Hundred and Sixteenth Street.*" A man's voice crackles over the speakers in the car as people push their way off the train. He sounds very bored. "*This is a Brooklyn-bound A train, running on the C line. Cathedral Parkway next.*"

Leo frowns. "I thought we were supposed to go from One Hundred and Twenty-Fifth to Fifty-Ninth."

"Me, too."

A woman stuffed into a seat nearby looks up from the novel she's reading, which seems to feature two very hunky shirtless guys on the cover. They might even be . . . embracing. Wait, is she reading a gay romance novel? On the subway, like it's no big deal? "They're doing construction on the downtown express track," she says. "All the downtown trains are making local stops."

Local stops? So we're going to stop at every single station we passed before?

I take it back. *This* is the last thing I need. I'm beginning to think New York City doesn't want us to get anywhere, and the Universe does not give a single fuck about me.

No, scratch that. I'm beginning to think the Universe actively hates me.

The train jerks forward again, and I check my phone. I'm going to be in so much trouble when I get back. The chaperones had to check everybody off their lists before we left the hotel this morning, and again when we got to Central Park. Sooner or later, they're going to figure out I'm missing.

The way this day is going so far, they'll probably send the NYPD out to look for me. And then I'll be *that* girl—the one who got so lost in New York that a whole police department had to scour the city looking for her. Forget Jared and his spectacular projectile vomiting. Everyone in school will be talking about *me.* How am I ever going to live this down?

I should text Kat again. Right? Tell her I'm going to be later than I thought?

"So. Uh. How'd you get shit on your shoe?"

I'm so far into my horrifying thoughts that it takes me a minute to realize Leo is talking to me. I look up. He's almost a head taller than me, and his face is too close, since we're still smashed up against each other. I'm practically looking up his nose.

He's not frowning, for once. He actually looks sort of awkward and uncomfortable.

Is he trying to make polite conversation?

I manage to blink my eyes clear and try to shrug. "I stepped in dog shit. In Central Park."

Leo chews his lip. "I guess people don't clean up after their dogs anywhere."

The train slows again. Cathedral Parkway. This is going to take forever.

"So how'd stepping in dog shit in Central Park make you get on the wrong train?" Leo leans one way as people go around us to get off the train, and another way as people get on.

I don't have the energy to tell him to mind his own business. "Because I was trying to clean off my shoe while everyone else kept going without me. So I just jumped on the first A train I saw, and it was the wrong one."

The train lurches forward again.

"Nobody noticed you were gone?" Leo says.

That stings. "I told my friend I would be there in a minute." I don't want to start crying again, so I wave my phone at him—in the extremely tight space between our two jackets. "She knows I'm on my way. Anyway, you're one to talk. Clearly nobody noticed you missing either."

His face snaps back into a scowl. "My friend Evan was texting me until I lost signal."

I can't think of anything smart to say in response. I'm too busy feeling hopeless. "Well. Great."

"Great."

I stuff my phone back in my pocket. We glower in different directions.

Stop after stop goes by, and the train gets more crowded. How did I find all of this exciting? The people, the traffic, the whole *big city–ness* of it. I'm getting jostled right and left. People keep stepping on my feet.

By the time we finally get to Fifty-Ninth Street again, I feel like I've been on this train for days. At least once we get to Forty-Second Street the train empties out a bit. By Thirty-Fourth Street, I have breathing room, and by Fourteenth Street, there's enough space that I can take a very large step away from Leo.

When we rumble into Chambers Street, I'm ready. Leo will not be dragging me anywhere this time. As soon as the doors open, I push for the platform and sprint for the stairs, Leo right behind me. We slam through the turnstiles, sprint up more stairs, reach the cold, open air . . .

I pull out my phone and fire off a text as fast as I can.

ME

Got to Chambers St.

Where are you guys

Next to me, Leo groans.

I ignore him, focusing on the dots that tell me Kat is typing back. Finally.

KAT

Chambers St!!

I don't see you???

I stand on my toes, turning in a circle, but all I see are tall buildings and cars and people walking. And none of the people are Kat.

Or anyone else from band. It's not nearly as crowded here as it was at Columbus Circle, but that only makes it easier to tell that Kat isn't here.

Where is everyone?

Next to me, Leo says, "We're at the wrong Chambers Street."

SIX

LEO

ABBY STARES AT me like I've announced the world is ending. "You said that train went to Chambers Street."

"It did. We're at Chambers Street. But my friend Evan says they transferred from the A to the J train. Look." I shove my phone under her nose and jab a finger at the tiny map on the screen. "It's a different Chambers Street stop."

"There are *two* Chambers Streets?"

"No!" I want to scream. "There is *one* Chambers Street with *two* different stops. Or maybe more than two, I have no idea. But *we* are at the *wrong one*."

Abby seems to deflate. She looks away, folding her arms tightly across her chest like she's cold. "Okay, fine, I get it. How do we get to the right one?"

"Uh . . ." Right, the million-dollar question. I look down at the map on my phone. Look up at the street signs. But nothing's making much sense. With Abby standing here, darting sideways glances at me, I just feel flustered. And kind of guilty. About the book, about kind-of-maybe-sort-of yelling at her . . .

Abby sighs. "Give me that." She takes my phone and taps the screen. Up pops an arrow, and the tinny little GPS voice says cheerfully, *"Head north on Church Street toward Chambers Street . . ."*

Cool. Glad to know I just completely forgot how to use Google Maps in front of a total stranger.

Abby turns around and starts walking.

For such a small person, she can walk incredibly fast. I guess I shouldn't be surprised. Nobody power walks like marching band people.

"Um." I clear my throat. "Can I have my—"

She silently holds out my phone. I glance at the directions, and then turn off the play-by-play, because that'll drain my crap battery in about five minutes. Anyway, it seems simple enough—just a straight shot along Chambers Street from here.

We half walk, half jog down the sidewalk, dodging around people, skirting grates in the pavement. Next to me, Abby wipes her eyes. Quickly, like she's hoping I won't notice. Maybe it's just the wind. The cold air is definitely making my eyes water.

But I have a feeling it's not the wind.

"Um . . ." We're under scaffolding now, built over a long stretch of the sidewalk, turning it into a janky-looking tunnel. "Maybe there's, like, a lost and found for the subway somewhere. I mean, there has to be, right? With a phone number we could call or—"

"Yeah, maybe," she says. Flatly.

I should give up. I can tell when someone doesn't want to talk to me. I could just put up with her until I find my actual friends, at which point I'll never have to see her again. Sure, we're staying at the same hotel, but it's a big hotel and we'll be busy. And there will be hundreds of people in the parade tomorrow. Maybe thousands. Plus all the people watching. I won't run into her.

But in my head, all I hear is Evan saying, *He's got the Face.*

And also, I still feel guilty.

We reach a crosswalk and stop to wait for the light, cars rumbling past us.

Here goes nothing. "Look . . . I'm sorry you lost the book. What, uh . . . what was so special about it?"

She looks at me and her eyebrows snap together—two chestnut paintbrush strokes above her light brown eyes. She's definitely sizing me up.

I stare back. Hoping I look neutral.

The crosswalk signal chirps, and we both look away. Halfway across the street, Abby says, "It's my favorite book. It's set in New York City and it's a romance with all these famous landmarks in it, and it was signed and had some . . ." Her voice wavers. "Some stuff in it that was a gift for someone."

A gift? Now I'm curious. "What kind of stuff?"

Is it my imagination, or did she just blush? "It's not your business, but I was going to tell my best friend that I . . . sort of . . . really like her."

She looks at me again. I realize her eyes have a little gold in them.

"Oh." Her meaning hits me like a brick. "You mean, *like* like."

(What's wrong with me? I sound like I'm in middle school.)

But she just looks away and says, "It's her favorite book, too. We read it at the same time, and we both love it, and I found this special copy signed by the author, and I wrote a bunch of notes to her in it, and I was . . . I was going to use it to tell her that I . . . *you know* . . . and now, thanks to you, I've lost it."

Oh, great. Back to this all being my fault. "I didn't even know you dropped your book, okay? I was just trying to get us both off the train."

She looks annoyed. "I didn't *drop my book*. You knocked it out of my hands because you have no sense of balance."

What? "Hey, I'm in marching band. I can pull off complex formations like you wouldn't believe. With a snare drum strapped to my front. I have *great* balance. Anyway, who gives their friend a *book* to confess their great, undying love?"

She's definitely blushing now. "It's special, okay? It means something."

"Okay." I shrug. "Still seems like kind of a cop-out."

She rolls her eyes. "Right, because underlining romantic moments and writing romantic notes in the margins of a romantic book set in New York City while on a magical trip to New York City is a *cop-out.*"

Ugh. "Happy-to-be-here, grateful-for-the-opportunity," I mutter.

She stops in the middle of the sidewalk and shoots me a slightly dangerous look. "What did you say?"

"Nothing." I plow on ahead. "We should keep going."

She jogs after me. "You got derailed by a FaceTime from your *sister,* and you're judging *my* plans for my day? My plans went wrong because of you!"

That is unfair. "Okay, first of all, fifty percent of your day going wrong was you getting on the wrong train, and that had nothing to do with me. And second of all, I wasn't *derailed.* My family is going to implode tomorrow, because of me, and my sister chose that moment to decide she wanted to discuss it. And I try to *listen* when people want to discuss things. That's the only reason I was late."

She raises her eyebrows. "You? Listen? *Wow.*"

Now I'm really angry. "Yeah. I listen. It's everyone else who doesn't listen to me."

"Can't blame them, if you're this judgy about everything they tell you."

"I'm not judgy!"

She stops again, this time right on the next corner, which is really annoying because if we don't hurry up, we're going to miss the walk signal. "Look, maybe you don't think books are important—or maybe you don't believe in handwritten notes and thoughtful gifts. Maybe where you're from, coming out to your best friend and going 'Oh, hi, I'm suddenly gay and super in love with you' is no big deal. But I'm from Westvale, Missouri, where it *is* a big deal, so sue me if I wanted to write her secret notes in our favorite book so I could hand her something romantic and special and not lose my nerve."

She's looking distinctly murderous, but all I can do is stare. I'm not sure what I expected, but it definitely wasn't all that.

We missed the walk signal. Traffic crosses in front of us again.

I clear my throat. "Well, I'm from Springfield, North Carolina, so . . . it's a big deal there, too."

"I'm not out," she says. It sounds defensive. And maybe a little afraid. She blinks again—fast. "I don't even know if my friend is . . . queer."

"I only know two other queer people."

"Two more than I know."

"We don't even have a Starbucks."

She gives me a weird look. That's fair. I don't know what point I was trying to make with that.

"So . . ." I rock back on my heels. "You wrote, like, love notes to your friend in this book, and you don't know if your friend is queer, and you were planning to give it to her on this trip."

She shrugs, looking uncomfortable. "Yeah."

"Why?"

She looks down at her shoes. "Because telling her here seemed easier than telling her in Westvale."

Oh. My stomach twists. That I get. Sure, I can be annoyed by all this "magic of New York City" crap, because this trip is anything but magical for me, but . . .

But I can understand how a confession like that would seem less terrifying in a city that acts like nothing's a big deal.

The light changes. We go back to speed walking.

"What are you gonna do now?" I ask.

Abby just says, "We should be there soon."

Okay, so her coping mechanism is avoidance. Or she wants to ignore me.

"Yeah, I think we're close." I pull out my phone, zooming in on the tiny map. "No, wait. We're here. I think this is the stop."

I look up, and so does she, both of us turning around in a circle. The mix of shiny skyscrapers and shorter brick buildings has given way to a massive and weirdly old-fashioned stone building that looks like it belongs in Ancient Rome. It has huge pillars and figures of people carved into the stone above them. Engraved in the middle of it all is NEW AMSTERDAM, MANHATTAN, NEW YORK. Plus a bunch of X's and I's and other letters that must be Roman numerals.

"There's the stop." Abby points to one side of the huge building. Green railing, white-and-green spherical lamp—that's a subway stop, all right. And the sign on the railing says CHAMBERS STREET.

So where is everyone?

I switch to my texts on my phone.

EVAN

Are you here? I think I can cover for u but we're leaving on the tour now 😣

Shit. The text is from ten minutes ago; we were probably arguing at that crosswalk and I didn't even notice my phone buzz. Or maybe my phone didn't buzz. It's such a piece of crap. "They already left."

Abby sighs. She's looking at her phone, too. "Yeah, same here."

I tap out a quick reply to Evan.

ME

We missed you. Where are you going next?

Please cover for me till I catch up?

I stare at my phone for ten whole seconds, but he doesn't write back.

He's on a subway tour. Underground. Maybe he doesn't have

signal, either. Is his phone as terrible as mine? It might be. It's pretty old.

Fuck.

I sling my backpack down from my shoulder and crouch down on the sidewalk, unzipping the main pocket.

Abby eyes me. "What are you doing?"

"Looking for my schedule for the day." I shove my sticks aside. I forgot I had all these loose papers in here. Why didn't I leave my Algebra II homework in the hotel room? "It's in here somewhere."

Abby crouches down next to me and opens her backpack, too. "I have an itinerary." She pulls out a folder that looks a lot like the folder I got yesterday—just purple and white, instead of black and gold, with *Westvale HS* stamped on the front. Her mascot looks like an aggressively cheerful bird.

"We're in different bands," I say. "We're not going to have the same schedule."

"Yeah, obviously. But right now our bands are on the same tour, which means they'll end up in the same place."

Oh. Right.

She pages through the folder. "Okay, the subway tour will finish near NYU, so I guess they aren't coming back here. *We will have a quick lunch in Washington Square Park*"—she must be reading from the itinerary—"*before heading uptown for our Broadway show at two o'clock.* What time is it now?"

I check my phone. "Just before noon."

Abby closes the folder. "I guess we go to Washington Square Park, then. Where's that?"

I pull up Google Maps. "Uptown from here. I think." (If that's how you use the word *uptown*.) "Looks like a ten-minute subway ride if we go back to the station we came from."

"What's your band doing?"

"What?"

She gives me a very patient look. "Well, both our bands are going to end up in the same place, but is yours staying there?"

"Oh, uh . . ." I fish around in my backpack some more and finally find my own folder. "We're also going to a Broadway show."

Abby looks mildly interested. "Which one?"

"A musical adaptation of *The Great Gatsby*."

She pulls a face. "I had to read that book for English last year. Nobody's appealing and everybody's selfish. Or, like, a metaphor for something."

Great. That sounds super fun. "What are you seeing?"

"*Wicked*." She shoots me a grin that somehow doesn't look totally convincing. "It's my friend's favorite. She knows all the words." She glances at her phone. "We should go so we don't end up missing lunch. Are you guys also doing lunch in Washington Square Park?"

I look back at the folder in my hands. "I don't know. It just says *lunch before Broadway show.*"

Abby's eyebrows jump. "That's . . . not very helpful."

"Yeah." I'm getting the distinct impression whoever planned Abby's trip is more organized than whoever planned mine. Mrs. Waggoner would be so miffed. "I guess we could head for Washington Square Park. See if Evan texts me at some point. Or I could go straight to the Broadway theater? But then I might not get lunch."

Right on cue, my stomach growls. Loudly enough that I can hear it over the sounds of Manhattan.

Abby shoots my stomach a surprised look. Apparently she can hear it, too. "Yeah, I think you better not miss lunch."

I glower. I ate as much as I could this morning. How am I already this hungry?

"I guess we don't know when our bands are going to get to Washington Square Park." Abby chews her lip, frowning at her phone. "And they'll still have to go from there to Broadway, so . . . what if we miss them?"

"Miss them?"

"At Washington Square." She glances up. "And then we end up missing lunch."

"What are you getting at?"

"Maybe we could find something to eat here"—she waves a hand vaguely at the streets around us—"and then go straight to the Broadway theaters, to make sure we don't miss them again. I mean, we could try to text, but maybe just to be safe . . . I think Kat could cover for me, and maybe your friend could cover for you? It wouldn't be for very long."

My brain takes a few seconds to catch up. "Right. Uh. Yeah, Evan could probably cover. That makes sense." I have no idea if it makes sense, but I can't think of anything better to do, and I really don't want to miss lunch. If I have to sit through a Broadway show on an empty stomach, I will probably murder someone.

"Okay. So." Abby looks around. "Should we start walking back the way we came? I mean, it's New York, so . . . we can probably find something, right?"

I shrug. "Sure."

We barely get three blocks before we find pizza.

The shop doesn't have an actual name, as far as I can tell. Just a green awning with PIZZA printed on it in big white letters. A neon sign in the window says PIZZA BY THE SLICE.

That seems easy. And cheap. "What about this?" I ask.

Abby cranes her neck to look up at the awning. "Okay."

The shop is about the size of my bedroom closet and packed with people, all crowding toward the counter at one end. Two tiny tables are stuffed in by the front window, with two chairs each, but this is clearly not a sit-down establishment.

Abby's eyes go wide. "It smells amazing."

She's not wrong. The shop is warm and loud and smells overwhelmingly of cheese and tomato sauce and salt and something frying. Way better than the Domino's we've got in Springfield.

It's crowded, but the line moves pretty fast. Everybody seems to be getting slices to go, carrying them past us toward the door in triangular cardboard boxes.

When we reach the front of the line, the guy behind the counter doesn't even look up from the pad of paper he's scribbling on. "Yeah?"

Abby stands on her toes and raises her voice. "Could I get a slice of plain cheese, please? To go?"

The guy nods and glances at me. "You?"

I clear my throat. My heart rate speeds right up, like it always does, every time I do this calculus—how low do I pitch my voice to pass before it's too low and either it sounds fake or nobody can hear me. "Same for me, I guess."

The guy just nods. Turns away and picks up a pizza cutter like nothing unusual happened.

My mom thinks people from the Northeast are "rude," which she bases (as far as I can tell) off one trip to Boston with my dad before Casey was even born. But honestly, if nobody in New York City ever says something to me like *And for you, miss?* I will consider them the politest people on the planet.

Being an anonymous rando is amazing. I never get to be that at home.

The guy behind the counter slides two triangular boxes toward us. Abby pulls some cash out of her wallet. I scrounge several bills out of my pockets. The guy gives us our change without a word, and we head back outside.

Eating a pizza slice while holding a cardboard box and walking at the same time is almost as hard as marching in formation. Especially with wind spiraling right at us down the street. Maybe I should have suggested we sit at one of the little tables instead of braving the sidewalk.

But everyone else took their pizza to go. So walking and eating must be possible.

"We can take the same A train to the Broadway theaters, right?" Abby says. There's a long string of cheese stretching from her pizza slice to her mouth.

"Yeah, I think so." I grip my pizza box in one hand and fish my phone out with the other. The battery is already down to fifty percent. Terrific. "There's a Thirty-Fourth Street stop on the A. That looks close enough."

"Well, if it *looks* close enough . . ." She side-eyes me, which is not very threatening when there's cheese hanging off her face.

"Uh, you've got some . . ." I point to my chin.

"Oh." She wipes at her face. She's turned pink again. "Thanks."

We keep walking, but now I feel awkward. Like I should make conversation. Say something else so I don't leave it all hanging on a comment about cheese on her face. "So, um . . . how long was your bus ride? Or did you guys fly here?"

She glances at me. I could swear she almost looks surprised. "We took buses. It was, like, nineteen hours or something. I think."

"Wow. Or, um . . . yikes."

Her eyebrows go up.

"I just mean . . ." When did I get so bad at normal conversation? "Our trip was more like ten and I was still kind of losing it by the end."

"Yeah." She looks down at her slice, fiddling with the crust. "I think that was the longest trip we've ever been on. I mean, my band. And also me."

"What do you even *do* for nineteen hours?"

Her eyebrows pull together. "I spent a lot of time thinking how this trip was going to be perfect and magical."

Oh, great. Not this again. For a split second, I'm tempted to yell at her, one more time, that I did *not* make her lose that book. That or just give up, turn around, and leave, although I'm not sure where I'd go. We're stuck going the same direction, to the same place. Given my luck so far, we'd probably run into each other again in, like, a block.

I take a slow breath. In through the nose, out through the mouth. "I'm sorry, okay?"

She narrows her eyes at me.

"I'm sorry for . . . accidentally falling over you, which was not my fault, but did cause you to drop your book and lose it."

For a second, her face is blank. Then her lips twitch into a tiny smile. "Thanks." The smile fades and her shoulders slump. "I don't know. If I don't have the book, maybe I should give up on the whole thing."

"Why?" It's out of my mouth before I realize it's a nosy question.

She shrugs. "Maybe this is the real sign from the Universe. I spent all this time making the perfect gift for Kat, and I had a moment to give it to her this morning—I think—but I blew it. I couldn't figure out what to say." She sighs. "And instead of giving me another chance, the Universe makes me miss my train and sends the book off to who knows where, but now I definitely can't give it to Kat." She stuffs the last bit of her pizza crust in her mouth with surprising violence.

So she's equating being stuck with me to being punished by the Universe? Wow, that makes me feel special.

Don't be a dick, Leo.

"Well, what if the Universe is actually looking out for you?" (It's not, because the Universe sucks, but I'm trying to be nice.) "Maybe the whole book thing was a terrible mistake, so the Universe got rid of it for you."

Her mouth is too full to reply, but she looks dubious.

"I'm just saying—maybe the Universe *is* giving you a second chance. Telling you there's a better way to do this."

She swallows and says, "Like what?"

I take a bite of pizza to buy myself some time. "You said that book was your favorite, right?"

"And Kat's favorite, too. My friend."

"Right. So ... maybe that's too obvious. Or, like, not unique enough."

I'm reaching, and Abby's face tells me she knows it. "How is a signed book that I personally annotated not unique enough?"

"It's not really *your* story, is it?" I'm completely improvising, but I feel like I might be on to something. "Like, sure, you can write your own notes in it, but that's just writing yourself into someone else's story." I toss my empty pizza box into a big metal trash can on the corner. "Why can't you just *tell* her your feelings, anyway?"

Abby tosses her pizza box after mine. We pause, waiting for another traffic light, and for a while, she's quiet. "Because I'm not out." Her voice is low. "I don't even really know who I am, half the time. I ... I wanted to tell her, but, like, without *telling* her. The book just ... felt romantic. But less scary." She shrugs, but it looks dejected this time. "That book is the kind of story I want to be a part of. I mean, the heroine—Clara Jane—she goes up to the top of the Empire State Building to meet her true love at the end. It's cheesy and stuff, but ... I guess I wanted to do something that felt like that. We obviously can't go to the top of the Empire State Building. It's not one of our sightseeing stops. But we both love that book, so giving it to her, with all this stuff I wrote ... That felt like the closest I could get to a big, epic love scene."

I've spent zero time thinking about romance. Not because I have anything against it—but I haven't thought about it. Maybe that's because I've never really had a crush on someone. Or maybe it's because except for her one kiss with Zuri, Gina hasn't had any romantic encounters and Evan's pretty much in a monogamous relationship with his tuba, so it's never been something I talk about with my friends, either. Plenty of other people in band hook up, or date, or make out under the bleachers during football games. Just ... not us.

Maybe, though, I haven't *let* myself think about it. Because I know, deep down, that there's no chance anybody will be interested in me. The one trans guy in Springfield? Who's going to go for that? If Gina can't even find a girl to date, what hope do I have?

Do I even like girls?

I don't know. I think so. Sometimes I think I might like guys, too.

And sometimes, I can't tell if I want to *be* a guy or if I also want to *be with* a guy and that's just . . . *ugh*. That is too much for my brain.

So I've never given a shit about romance before. Or I told myself I didn't.

But staring at Abby staring at her shoes, thinking about this book she spent so much time on getting trampled by a bunch of people on the subway . . .

Well, maybe it's guilt, but I want her to have that big, epic love scene.

Anyway, she's queer and from a small town, and so am I, and one of us might as well have a good time on this trip.

"What other places are in the book?" I ask.

Abby looks confused. "What do you mean?"

"That book. Your favorite."

"The Hundred Romances of Clara Jane."

"Yeah, that one. You said it's set in New York, right? So the last scene is on the Empire State Building, but where does the rest of it take place?"

She looks at me doubtfully. "Kind of all over, I guess? Chinatown, Union Square, this café in Brooklyn . . . although that might be made up. There's a scene in Grand Central . . ."

How many times has she read this book? "Okay, so what if . . . If you can't get this book back, maybe you could find something that represents each of those places. You know, like souvenirs or something. And then you could give those things to, um . . ."

"Kat."

"Yeah, Kat." The light changes, and we start walking again. "If you found her a souvenir from each of those places, that's still sort of about the book, but also more about you guys, right? More about this trip. I mean, you could've gotten that book anywhere, but you can only get New York souvenirs in New York."

Abby frowns. "I guess . . ."

"You'd still have to actually tell her your feelings, but giving her a souvenir from every place you visited in honor of y'all's favorite book seems pretty epic to me."

"Yeah." Abby grins, briefly. "It does." The grin fades. "I don't know when I'd have time for that, though. We're basically scheduled for the entire day, and then we've got this rehearsal and run-through before tomorrow . . ."

I bite my lip. Pull out my phone to check the time. And then I throw caution to the wind and say, "How about now?"

SEVEN

ABBY

IS HE SERIOUS?

I stop walking. He stops with me. He doesn't *look* like he's joking. He's not even frowning—much. He's just standing there, hands in his jacket pockets, staring back at me.

"We have to go to Broadway," I say. "The theaters." Because I'm supposed to see *Wicked* with Kat. Because Kat loves *Wicked,* and I love Kat . . . "Before people realize we're gone and we get in trouble."

He shrugs. "Yeah, but the shows don't start until two, right? We've got some time."

An hour. Maybe a little more. "Where would we even go?"

"Well, let's see . . ." Leo types on his phone, squinting at it. "How about Chinatown?"

My head spins. "Chinatown?"

"That was in the book, right? And it's pretty close." Leo holds up his phone. "Ten-minute walk. I bet we could shave it down to five if we walk fast. And it looks like there are a bunch of subway stops around there, so we could hop a train that would get us close to the theaters, and it probably wouldn't take that much longer."

I chew my lip.

We should go to Broadway. Make sure we get there with plenty of time to spare, make sure we're in exactly the right place, make sure our bands can find us. That was the plan.

But if we do that, then I'm giving up. Giving up on the epic, romantic confession, giving up on the fantasy of telling Kat here, in New York City, in the magical way I had planned.

Giving up on the Universe.

Anyway, what if Leo's right? What if this is the Universe telling me I shouldn't give up?

My heart drums in my chest, and suddenly I'm saying, "Yeah. Let's do it."

For a second, Leo just stares at me. And then he grins—a real grin. Wide enough that I notice he's got a tiny gap between his two front teeth. "Cool. This way."

And he starts walking in the same direction we've been walking. It's kind of anticlimactic. "Are you sure this is right?"

He looks miffed. "Yeah, I'm sure. I looked it up." He glances at me. "For the record, I *can* read maps. Usually."

I look away so he doesn't see me smile.

After a block, just as we're turning down another street, Leo looks at his phone again. I realize it's buzzing in his hand.

"Sorry." He waves it at me. "FaceTime. Hang on." He doesn't stop walking, though. Just holds up the phone and answers it. "Hey."

"Leonardo Brewer," says the voice on the other end. "You missed the tour and now we're in Washington Square Park and I still don't see you."

My stomach drops to my knees. One of Leo's chaperones found out. We're busted. This will be the shortest adventure ever because we'll have to head for Washington Square Park immediately. Or even worse, they'll send the police for us. The voice on Leo's phone sounds really intense.

But Leo just sighs. "Yeah, I know. We missed you at Chambers

Street, and then we decided to get lunch and meet you at the Broadway theater to be safe."

"We?"

Leo tilts the phone my direction. "Evan, meet Abby."

For a split second, I debate flinging myself behind a parked car, because *why is Leo showing me to his chaperone?*

But the person on the screen is a blond guy who doesn't look any older than us. He has messy hair and a square-ish jaw that looks like it belongs on a superhero, and he's giving me a friendly grin. "Hey, Abby. I'm Evan."

Wait. Leo mentioned an Evan, didn't he? His friend. "Um. Hi, Evan." I manage an awkward wave. "Nice to . . . meet you."

"Speaking of meeting," Evan says, "how'd you two meet?"

Leo turns the phone away from me and gives it a frown. "We both got on the wrong train."

"Ah, most serendipitous! I see you haven't left the Face behind."

Leo gives him the finger. "You are such a jerk."

I realize my own phone is buzzing and fish it out of my pocket. It's Kat. FaceTiming me.

Crap. What do I do? I can't ignore her. She's probably freaking out.

I glance at Leo, but he's in the middle of grumping at Evan, who's laughing.

So I take a deep breath and answer the FaceTime. "Hi."

"Abs, where are you?" Kat's forehead is puckered up and she's leaning close to the phone, like she's worried someone might overhear. "Are you okay?"

"I'm fine." I try to make my face look fine. Or as fine as it would look if I hadn't just lost a book full of confessions that Kat knows nothing about. "I'm sort of near Chambers Street? I'm sorry, I know we missed the tour."

"God, you should have seen the stunt I had to pull with Morgan before the subway tour." Kat rubs her eyes with one hand. "Both of us pointing like you were somewhere else in the crowd. But they bought it—it's lucky you're so short." She leans close to her phone again. "Also, Mrs. Gunnerson is definitely in over her head. She actually *left* Amira in a bathroom."

"What?"

"Like . . . she forgot Amira was still in the bathroom and started taking the rest of our group back to the park. I had to remind her we didn't have Amira. I guess Mr. Rosinsky got food poisoning, so now everybody else has more to do or something?" Kat lets her breath out. "Anyway, how far away are you? Are you getting here soon?"

"I'm working on it." That's not a lie, at least. Technically. "Leo and I are, um, going to head straight to Broadway for the show and meet you there. Can you cover for me, just until then? It won't be that long."

Kat blinks. "Who's Leo?"

"Oh." I tilt my phone until Leo's in the frame. "That's Leo. Leo, this is my friend Kat."

Leo glances away from his phone. "Hi, Kat."

"Who are you talking to?" It's Evan's voice, from Leo's phone.

Leo tilts his phone until it's pointed at mine. "Abby's friend Kat."

Kat looks confused. "Who are these people?"

"Hi, Abby's friend Kat," says Evan. "I'm Evan."

"I ended up on the wrong train with Leo," I say. "He's in that other band that you went on the subway tour with. You know, the one we saw at the hotel yesterday? His band is going to a Broadway show, too, so we thought it might make more sense for us to get something to eat and then meet you guys near the shows, so we don't accidentally miss you—"

"Wait, wait, wait." Kat looks away from her phone, squinting into the distance. "Is Evan in the other band, too?"

"Yup," Evan says cheerfully.

"Wave at me," says Kat.

"I'm waving," says Evan.

Kat snorts out a laugh. "I totally see you." She waves at someone I can't see. "Well, now I know who Evan is. He's tall."

"Extremely," Leo says grumpily.

"You're still with the other band?" I ask.

"Kind of." Kat's still not looking at me. "They're across the park. Hey, Evan, did you get any good pictures of that City Hall station we went through? All mine turned out really dark."

"I think I got one that's pretty okay." Evan's voice filters from Leo's phone speakers. "You want it? I could text it to you."

Why does she need pictures from Evan? "I bet Morgan or Amira got a good one—"

"Yeah, that would be great!" Kat says, like she didn't even hear me. "I really wanted a good picture for my Tumblr. That station was amazing."

"Leo, the acoustics were bonkers," Evan says. "It would have been such a cool performance space . . ."

Kat's still glancing around, like she's avoiding looking at me. Or maybe she's just taking in the sights of the park. Maybe she really didn't hear me.

I wish I hadn't missed the tour. I wish I'd been there to take pictures with Kat.

Well, I may not have The Book anymore, but I'm going to find her perfect souvenirs in Chinatown. I'm getting a second chance, and I'm not going to mess it up. "So, um, do you think you can cover for me?"

Kat's eyes finally come back to her phone screen. "Yeah." She lets her breath out and shrugs. "I think so. Everybody's eating these box lunches with sandwiches and stuff right now anyway. I honestly don't think Mrs. Gunnerson is even paying that much attention."

"Oh." I'm not sure whether that makes me feel better or worse.

Kat hesitates. "Want me to try to save you a sandwich?"

For a second, I'm tempted to say yes. Even though I'm not hungry.

And I'm sure the sandwiches aren't anything special. "That's okay. I had pizza. So . . . I'll just see you at the theater?"

"Okay." Her image turns a little pixelated, but I think she smiles. "See you soon." The call ends.

I tuck my phone back in my pocket. My stomach is knotted up, just like it was this morning on the boat ride.

On Leo's phone, Evan is saying, "Not my fault if you get his angry librarian look later. But I'll do my best. I better go."

"Yeah, okay." Leo ends the call.

"Who has an angry librarian look?" I ask.

"Our chaperone, Mr. Corbin. He is, uh, an actual librarian." Leo clears his throat. "So that was your friend Kat."

I glance at him. I think he might be baiting me, because that didn't really sound like a question. I'm not going to fall for it. "So that was your friend Evan."

His mouth twists. "Touché."

"And your full name is Leonardo?" I need a distraction from the ball in my stomach.

He gives a long-suffering sigh. "No. It's Leo. Evan just likes making up pretentious names for me." He pauses. "Kat seems nice. She's . . . pretty."

I look up at him. My heart does a strange little hiccup.

"Sorry," Leo says quickly. "Maybe that was weird."

Was it? I don't know. "It's . . . it's fine."

I'm suddenly stuck wondering what kinds of people Leo finds attractive.

As far as I can tell, Leo literally typed *Chinatown* into Google Maps and left the rest to the algorithms, but somehow, ten minutes later, that's exactly where we end up. On a narrow street, full of short, red-brick buildings packed closely together, with storefront awnings in Chinese. Some of them don't even have English translations underneath the Chinese characters. There are hair salons, nail salons, hot pot, a supermarket spilling out onto the sidewalk, tables crowded with fruits and vegetables. There are restaurants promising KOSHER CHINESE DIM SUM and VEGAN NOODLES—and also Vietnamese pho, Indian food, sushi, bubble tea . . . there's even an Italian restaurant. (Its sign is not in Chinese.)

Above it all, the redbrick buildings are lined with black fire escapes. Some have round red lanterns hanging from their railings.

I hear plenty of Mandarin, which I can sort of recognize, because I've heard Kat speak it with her family so many times. But not everyone is Chinese. Not everyone is even of East Asian heritage. The people carrying shopping bags or pushing little carts full of groceries are white, Black, Latine, South Asian. I hear French, Spanish, something that might be Russian . . . I can't even begin to recognize every language around me. And some of these people seem like they might be tourists, the way they're walking slowly and looking around, but others are definitely running errands or picking up takeout for lunch.

The knot in my stomach disappears. I'm standing where Clara Jane stood. The lanterns are here, just like the book said they would be. In chapter four, Clara Jane gets bubble tea with one of her dates—maybe they even went to that place *right there* . . .

"So," Leo says, "what now?"

Oh. Right. I can't stand here and stare all day. We have to get moving. "Um . . . what do you think would be a good souvenir?"

Leo shrugs. "You tell me. What's in the book?"

I guess that's fair. I can't really expect him to be helpful. He hasn't read the book. And he doesn't exactly know Kat.

I chew my lip, turning in a slow circle. It's so bright and busy. I don't even know where to start. "Maybe we should just walk and . . . see if the Universe points us toward something?"

I regret it as soon as it's out of my mouth. I glance at Leo, waiting for him to look grumpy or roll his eyes.

But he doesn't. He just says, "Okay," and starts walking.

We walk (quickly) past the bubble tea and a clothing store featuring beautiful silk dresses, past a banner for a city council election (in both Chinese and English), around bags of trash crowded near the curb. Halfway across a grate in the sidewalk, I get a blast of hot air from underground, strong enough to blow my hair away from my face.

Where's that from? The subway? The sewers?

I really hope it's not the sewers.

Leo keeps getting ahead of me. He's not ridiculously tall or anything, but his legs are longer than mine. I have to take twice as many steps to keep up with him.

After the third time I break into a jog to catch up, I say, "Do we need to walk this fast?"

He slows down, so suddenly it's like he walked into molasses. "Sorry."

"It's okay, I know we're trying to rush and I'm short, but ... I need to conserve *some* energy for the parade tomorrow. Our band director basically tried to pack a whole halftime show into one minute." We pass a Chinese bakery advertising hopia. I don't know what hopia is, but the smell makes my mouth water. "We're playing this jazzy Christmas medley. 'Deck the Halls,' 'Jingle Bells,' 'Joy to the World' ... if it can be pepped up, we've pepped it."

"That's cool." Leo looks decidedly un-pep.

"What about you guys?" I dodge another grate in the sidewalk. "What are you playing?"

Now he frowns. "'Seventy-Six Trombones.' From *The Music Man*."

"Oh, yeah, we played that last year for regionals." We pass a jewelry store, a florist, a sign that says CANDY BEAUTY SKINCARE. Nothing that seems very souvenir-oriented. "At least you weren't practicing Christmas songs in the middle of July. That was weird."

Leo just grunts.

Okay, that's it. "What's the matter with you?"

"Nothing," he mutters.

"Then how come every time I say something about the parade or New York City, your face does *this*?" I pull the biggest grimace I can manage.

He glowers. "I told you, my family is going to implode tomorrow."

I'd forgotten, but I'm too embarrassed to tell him that. "What does that have to do with the parade?"

He looks down at the sidewalk. He's quiet for so long that I start to wonder if he's not going to answer.

And then he says, "My parents have been telling my extended family that I'm just a tomboy. They all use my deadname. So tomorrow, thanks to this parade, they're going to find out I'm trans, because they'll be watching the local news coverage at my house. And the news has this whole documentary segment thing they're going to show, and I'm in it. As . . . me."

Oh.

I want to ask what this means. What it means for Leo's family to call him by his deadname. What it will mean for them to see him as *Leo*. Why the news segment will be the tipping point and how Leo feels about any of this.

I want to ask whether people talk about this, where he's from. I want to ask if he worries about legislation, like I do. If legislation is already there.

But I'm not sure what I should say. What's too private and what's too . . . real. "Your parents can't explain to them tomorrow? When they see you on TV?"

Leo's look is pure vitriol. "Wow, thanks, not-remotely-out person. I'd never thought of that. Super easy. No big deal."

I open my mouth to snap back at him, but I bite my lip. Because he's right. "Sorry. You don't really owe me an explanation."

Leo's eyebrows jump. "Uh . . . no. I mean, yeah. Or . . ." He looks away again, back down at the sidewalk. His breath clouds in front of his face. "My parents think nobody else in the family is ready for it, whatever that means. Like, my parents get it, but my extended family won't, so they refuse to tell them."

I try to imagine that—coming out to my parents, and them responding, *Great, you're gay, now don't tell anyone.*

I don't know what I would do.

"That sucks." I know it's not enough—but maybe nothing's enough. Nothing I say will really fix it. I don't even know how to try. I've never met someone I knew was queer, let alone trans. I don't know what I'm supposed to say to any of this.

Leo shrugs, but it looks half-hearted. "I should probably just be grateful my parents get me."

It sounds like a line. Something to say even though he doesn't really believe it. "Kind of seems like if they won't tell anyone, then they don't. Get you, I mean."

He frowns at the sidewalk. "Could be worse."

I know that's true. I mean, for all the positive *I came out and my parents were totally cool with it* posts I've seen on social media, I've also seen the awful ones. I don't think my parents would be awful. I'm pretty sure they wouldn't, actually. It might take them some time to get used to it, but I think they would. I think my older brother would, too.

But even so . . . there's still that *but.* That tiny, terrified voice in the back of my mind. Just knowing those awful things are happening to someone . . . It's hard not to let it settle inside of you, undermining every single thing you hope for, until the bar just drops lower and lower.

Until we get here. Feeling like we're supposed to be grateful anyway.

"Was that why your sister called?" I ask.

Leo lets his breath out with a grunt. "She thinks I should tell the whole extended family myself."

I grimace, for real this time. "Oh. Wow."

He shrugs one shoulder. "She doesn't think me coming out to

them should be a big deal, because it wasn't a big deal when I came out to her. My identity is just my identity, so why should it be a big deal to anyone?"

"But . . . it *is* a big deal to you. Isn't it?"

"Yeah. No. I don't know. I don't know what it's supposed to be."

"Is it supposed to be anything?"

He looks at me. He's frowning again, but it looks more . . . confused.

"I just mean . . ." I swallow. What *do* I mean? "I just mean, I could see how, like, it's a big deal and not a big deal. Or feels like it's supposed to be a big deal but you don't want it to be a big deal. Or something. Sorry." I shake my head. "That doesn't make any sense."

"No, it . . ." His voice is quiet. Almost a mumble. "It does." He looks away, at the stores we're walking past. And then he says, a little louder, "See anything yet?"

"Um . . ." I glance around. Trying to focus. "What about that store over there?"

I point at what looks like a very touristy gift shop, crammed full of knickknacks, with I 💚 NEW YORK T-shirts swinging on hangers under the awning. Kat definitely wouldn't want a basic I 💚 NEW YORK T-shirt, but it's the first place I've seen that has obvious souvenirs.

"Sure," Leo says.

Up close, the storefront is even more crammed. Rotating stands of sunglasses and postcards, crates of flip-flops (in November?), shelves of shot glasses and tiny snow globes, baskets of magnets and phone cases. Every square inch of shop space has been filled up with things that have NEW YORK CITY stamped on them somewhere.

I run my fingers through a bunch of keychains so they rattle like clunky wind chimes. There's no way you could look at them and think they were anything other than New York City souvenirs. But they don't feel right. They don't feel like *Kat*. Neither do any of the magnets.

None of it feels exciting enough. None of it feels magical.

"Hey, how about these?"

I turn around. Leo is standing behind me, face perfectly blank, wearing heart-shaped, bright pink sunglasses.

I burst out laughing. It's such a sharp turn from everything we were talking about five minutes ago, and maybe it's not even that funny. Maybe we just both need a break.

Leo looks offended. "Excuse me, *I* think I look pretty."

I try to stop laughing and keep a straight face. But I'm never good at keeping a straight face. "I'm sorry, you *are* pretty. The prettiest."

"Thank you." Leo takes off the sunglasses. "These are perfect. Just hand them to her and say"—he lays one hand on his chest—"*These have two hearts, side by side, just like our hearts, beating only for each other.*"

Is he teasing me? "What?"

"No, you're right. We need something else." He turns around, fiddles with the sunglasses stand, and turns back, wearing another pair, this time with round yellow lenses. "*You are my sun, and I am your sun, and we are like two suns who also like the same book.*"

It doesn't seem mean, though. He's not even frowning. "Okay, that makes no sense, and also, you should clearly write greeting cards for a living."

Leo switches sunglasses again. The third pair doesn't even have lenses—just horizontal white stripes of plastic. "*Without your love, I am in a prison.*"

I bite my lip to keep from grinning. "How are those even effective?"

Leo scrunches his face up. "It is kind of like looking through window blinds."

I roll my eyes. "All right, let's keep going. I'm not getting Kat window blinds for her face."

Leo takes off the sunglasses and our eyes meet, for a second, before he looks away. His eyes have a little green in them.

"Okay, sure." He almost smiles. Almost. "Let's go." He sets the sunglasses aside and we duck out, back onto the sidewalk.

On the very next block, I see a handwritten sign in a store window: FABRIC, BUTTONS, ALL SEWING SUPPLIES. I can't read the larger Chinese characters on the awning, but it doesn't matter.

"That's it." I poke Leo's arm to get his attention. "Kat sews. She makes her own dresses."

Leo nods. "Works for me."

The storefront is narrow, sandwiched between a nail salon and a small pharmacy. A bell jingles when I open the door. Inside, it's warm and musty, with bolts of fabric piled on shelves all the way up to the ceiling. Most of the counter by the cash register is taken up by racks of buttons, scissors, and spools of thread.

It's not fancy, but *wow*. Kat would love this place. It feels like it belongs in *THRoCJ*. I can just picture Clara Jane stepping in, bumping into some handsome stranger in the single, narrow aisle . . .

"Hello!" A curtain at the end of the aisle moves, and a middle-aged Asian woman with big round glasses appears. She's wearing fuzzy slippers. "We're closing soon."

"Oh, sorry!" I automatically step backward and bump right into Leo. He lets out a very soft *oof.* "I was just looking for a gift for my friend . . ."

She beckons. "It's fine! Day before Thanksgiving, we always close up early. But I can give you a few extra minutes. Looking for anything in particular?"

"Um . . ." Somehow I feel like most people don't wander into sewing stores and say, *Yes, I'm looking for a souvenir so I can confess my love to my best friend.* Most people probably don't go to sewing shops for souvenirs in the first place. "Could we look around a little bit?"

The woman waves a hand. "Yes, of course. Let me know if you need help."

She disappears back behind the curtain.

Leo glances at me, eyebrows raised. "So, are we looking for fabric, or . . . ?"

"I don't know. Maybe?" I start down the aisle. Leo trails after me.

I've been to the sewing store in Westvale with Kat a bunch of times. It's staffed by these three old ladies and stocks a lot of fabrics that Kat calls "grandma patterns." In the store's defense, though, most of the customers are grandmas, and most of them seem to make quilts.

But the fabrics in this store are modern and beautiful. Silks and cottons. Plain and patterned. Vintage polka dots, sharp stripes, lush, dark florals that look chic instead of like a tablecloth.

It's all exactly like Kat's Pinterest boards. I could see her making dresses out of every single fabric in this store.

But I can't get her fabric. I have no idea how much would be useful, and I can't carry a ton of fabric around all day.

So I go back to the counter, leaving Leo contemplating rolls of colored ribbon, and slowly turn the spinning racks. Thread is too silly. She doesn't need a thimble. Or scissors. None of those things feel like a souvenir.

And then my eyes catch on a button in a tiny plastic bag. It's hanging on a rack full of buttons, but it jumps out at me because it's shaped like a pig.

A cute, pink pig.

My stomach flips. "Hey, Leo?"

"Yeah?"

I slip the tiny bag off its hook and turn around, holding it out. "What about this?"

He leaves the ribbon and comes over to frown at the button. "Kat likes pigs?"

"She was born in the Year of the Pig. Or . . . Boar. She said it depends on the translation. She's had this stuffed animal pig since she was a baby. I actually . . ." Heat rises up my neck. "I stopped eating bacon because Kat thinks pigs are really cute. Not that I ate bacon very much before that . . ."

The corner of Leo's mouth turns up. "A button is good. She could use it in a sewing project."

"Yeah. Exactly." My stomach is fluttering now. *I found a souvenir.* And yeah, it's just a button. But it's a start.

I tap the silver bell next to the cash register.

"Coming!" The owner reappears from behind the curtain and shuffles to the cash register. "Find everything?"

"Yeah." I slide the button across the counter. "Just this, please."

The woman glances up at me. Oh, no. She's going to ask me why on earth she kept her store open so I could buy one single button.

But she straightens her glasses and rings it up. "Two ten, please."

I fish my wallet out of my backpack and hand her a few dollars. She gives me change and puts the button in a little paper bag, stamped with a needle and thread in purple ink. It's kind of unnecessary, but nice.

I stow the paper bag in my backpack. "Thanks. Happy Thanksgiving."

She nods and waves at us, and I push my way out of the shop, Leo right behind me. The bell tinkles again.

As soon as we're on the sidewalk, the woman turns the sign in the door to CLOSED.

"Wow." Leo's eyebrows jump. "Guess we were just in time."

"Yeah." My skin prickles. "I guess so."

And then my phone buzzes.

EIGHT

LEO

ABBY PULLS OUT her phone and her eyes go wide. "Oh, shit."

"What?"

"It's Kat. We lost track of time . . ." She's texting madly.

I pull out my own phone. I have a text message, too. From five minutes ago.

EVAN

Wtf where are you

Crap. I could swear none of that took very long. How has so much time passed?

I open Google Maps. The show starts at two. And it's . . . where is it again?

"We should go, right?" Abby is still texting. Her voice has an edge of panic. "I mean, they must let people in even if they get there late . . ."

I find the theater I'm about seventy-five percent sure I'm supposed to be at, and look up directions. Twenty-five minutes on the subway. Minimum. We definitely won't make it in time.

My phone buzzes. The continuous buzz of FaceTime.

I answer with the best innocent grin I can muster. "Hey, Evan."

Evan does not frown very often. He's usually pretty stubbornly sunny. But he's frowning now, which makes his jawline look even more chiseled. It's like being glared at by Thor. "Where are you?"

"Uh . . . Chinatown."

"Chinatown?"

"We lost track of time. A little."

"Leopold, I am standing here holding a ticket for you, which I only have because I convinced Mr. Corbin that you were in the bathroom."

I've always known Evan was the dad of marching band, but his Disappointed Voice is a real guilt trip.

"We didn't do this on purpose!" I look around, praying there's a subway stop on this block. There isn't. Of course. "Look, we can go get on a subway train now, but we won't get there before the show starts."

Evan sighs heavily. "I guess I could tell Mr. Corbin you're having violent diarrhea—"

"Evan."

"—and someone needs to wait with your ticket, but he won't be super impressed when you walk in through the front door. Something tells me he won't buy you running to another building to have violent diarrhea."

"Would you *stop* saying *diarrhea*?"

Abby looks up from her phone. "Maybe we should just tell our chaperones. They're going to find out eventually anyway."

I groan. She's probably right. Mr. Corbin will find out I'm not in the bathroom and Abby's chaperone will find out she's not wherever Kat said she was. The only thing we'll have accomplished is getting lost, losing her book, upending all her plans, and finding one pig-shaped button . . .

And *fuck*. Why do I care? Why did I suggest this whole epic confession of love? I don't believe in the Universe. All it's done so far is screw me over.

But I do. Care. Because it's a distraction, or because I still feel guilty, or because for some reason I decided to try to make her laugh by putting on those sunglasses, and then she *did* laugh, and for the first time today, I forgot about tomorrow.

Maybe it's just that if Abby's bonkers plan actually results in a happy ending, I'll feel less like I'm doomed. Or I'm hell-bent on being obstinate. I don't know.

"Evan," I say, "I'm gonna text you something in a sec." And I end the call, right as he's opening his mouth to protest. Turn to Abby. "We're going to miss the beginning of the shows."

She blinks at me. "Yeah, I know."

"If we go now, somebody will have to wait to give us tickets, which means our cover will be blown and we'll be busted."

"Yeah, I *know*."

"So . . ." I swallow. "What if we skip the Broadway shows?"

"Skip . . . What?"

"Skip the shows. All you've got is a button. If we skip the shows, we'll have—I don't know—two or three more hours, right? We can hit those other book locations you talked about. We could actually *do* it—find Kat a souvenir from every place. Plan your whole epic scene." My pulse races. This is nuts. "If Evan can cover for me and Kat can cover for you, then we can meet them after the shows end and nobody will be the wiser."

Abby's mouth is open. She gapes at me for several seconds before she finally manages to say, "How would Evan and Kat cover for us? There are tickets. The chaperones have lists. If there's a literal empty seat in the theater, they'll notice."

"I . . . have an idea about that." (A nuts idea.) "Do you think Kat would cover for you?"

Abby chews her lip. She looks back down at her phone. One thumb hovers over the screen, like she's trying to decide if she should text Kat. Tell her I'm officially off my rocker and she's ditching me right now.

Then—"Yeah," Abby says. "I think so."

I look back at my phone. "What's your number? And Kat's? We should start a group chat."

In my imagination, the next several minutes go like this:

Evan, face carefully arranged into an expression of uncomfortable concern (which is pretty much how he looks every time he empties his tuba spit valves), informs Mr. Corbin that he gave me my ticket, but I'm still in the bathroom.

Mr. Corbin offers to check on me, pauses, looks even more uncomfortable than Evan, and asks if Mrs. Waggoner should check on me instead.

Evan, now looking deeply offended, makes himself as tall as possible and says in a surly voice that maybe nobody should check on me and just trust that I can find my own way into the theater because I'm almost seventeen years old. And also because he's already told me to find an usher to show me to my seat when there's a good break.

Mr. Corbin takes the easy way out and admits this is actually a perfectly fine plan. Because the only alternative is dealing with the Logistical Headache, and that's the last thing he needs right now. Which bathroom is the Logistical Headache even in? Nobody wants to know.

Meanwhile, Kat informs her chaperone that Abby isn't feeling well and is also in the bathroom. Kat's chaperone also asks if she should check on Abby, but Kat sweetly informs her that it's okay, she's already asked *another* chaperone to check on Abby.

If everything goes according to plan up to this point, Evan and Kat will be in the theater, enlisting some help. Abby assured me her friends Morgan and Amira would be on board, and I know Gina will have my back, since Gina's always down for sticking it to anybody who makes rules, as a general principle.

Plus, when you're in marching band, you stick together. That's what gets drilled into us during every single rehearsal.

I'm hoping it applies outside of rehearsal, too. Because for this to work, we kind of need a chain of seat switching. However much switching it takes for the seats that are supposed to belong to me and Abby to be as far away from any chaperone as possible.

And then, with the help of some well-timed diversions right before the show, Kat and Evan will rig up—employing backpacks stuffed inside sweatshirts and sweatshirts stuffed inside band jackets—a fake me and a fake Abby to sit in our seats.

Then we hope the chaperones are tired. Too tired and too far away to look that closely in a darkened theater. Too grateful for the chance to sit down and zone out for three hours.

Given how overwhelmed Mr. Corbin looked, even before I got lost, this seems plausible. Especially since Abby said her band is down a chaperone, thanks to food poisoning.

So now Abby and I are standing awkwardly on a street corner, watching our phones. Waiting to find out if any of this has worked in real life.

Maybe we should have headed for the subway, just in case. Abby glanced at me, a few times, and I wondered if she wanted to suggest that. If she was waiting for me to.

But neither of us said anything. So here we are. Abby chews her lip. I chew my nails, bouncing my leg up and down, hitting my heel against the pavement.

This is a terrible idea. Complete lunacy.

We're about to be super busted. I can't even begin to imagine what my family will say when the school calls them. On the plus side, it might be a nice distraction from the forthcoming Outageddon.

On the minus side, I'll definitely be grounded for months.

Abby opens her mouth, and I'm convinced she's finally going to say it. Say we should quit now and hop on a train and face whatever's waiting for us . . .

And then our phones buzz. In perfect unison. A text on the new group chain.

EVAN
Guys I think it worked

Five seconds later, a text from Kat:

KAT
Morgan just faked an epic meltdown on the condition Amira film it for TikTok

EVAN
Nice! Did it work?

KAT
Say hello to fake Abby

She's included a very dim selfie of her pointing to a lumpy stuffed band jacket. On top of the band jacket is someone's purse, a thick winter beanie pulled over it.

EVAN
I'll see ur fake Abby and raise u fake Leo

He sends a picture of a backpack-stuffed hoodie, another sweatshirt stuffed in the hood to make it stand up like a head. In the seat next to the thing is Gina, stony-faced and giving a thumbs-up.

KAT
Wow we are artists

It worked.

This is the weirdest group text. But it worked.

ABBY
Thank you!! You guys are the best

I look up at her. She's looking back at me. A smile creeps slowly onto her face.

"They did it," she says.

"Yeah." My heart hammers.

KAT
Show is starting

EVAN
Godspeed and see y'all on the other side!

Abby lets her breath out, slow and shaky. "So . . . we have more time."

We have hours. Hours of time, just us.

"Where next?" I ask. "What's another place in the book?"

Abby looks down at her phone, pulling up a map. She's quiet for so long that I wonder if she's having second thoughts.

But then she grins. "Let's go to Union Square."

NINE

ABBY

"OKAY," LEO SAYS. The words *Union Square* clearly mean nothing to him. "Where's that?"

"Really close." I hold up my phone, hoping my hand doesn't shake. I feel almost light-headed. "Fifteen minutes on the subway. It's just a little farther up . . . like, up on the map. Is that what uptown means?"

Leo frowns. "I haven't heard of Union Square."

"It's where Clara Jane goes after Chinatown. Stop frowning."

"I'm not frowning," he says, still frowning.

I roll my eyes, but I'm smiling as I go back to the map on my phone. "We should still have some fare left, right? Both our bands were taking the subway to the shows . . ."

"Yeah. I think so."

"Okay. Then we should be able to get up to Union Square, and then one more trip after that, since we didn't use the fare that was meant for the subway tour itself. So that should get us to the theaters—assuming we can't walk."

He blinks, looking totally lost. "Um. Great. Good plan."

I can't help grinning. "Did you say you play drums?"

"Yeah." Now he looks suspicious. "So?"

I nod sagely. "That explains it."

He blinks at me. "Explains what?"

"Why you don't know how to plan."

He glowers. "Okay, first of all, I just planned a whole lot of stuff, remember? And second of all, what do you play?"

I have a nasty feeling I've walked into a trap. "Clarinet..."

Leo huffs. "Well, that explains that."

"What?"

"Why you're a giant nerd."

"Um, seriously? That's the best you can come up with? You know we're both band nerds, right?"

For a few seconds, he just stands there. I can practically see the gears turning in his brain while he tries to form a comeback. In the end, he shrugs. "Fair."

He starts walking.

"We're actually going this way." I fight to keep a straight face and point over my shoulder, toward what my phone promises me is Canal Street.

Leo silently turns on his heel and stalks past me in the other direction.

The Canal Street station has the same tile-lined passageways as every other subway station I've seen so far, but it's way more confusing. Tunnels split off in multiple directions, some going down, some going up, and the whole place rumbles—trains coming and going on platforms I can't see. It's like a labyrinth.

We follow signs for the 6 train. The *uptown* 6 train toward Pelham Bay Park, because I'm not making *that* mistake again. We reach the platform just as the tunnel begins to glow, and a moment later, the train roars out, sending a blast of warm wind into our faces. The timing is so perfect I shiver.

It's four stops to Union Square. I stand next to Leo, both of us grasping the pole in the middle of the train car. I can't stop fidgeting, and I can't figure out what to say to make conversation. We're on our way, and I'm suddenly a jumble of nerves.

I pull out my phone to check the map, and then the time, and somehow I end up in my text messages.

KAT

Are u sure u don't want to try to sneak in late??

It's the last text she sent on the chain that's just the two of us, before Leo started the group chat to explain his whole wild plan.

I didn't reply. I couldn't figure out what to say in the moment. I jumped on the group chat instead.

My thumbs hover over the keyboard. The show's already started, but she has notifications silenced . . .

ME

Sorry I'm missing it. Thanks for covering. I'll explain more later!

I stick my phone back in my pocket. A twinge of guilt goes through me—Kat was so excited for *Wicked*. But she's still seeing it, still seeing a real Broadway show, even if I'm not with her. She can tell me all about it later.

And the truth is . . .

The truth is I feel just like Clara Jane felt in chapter twenty-one. *Giddy and hopeful, and in the right place.*

I glance at Leo. He's tapping his fingers on the pole, drumming out a rhythm, eyes bouncing around the train car.

A little bubble of warmth rises in my chest. He's as fidgety as I am.

The Union Square stop is also called *14th Street*, apparently, because New York City isn't confusing enough. At least the station is less of a maze than Canal Street, so Leo and I find our way out pretty easily. Up the stairs, through the turnstiles, up some more stairs to the street . . .

And right into Christmas Central.

I don't know what I was expecting—there's not a whole lot of description of Union Square in *THRoCJ*—but it wasn't rows and rows of red-and-white-striped tents, packed all around us, edged with fake evergreen garlands and red bows. Twinkling white lights crisscross between the tents, which themselves are packed with stuff. Candles, Christmas ornaments, potted plants, stacks of chocolates, knitted hats . . . I even see sock puppets. And the whole place smells like sugar, and cinnamon, and roasting nuts. Which is wonderful, and also oddly specific. Are they really roasting nuts somewhere around here?

Above the tents is a banner that reads UNION SQUARE HOLIDAY MARKET.

"What," Leo says, "is this."

He's looking at the tents like we've come out of the subway onto an alien planet. I can't help grinning. "Your worst nightmare. Magical happiness."

Leo groans. "I don't hate happiness, okay?"

I grab his sleeve. "Sure, okay. Come on."

He sighs but lets me pull him into the maze of tents.

The holiday market is bright and colorful and crowded, in a comfortable way. Enough people to make it feel bustling and alive, but not so many that we end up getting jostled around.

So . . . I don't really *need* to hang on to Leo. But there are so many things I want to look at, and I don't want to rush into the crowd without him, so I grasp his sleeve and pull him over to a stand selling chocolates as big as ping-pong balls. And then I tug him over to a booth with pendants made of flower blossoms pressed into glass. And by the time we're taking in a wildly colorful display of painted lanterns and twinkling suncatchers, my arm is looped through Leo's, and it just seems easier to leave it there.

Anyway, he doesn't seem to mind.

Just like he didn't seem to mind when I told him about the time I tried to press flowers and they turned all moldy, while we were in the booth with the glass pendants. Or when I babbled about the Chocolate Chip Incident of Doom at our pancake breakfast fundraiser, while we stared at the giant chocolates. (There was a five-pound bag of chocolate chips. It did not have strong seams.)

Every time I start to worry I'm talking too much, Leo drops in a comment. Agreeing with me. Or poking fun (in a gentle way) at whatever I'm looking at. The kind of comment that means he's actually listening to me; the kind of comment that means he's not bored.

He's a lot different than the asshole I thought he was a couple hours ago.

Eventually, Leo and I get through one whole row of tents and come out the other side into the rest of Union Square. Which . . . isn't quite as magnificent as I thought it would be. It's nice, but it's really just a mostly paved park, with bare trees standing on islands of slowly browning grass, surrounded by black iron benches. I guess it probably looks nicer in the summer, when everything is leafy and green.

It's clearly not the sort of place that has a gift shop.

"I guess we could look for an acorn," Leo says. "Maybe a blade of grass."

I snort. "Right. We definitely don't have those things in Missouri."

"Some dirt?"

I roll my eyes.

"Yeah, you're right." Leo nods his head, serious. "New York City dirt is probably unnecessarily pretentious."

Somehow, I manage to keep a straight face. "So we should probably go back and look at more of the tents, right?"

"The only way I'm putting up with that much twinkly stuff is if I also get some hot chocolate," Leo says.

"Okay. That seems fair."

We turn back around and walk back into the rows of tents, stopping first at a stand selling roasted nuts, warm apple cider, and hot chocolate. It smells so good that I can't resist either, so Leo and I both get little paper cups of hot chocolate, and a small pastry bag of nuts to split. It's kind of expensive—six dollars for each cup, plus another four for the nuts. The coffee shop in Westvale sells hot chocolate for $2.50. But at least the stand takes cards, which means I can use the debit card I got after I started working at Sundae Fun Day.

Leo pays for his hot chocolate with a wrinkled ten-dollar bill scrounged out of his pocket, and then holds out two dollars to me when he gets change.

I'm holding hot chocolate and nuts. I don't have a free hand. "I can cover these, if you want." I wave the bag of nuts.

"Nope." He carefully tucks the crumpled dollar bills into the pocket of my band jacket.

We can't really walk arm in arm when we're both holding hot chocolate, and we have to keep passing the bag of nuts back and forth so whoever has a free hand can eat some. It could be awkward, both of us trying to hold the bag while the other person gets a handful. But instead, it makes me laugh. Even Leo grins.

And anyway, it's worth it. The hot chocolate is delicious, and the nuts are warm and sticky and sweet.

We both have to lick our fingers when we're done, trying to get rid of the leftover tackiness.

"I didn't think this through," Leo says, frowning and rubbing his fingers together.

"Maybe there are napkins somewhere?" But something catches my eye, and I'm suddenly distracted. "Hey, what about this?"

Leo follows me to a tent selling hundreds of Christmas ornaments in a swirling mess of gold and silver, red and green, glitter and crystals. "I don't see napkins—"

"No, I mean—a souvenir, look." I pull him into the tent, toward the ornament I've spotted. "It doesn't exactly scream *Union Square,* I guess, but Kat plays flute . . ." I carefully lift the tiny silver flute ornament off its hook and hold it up. It's delicately beautiful, with a pinpricked hole for the mouthpiece and perfect renditions of all the keys.

Leo leans down and squints at it. "Yeah. That's really pretty."

He's suddenly close, studying the ornament dangling off my finger, his face level with mine. I could count the freckles on his nose.

He catches my eye, past the ornament, and smiles. A real smile. All the glitter and crystals around us dance in his eyes.

And just for a second, my breath hitches. A catch in my lungs, as though they forgot how to expand.

I quickly look back down at the ornament. "Yeah. I'll . . . I'll get this." I lay it carefully on my palm and turn around to join the line by the cash register, pulling out my wallet.

At least my lungs are working again, even though Leo's smile is still stuck in my mind.

The woman behind the register wraps the ornament in another tiny paper bag, which I tuck into an inside pocket of my backpack, right next to the button. I turn back to the hooks of ornaments, where I left Leo.

He's gone.

Crap. How did I lose him? Or did he lose me? Was I actually driving him up the wall the whole time I was babbling and now he's decided to ditch me?

I turn in a circle, standing on my toes, trying to see past the other customers in the tent.

And there's Leo. Waiting for me outside, squinting up at the cloudy sky.

Oh, thank god.

"Hey," he says, when I duck out of the tent. "I got some bad news."

Oh, no. The chaperones discovered the fakes. It's over.

He points up to the sky. "I think it's starting to rain."

As if on cue, a drop of water lands on my nose. Another one hits my forehead. The clouds have turned a heavy, grayish blue and it's starting to sprinkle—barely.

"Seriously?" I whack his arm. "You lead with *I have some bad news* when it's just some drizzle?"

Leo looks down at me and opens his mouth.

And that, of course, is when it starts to pour.

TEN

LEO

"**OH, COME ON!**" I squeeze my eyes shut. My face is getting assaulted. This rain is torrential—hundreds of tiny daggers slicing down from the sky. "Give me a break, New York!"

Around us, the whole holiday market devolves into chaos and cursing. Everyone scrambling under the tents for cover, stepping on each other's feet. Vendors throw towels over their merchandise as their tents start leaking at the seams.

Abby bursts out laughing.

I squint at her, holding my hand up to shield my eyes from the downpour. We're getting drenched. I'm already freezing.

But Abby is standing there laughing, water dripping down the ends of her curly hair and darkening the shoulders of her jacket. "This is my fault!"

Wait. What?

"I just had to say *drizzle,* and this is what we get." She wipes rain out of her eyes. "What is even going on today?"

I stare at her. She's slowly turning around in a circle, holding her arms out, laughing, like this sudden downpour isn't ruining all our plans.

Laughing just like she did back in Chinatown, when I put on those sunglasses. Laughing like she really doesn't give a fuck who sees her or what they think.

And watching her, I feel suddenly weightless.

We're getting poured on, in the middle of Manhattan, after getting on the wrong train, ending up in the wrong place, and skipping out on two Broadway shows while stuffed versions of ourselves sit in the theater. This day is ridiculous.

I can't help it. I start laughing, too. For a moment, the cold fades to the background, and the rain running down the back of my neck isn't so annoying.

And then . . . okay, it's actually getting under my binder now. "We should probably get somewhere dry!" I yell.

Abby lowers her arms. "Where's the subway?"

I look around, but I have no idea. I've gotten completely turned around in all these rows of tents, and the rain is turning everything into a grayish blur. "Uh . . . let's try this way."

I take off, jogging awkwardly through the tents. My sneakers are so soggy they squish on the pavement. At least my fingers are very definitely not sticky anymore.

Abby follows me. "Maybe up there?" She points to the gap at the end of the row.

But instead of the subway station, this row dead-ends in an intersection. Must be one corner of Union Square. Skyscrapers loom across the street and a city bus rumbles slowly past. I turn around. The tents are all behind us now, which probably means the subway station is somewhere back there, too.

"I think I see another entrance!" Abby elbows me and points. Across the street in front of us is a green-and-white lamp, and a dark green railing . . .

The light changes. We have the walk signal. And at this point, that entrance across the street is probably closer than the subway station behind us.

"Let's go." I jump the puddle forming near the curb and jog across the street, Abby right behind me.

But when we get to the subway entrance, it's blocked off with yellow tape. A plastic sign reads TEMPORARILY CLOSED—PLEASE USE ANOTHER ENTRANCE.

Abby grabs my arm. "Come on." She pulls me around the corner and down the side street. For a second, I think maybe she's seen another entrance or something, until I realize she's heading for the movie theater at the end of the block, and the big awning stretching over the sidewalk, showtimes blinking in a digital stream around its edge.

We duck under the awning and immediately get hit with the warm, salty smell of popcorn.

Great. Now I'm hungry.

"So . . . now what?" My teeth are chattering. "We wait until this lets up?"

Abby is shivering, too, poking at her phone, eyebrows pulled together. "We can still go to another place from the book. We just need one that's inside, out of the rain."

"Uh, unless it's literally this movie theater, we still have to go out in the rain to get there."

"We could take the subway." She looks up with a grin. "Chelsea Market."

"What's that?"

"Another place from the book! And it's inside—at least, I'm pretty sure it's inside. It's inside in the book. Anyway"—she goes back to her phone—"it looks like we can take a train straight there."

I groan. "So now we have to go all the way back through all those tents?"

"No, there's another stop. Look." She holds out her phone and points at a little blue dot on the map. "We're on this corner, and here's the train." She points at a blue square with an *M* in the middle. "We just have to go down Thirteenth Street, and then up a little bit."

It *looks* close enough. Not really any farther than going back the way we came.

"Okay." It's not like I can get *more* soaked. "Let's go."

We duck back out into the rain, jogging across the street. At the end of the next block, I glance up at the street signs, posted perpendicular to each other on a lamp post.

Wait a minute . . . I grab Abby's jacket sleeve and pull us over, under another awning—this one bright red. "I thought you said we were supposed to go down Thirteenth Street."

Abby looks confused. "Yeah."

"I think this is Broadway."

She looks up. Narrows her eyes at the signs. BROADWAY and E 12 ST. "But I thought we were . . ." She pulls out her phone. "Oh, crap. Sorry, I got turned around. I thought *this* was Thirteenth Street . . ."

"It's okay." I probably would have gotten turned around even worse, but I'm not going to tell her that. I just wave a hand at the storefront next to us. "Look, let's go in here, find a bathroom with paper towels, or a dryer, or something, and dry off a little bit. Maybe the rain will stop soon."

We both look out past the awning. It's still pouring.

Abby sighs. "I guess it wouldn't be great if we woke up with colds on parade morning."

Yikes. I hadn't even thought of that. Sure, my family might implode once they find out I'm trans, but honestly, I think Grandma Brewer will be even madder if she doesn't get to see me in the parade at all.

I lead the way to the store entrance, pulling open one of the glass doors. Through a second set of glass doors and then we scuff our shoes on the long black mat. And Abby's jaw drops.

We're in a bookstore. The biggest bookstore I've ever seen. The floors are worn wood, the ceiling soars high above our heads, and every square inch of space is packed with books. Books on tables. Books in boxes. Books on shelves so tall that anything near the top would be impossible to reach without a ladder. New books, worn and used books, huge textbooks and tiny paperbacks. And it all just keeps going—like a warehouse of books. There's even a Christmas tree made out of books with green covers, draped in white twinkling lights.

"This place is amazing," Abby whispers. And then she shivers. "Let's look for the bathroom, though."

Right. I go up to the counter with the cash registers. "Um, excuse me?"

A woman turns around. Her blondish brown hair is twirled up on her head with two sticks and she's wearing a shirt that says STRAND in stark red letters. Maybe that's the name of this store. "Can I help you?"

"Yeah." I wave my hand vaguely toward Abby. "We were just wondering where—"

"Oh." The woman looks at me and then at Abby. "Yeah, go straight to the back and then take the elevator to your left up to the third floor, and then you'll be all set."

"Great." How'd she guess so fast? Do we really look that bedraggled? "Thanks."

"You bet." And she winks at me.

Uh.

What?

I go back to Abby, who has her phone out and seems to be taking pictures of a bulletin board full of flyers near the door. "I think that lady was flirting with me."

Abby looks up and quickly shoves her phone in her pocket. "What? What lady?"

"The one behind the desk."

Abby looks past me. Her expression turns doubtful. "Kind of just looks like she's unpacking books, Leo."

"She *winked* at . . . Never mind. Were you taking a picture?"

"No." She shifts. "Yes. Just a funny notice. On the board." She flaps a hand at it. "Did you find out where the bathroom is?"

"Yeah. This way."

We drip our way through the bookstore, under evergreen garlands strung from the ceiling, shoes squeaking on the floor, while weird indie songs with sleigh bells in them filter through the speakers. Sure enough, there's a lone elevator, all the way at the back of the store, next to a shelf of used self-help books.

The doors creak open as soon as I hit the button, like the elevator was waiting for us. It's old inside and kind of janky, the complete opposite of the slick elevators with their TV screens back at the hotel.

This elevator groans its way up to the third floor. When the doors open, I'm expecting another giant room full of books, but the room we get is much smaller. It looks more like the stuffy library of some reclusive professor. The walls are wood paneling, there's a dark Persian rug on the floor, and the built-in shelves are lined with old books in various shades of brown and blue and black. I half expect a guy in tweed to be sitting and smoking a pipe in an armchair.

There are several armchairs, but no guys in tweed. Just a bunch of teenagers, all around our age, and all staring at us.

"Oh, *hell* yeah!" The closest one, who's incredibly pale, with short, bright blue hair and equally bright red glasses, pops up from their chair like someone lit a firecracker under their butt. "You are *just* in time, we really need more people for this."

"Wow, real welcoming, Rae." A tall, lanky Black guy in a gray sweater stands up in the corner. "Hey, I'm Oliver. We're glad you came."

He sounds like my guidance counselor.

"Rae planned today's activity," says the Black girl next to him, "so they're a little hyper."

"Um . . ." Abby looks as lost as I feel. "Rae?"

"That's me!" The blue-haired person gives Abby a huge grin and points to the nearest armchair. "You can dump your coats there, if you want."

"Is it raining outside?" says a fourth person with light brown skin, whose black hair is pulled up in a knot. The sides of her head are shaved.

Rae gives her a look. "Uh, *yeah,* don't you hear it?"

"Is that what that pounding noise is? I thought maybe it was the radiators."

"How about we introduce ourselves?" Oliver says mildly.

"Sorry!" Rae gives us an apologetic look. "We haven't had anybody new join in a few months. I'm Rae. They, them pronouns."

"Oliver," says Oliver. "He, him."

The Black girl next to him says, "I'm Delia. She, her."

The girl with the cool haircut says, "Gabi. She, her, or sometimes they, them."

There's also a white girl with purple hair down to her shoulders ("Skye, she, her"), a person with a straight black ponytail and an earring ("Dylan, they, them"), and a blond girl in bright yellow overalls who has her arm looped through Dylan's ("Ida, she, her.").

It all goes by so fast that for a second, all I can do is blink.

Abby recovers first. "I'm, um, Abby. She, her. And this is Leo—he, him—and we were, uh, looking for the bathroom?"

"There isn't a bathroom up here," Rae says, like this should be obvious.

"Aren't you guys queer?" says Dylan.

Oliver immediately shoots them a Look. "We don't make people choose labels, Dylan, remember?"

"I was just asking!"

"Why are you up here if you were looking for the bathroom?" Rae says.

What is going on? "Because we got soaked outside," I say, "so I asked the cashier—"

"*Oh*," says Delia, like everything has been revealed, "you just wanted a bathroom where you could dry off before you came up?"

Now I'm even more confused. "What?"

"There's a bathroom on the second floor if you want to dry off before we start," Skye says cheerfully.

This makes no sense. "The cashier sent us up here," I say. "When I asked for a bathroom."

Everyone stares at me.

Finally, Oliver says, "You mean you're *not* here for the QYBC Triple-A?"

"The what?"

"Queer Youth Book Club And Additional Activities," Rae says helpfully.

Are they joking? "That's a terrible name."

Abby elbows me in the ribs. (Ouch.) "He didn't mean that."

Gabi raises an eyebrow. "He looks like he did."

Abby sighs. "That's just his face."

"I wanted to name it Quibble," Dylan says. "Queer Inclusive Book Babes Love Everything."

"We *know,* Dylan," says Oliver, the mild facade cracking.

Abby leans closer to me. "Leo, did you actually *say* we were looking for the bathroom?" she whispers.

"What do you mean?"

"To the cashier? Like, did you say *bathroom*?"

"No . . . I started to, but she seemed to get it and told us to take the elevator, and then she *winked* at me, and I told you, it weirded me out that she was flirting with . . ." My brain suddenly catches up. "Oh."

Hits like a brick. She thought I was asking about the queer book club or whatever this group is. I thought she got it, but *she* thought she Got It and was saving me all kinds of awkwardness.

Great. Do I really look that queer? Or trans?

I can't decide how I feel about that. Nobody's ever looked at me and immediately directed me toward a group of queers, but then again . . . there *aren't* any other queers in Springfield to be directed toward. Except Gina. And Zuri, but nobody knows that except me and Gina.

Rae claps their hands together, interrupting Oliver and Dylan, who are now arguing over why the club can't be called Quibble. "Look, you guys are here now, and I planned this activity for eight people, and Jude and Mateo clearly aren't showing up because they are *flakes,* so as long as you're not raging homophobes, can you stay?"

"Um," Abby says.

"Rae," Gabi says, "if they aren't queer—"

"We're queer," Abby says defensively.

Gabi looks at her in surprise. So do I.

Abby fidgets with a snap on her jacket. "Well, I'm pretty sure I am. I think. I guess I shouldn't speak for anyone else . . ." She glances at me.

I groan inwardly. Way to put me on the spot, Abby.

But at the same time, I'm staring back at the biggest group of queers I've ever met. If I can't say this stuff here, where can I say it?

Why is this so complicated?

"I'm trans," I say.

Oliver shrugs. "Cool."

Dylan gives me a little *what's up* chin jerk. "Me, too," they say.

"And me." Skye grins.

It's the most non-reaction reaction I've ever gotten. It's actually kind of nice.

"Okay!" Rae pulls out a notebook covered in unicorn stickers out of their bag. "So, subbing you two in for Jude and Mateo—"

Wait a minute.

"—that means Team One is Delia, Skye, Ida, and"—Rae squints at Abby—"what's your name again?"

"Abby." She's back to looking confused. "But—"

"Great! And then Team Two is Oliver, Dylan, Gabi, and the Grinch."

"Hey!"

Rae waves me off. "I'm kidding, I know your name is Leo. Okay, so I've prepared several categories, and once you find a book that matches a category, you have to take it off the shelf so the other team can't claim it. But take a picture with your phone of where it goes on the shelf so we can replace all the books when we're done and nobody in the store will get mad at us. Like last time." Rae shoots Dylan a pointed look.

Dylan stares very intently at their fingernails.

Rae pulls several index cards out of their unicorn folder. "The categories are fantasy, science fiction—"

"Which are *not* the same thing," Delia says, sort of menacingly, looking right at us like we might be inclined to disagree.

"—historical fiction, and romance. Young adult and adult books both count, but no nonfiction. For romance, you have to find a book that features a shirtless guy on the cover—"

"Of *course*," Ida groans.

"Rae loves shirtless guys," Skye says to us.

"For historical fiction"—Rae scowls at Skye—"you need a book featuring two of the three following subjects: ships, war, or romance forbidden by class difference."

"Oh my god, Rae," says Gabi, "you sound like my English teacher."

Rae looks unfazed. "For fantasy, the book *must* feature a female protagonist—trans women included, of course—and must also have a dragon or a sword of significance on the cover. For science fiction, it must be written by a woman, or a trans or nonbinary individual, and must feature either spaceships *or* robots, but not both. And the last rule: If any of the books you find have queer characters, your team gets an extra five points." Rae places a hand dramatically on their chest. "Points to be awarded by me as the scorekeeper, obviously."

"So basically," Oliver says, "if you find a queer book, you automatically win."

Rae thinks about this for a minute, tapping their chin. "Yeah, pretty much."

Delia grins. "Awesome."

"So how long do we have to find these books?" Ida asks.

"Thirty minutes to find all your titles," Rae says. They hand out two index cards, one to Oliver and one to Ida. "We can all set timers on our phones so we're synced up. I've made these cards with all of the categories and rules on them, so you can make sure you've got everything covered."

"Wait a minute." This is getting out of hand. "What are we doing?"

Rae huffs, like I haven't been paying attention. "It's a book scavenger hunt! Are you going to take off your coats or just keep dripping everywhere?"

I open my mouth, but Abby's already ditching her backpack and shrugging out of her drenched band jacket.

Wait. We're doing this?

"Phones out!" Rae yells.

I guess we're doing this. I dump my backpack on the floor, pull off my damp beanie, stuff it in the pocket of my jacket, and fling my jacket at one of the armchairs.

"Go!" Rae shouts.

The members of The-Club-That-Should-Be-Known-As-Quibble thunder for the elevator like this is an actual race. Abby shoots me a grin and dashes after them.

I'm a little tempted to plunk down in an armchair. I hate any group activity that isn't a marching band practice or performance. Just ask Evan. He had to drag me through every game of Capture the Drum Major Mace at band camp. I don't care what Ms. Rinaldi says—there's no way that's a "band camp tradition" anywhere except Springfield.

But I'm not that much of a jerk. And curiosity gets the better of me.

So I crowd into the elevator along with everyone else, pulling out my phone. I manage to wedge myself into a corner where no one can see my phone screen and pull up a text message.

ME
What are we doing?

On the other side of the small elevator, Abby jerks and reaches into her pocket. She glances up at me, and then looks back at her phone. Is it just me, or is she biting back a grin?

ABBY
I know but it's only 30 minutes.

And it's with queer people

I suddenly feel like an asshole. Of course she wants to hang out with other queer people. At least at home I've got Gina. Abby doesn't know anyone else who's out.

And Abby's right, it's only thirty minutes. And it's clearly making her happy, so . . .

ME
OK fine. I'm in.

ABBY
Get ready to have your ass handed to you, book-nerd style!

I glance at her. She's still looking at her phone, but she's definitely grinning now.

ELEVEN

ABBY

THE SECOND THE elevator doors open on the first floor, Ida and Delia grab my arms and pull me over to a table full of beat-up paperbacks under a sign that says $1 BOOKS. Skye is right behind us.

"I think we should split up," Delia says. She's practically vibrating with excitement. "That way we can cover more ground."

"Yeah, but what if we all end up finding books in the same category?" Skye says.

"Well, we could coordinate . . ."

"That'll take too long," Ida says seriously. "We should stick together and all look for the same category. More eyes in one section will help."

Delia sighs. "Okay, fine, but I know the perfect fantasy book. Girl with a sword on the cover and everything . . ."

Ida shrugs. "Go grab it."

"*Yes.*" Delia blows us a kiss and disappears into the stacks.

"Where should we start?" Skye asks.

"Historical fiction," Ida says. "That's closest."

I trail after them, completely in awe. They actually know this bookstore—this huge bookstore in Manhattan—well enough to know exactly where the historical fiction section is. They must come here all the time. I imagine them riding the subway, or walking down the street, dodging through the holiday market, or whatever else happens in Union Square. Maybe on Saturdays, or maybe after school, like now. They must have come here right after school, right?

Imagine being able to just go to a bookstore in Manhattan, right after school.

"Here we go." Ida leads us into an aisle between two teetering shelves, so tall that a good half of the books crammed onto them are completely out of my reach.

I wonder if this store has those ladders on wheels. The kind that attach to the shelves, like in fancy libraries. That would be so cool. My fantasy house (the one I sometimes design in my head, imagining I'm super rich) definitely has a library with rolling ladders.

"Okay." Skye grabs the index card of categories from Ida. "Ships, war, and forbidden romance." She marches to the end of the aisle.

I don't even know where to start, but Ida's just pulling books off the shelves and inspecting their covers, so I turn to the shelf opposite her and start doing the same. Pull out a book, open the cover, skim the description to see if it might have anything we're looking for . . .

"So how long have you and Leo been together?" Ida asks.

The book I'm holding slips right through my fingers and hits the floor. *Thunk.* "Oh, uh . . ." I try to laugh. "We're not dating."

Ida glances at me. "Sorry. I just assumed, since you guys came in together and, you know, seem really comfortable."

Comfortable? Like . . . generally? Or around each other?

My mind goes back to Union Square, to walking through those tents with my arm through Leo's. Was that *comfortable*?

It felt easy. Like I could have been doing it all my life.

"Well, Leo's cool." I pick the book up off the floor and brush off the cover. "But I'm actually into . . . or . . . kind of in love with a girl."

My heart pounds, but all Ida says is "Gotcha." She flips through a book, sticks it back on the shelf, and pulls out another. "How long have you been with her?"

Oh, no. I'm handling this all wrong. "I'm . . . not with her, either, actually." I look down at the book in my hands. Does this have war in it? I have no idea. I can't focus on the description. "She's my best friend."

Ida gives me a knowing nod. "We've all been there."

Oh? "We have?"

She grins. "Pretty sure falling in love with your best friend is, like, a queer rite of passage."

It is?

I look back at the book I'm holding and force myself to read the description. No war. Or ships. The romance seems solidly permissible. I put it back on the shelf.

"Does it ever work out?" My voice sounds small, in my own ears. Small and kind of desperate.

Ida looks at me again. "Is she queer?"

I pull down another book. "I don't know. Maybe. I think she might be."

"Why don't you just ask her?"

Ida says this like it's the simplest thing in the world. For a second, I don't know how to answer.

Because nobody's out, where I'm from.

Because nobody talks about this stuff, unless they're trying to ban talking about this stuff.

Because if anyone is talking about this stuff, like this, I haven't found them, and I don't even know where to start looking.

But I'm not sure how to explain this to her, this girl in bright yellow overalls and pink eyeshadow, with three earrings in each ear, her dark blond hair twisted up into two pigtail knots on her head. This girl who's wearing Doc Marten boots and clearly doesn't care if people look at her, or probably what they think when they do.

This girl in New York City, who hangs out with her queer book club in a bookstore.

"I haven't felt ready to do that," I say. That, at least, is true.

"Got it!" Skye shouts. She triumphantly holds up a book featuring a sailing ship on the cover. "Boats and war. And bestie dude friends but unfortunately it does not look queer."

"Nice." Ida skips over and plucks the index card out of Skye's hand. "What should we do next?"

"Sci-fi," Skye says with determination. "This way."

I slip the book I'm holding back onto the shelf as carefully as I can and jog after them through the store, glancing around for Leo. But I don't see him; he must be hidden somewhere in the stacks.

I wonder what kind of book he's looking for.

I wonder if he's frowning yet.

"Thinking about your gal pal?" Ida nudges me with her elbow.

"What?"

"You were smiling." She waggles her eyebrows at me.

Was I?

"What gal pal?" Skye asks.

"Abby's crushing on her best friend," Ida says.

"Oh, *no*." Skye's eyes widen. "Tell me the bestie is not straight."

We pass under the big SCIENCE FICTION sign hanging from the ceiling and into another aisle.

Where we come face-to-face with Dylan, who seems to be trying to look through three enormous books at once. "I got here first," they say.

Skye laughs. "You don't own the science fiction section." She grabs one of the books out of Dylan's grasp.

"Hey!" Dylan makes a grab for it and drops their other two books. *Thunk-thunk*. A nearby patron gives us a disapproving look.

"Aw, my babe with the butterfingers," Ida says. She kisses Dylan's cheek.

Dylan looks miffed and leans down, scrambling for the books on the floor. "You could give me a hand here."

"No way," Ida says. "I'm out to win this."

Dylan groans and scoops up the books, shuffling awkwardly to the end of the aisle to keep browsing.

"So tell me about this girl," Ida says, while Skye pages through the book she grabbed from Dylan.

"Oh. Um . . ." I pull out a random paperback. The author's first name is John. I flip to the bio just to make sure and, yeah, definitely a man. "Her name is Kat. We've been best friends since middle school and . . . we were at this bonfire thing for the end of school in May, and ended up holding hands and it was . . ."

Perfect. Magical. A moment I never wanted to end.

Except right now, in this moment, it feels . . . distant. Far away. Almost like it happened to someone else. All I'm thinking about is the reflection of all those crystal ornaments, dancing in Leo's eyes.

Ida glances up from a huge tome with a spaceship on the cover. "It was what?"

"Oh." I push Leo's smile out of my mind. "It was nothing. Or, I mean, nothing happened." My face heats up. "But I'm going to tell Kat that I like her—on this trip. In New York. That's the plan, anyway."

Ida's eyebrows jump. "You're not from New York?"

Crap. Maybe I shouldn't have said that. "No . . . I'm just visiting. I'm from Missouri. Near Kansas City?"

Ida narrows her eyes. "I'm not gonna lie to you, I have no idea where that is. Sorry."

"It's okay." I'm not sure if it is, but what did I expect? People in New York City probably don't think about anywhere else. "It's not really a place with other queer people."

Ida raises an eyebrow. "That's definitely not true."

I look at her in surprise. "Um, no offense, but you haven't been to the suburbs of Missouri."

"I know, but . . ." Ida grins. "There are always queer people."

How can she sound so sure? "Suburbs," I say again. "Of Missouri."

"There are *always* queer people." Ida's grin fades, but she's looking at me intensely. "Just because you can't see them, doesn't mean they aren't there. It's not like we all wear a pride flag on our foreheads or something."

Well, that's true, since I obviously don't.

I chew my lip, sliding one book back onto the shelf and pulling down another. I wonder if anyone else at school browses queer hashtags on Tumblr alone at night. I wonder if I might be able to find them somehow.

Or maybe there's a club like this one in Kansas City. I haven't really tried looking that hard. It felt like such a big thing to look for by myself. But I can drive now. I've borrowed my mom's car to drive me and Kat into Kansas City on the weekends.

Maybe my mom would let me borrow the car to drive by myself. I could say I was going to the bookstore. She wouldn't have to know—not right away.

"You should tell your best friend." Ida's gone back to pulling out books. "Or at least . . . think about it."

I want to ask whether she means *tell Kat I'm gay* or *tell Kat I'm in love with her*. There's sort of a big difference.

But before I can figure out how, Dylan lets out a whoop and holds up a book. "Victory is mine!" they shout, and dash away.

Ida grins after them.

Something catches in my brain. "Um, Ida?"

"Yeah?"

"How do you . . . identify?"

"Like . . . sexuality or gender identity?"

I swallow. "Both?"

She runs her fingers over the book spines. "I'm a girl and I like people," she says.

I feel slightly disappointed. "So, you don't feel like you're . . . gay?"

Ida shrugs. "Gay can mean a lot of things."

"Yeah. Yeah, totally. I was just wondering, because you're with Dylan . . ."

Ida looks at me. A little challenging. "So, you're asking, since Dylan is trans and nonbinary, what does that make me?"

I have a sudden desire to disappear into my hoodie like a turtle. "Yeah. I guess so."

Ida sighs. "I don't really like labels," she says. "I guess you could say I'm pansexual, because I like people, not genders, but . . . I like to say I just like people."

"So, theoretically . . ." My mouth has gone dry. "If I was definitely in love with my best friend but was also kind of attracted to, like, this trans guy . . ."

"You'd still be queer," Ida says. Her eyes narrow. "Wait a minute. You totally think Leo is hot."

"No!" It comes out louder than I mean it to. I look around, but the only person nearby is Skye, and she's still scouring the shelves. "Maybe. I don't know."

Ida frowns. "Hang on, is Leo from Missouri, too?"

"No, he's from—"

"Yes!" Skye holds a fat paperback above her head. "Got one! Lady author. Robots."

"You're on fire," says Ida. "Let's go find Delia."

We find Delia near the cookbooks, where she's using a particularly sturdy copy of *Joy of Cooking* as support for the book she's paging through.

"Where have you been?" Ida says.

Delia looks annoyed. "I couldn't find the book I had in mind so I had to keep looking. Took forever." She holds up the book she was paging through. "But I found one. Girl with sword, plus a dragon for good measure."

"So that just leaves romance," Skye says.

"Does the fantasy book have queerness in it?" I ask.

Delia freezes. Skye and Ida look at each other.

"Do we not have a queer book yet?" Delia says.

Skye digs her fingers into her purple hair. "I forgot. I can't believe I forgot a *queer book*. I'm *self*-erasing!"

"We can look for a queer romance book," Ida says.

"But we need a romance book with a shirtless dude on the front," Skye wails. "You really think we're going to find a book with a shirtless dude that's *also* queer?"

Wait. Shirtless dudes. Romance novel . . . "I think I know a book."

Skye looks at me like I've just told her there's a Santa Claus. "Really?"

I hope I haven't made a big mistake. "I mean, I can't guarantee I'll actually *find* the book . . ."

"I'll go back to fantasy," Delia says. "Maybe I can find a different queer book. Just in case."

"I'll go with you," Skye says.

Ida throws an arm around my shoulders. "Let's do this."

My stomach is a ball of anxiety as she steers us both toward the romance section. I really hope I'm accurately remembering the book I saw on the subway train this morning—the one that lady was reading, the lady who told us that the downtown A train was making local stops. That book had two shirtless guys on the cover. Embracing. That's a good sign, right?

A queer sign?

But I don't know the author's name. The lady's fingers were covering it up as she held up the book. I'm not even sure I can remember the title. It had the word *His* in it, right?

That's probably not helpful. The word *His* could be in hundreds of romance book titles.

"All right." Ida's arm slips away. "Here we are. What are we looking for?"

The romance section looks like every other section we've been in, except that more of the books are small paperbacks. Two women are browsing at the other end of the aisle, but they don't even look up.

I take a breath. "I'm not actually sure."

Ida looks confused. "I thought you said you knew what book to look for."

"I *do*, but I . . . can't totally remember the title. And I don't know the author." I brace myself. Everyone seems to feel so strongly about this scavenger hunt, and I don't want to let them down.

But Ida just says, "Okay. What kind of cover are we looking for?"

Of course. We can at least look at the spines. I close my eyes. "Gold letters for the title. White background. It was called something like *His . . .*" Come on, Abby. "*His Fair . . .* or no, *His Faithful . . .*"

"Start looking," Ida says. "Maybe it'll come to you."

We turn to opposite shelves. It seems like every third romance novel has gold lettering for the title, and a lot of them have white backgrounds. This might be tough. I let my eyes skim, looking for *His . . .*

Footsteps pound closer, and Delia and Skye come careening around the corner of the shelves.

"No dice," Delia says grimly. "We couldn't find anything that was queer *and* had a girl *and* a sword of significance."

Skye looks grumpy. "Who *wouldn't* want to read about lesbians with swords? Seriously, what's wrong with people?"

"How much time have we got left?" Delia asks.

"Four minutes," Ida says.

I tune them out. My eyes itch because I'm refusing to blink. I'm going to find this book and I'm going to win this scavenger hunt. I don't care if it's silly. I really want to win, because . . .

Well, I want to belong here, even just for this one half hour. I want to belong in this queer book club in a city I don't live in.

There.

It's right there, on the shelf in front of me: *His Fairest Prince,* shimmering in gold letters on the white spine. I pull the paperback out. It's creased and the corners are dog-eared—a used copy, definitely—but it's the right book. Two shirtless guys on the cover, gazing longingly at each other against the backdrop of a gleaming castle.

I flip the book over, scanning the description. It seems to be about a lonely baker who gets commissioned to make a cake for the queen's birthday celebration, but when he delivers it to the castle, he falls in love with the queen's son . . .

Yes. That's queer, all right. "I got it!"

The women at the end of the aisle look up in alarm, but Skye, Ida, and Delia rush over. Ida snatches the book out of my hands and reads the description herself. "Oh, *hell yeah.*"

"It's queer?" Skye asks.

Ida passes the book to her and drapes her arm around my shoulders again. "My girl Abby, coming in with the win."

"Oh my god, you're never leaving," Delia says, leaning over Skye's shoulder to read the book's description.

Ida's weight against me is warm and solid. Skye and Delia are smiling so big you'd think we'd won, like, the Midwest Marching Championships. I never want this moment to end. All of us here, looking for books on a rainy afternoon, being queer like it's no big deal, like it barely even registers.

Even if it also means so much at the same time.

"Okay, back upstairs, come on." Ida's arm slips off my shoulders, and she shoves Delia and Skye down the aisle. "We've only got two minutes left."

I pull out my phone to check the time. I've got a text notification, sitting there on the screen. I must have missed the vibration, too caught up in the scavenger hunt.

KAT

Got to intermission. Can't believe you're not here.

The magical moment breaks like a rubber band, sharp and sudden.

I'm supposed to be looking for souvenirs for Kat. Supposed to be planning an epic confession.

And instead, I'm ignoring her. Instead, I got swept up in a silly scavenger hunt with people I barely know.

I unlock my phone and tap on the Messages icon, but I can't think of anything to type. My mind goes to the flyer I saw on the bulletin board at the front of the store, while Leo was asking about the bathroom. The one I took a picture of, and then pretended I wasn't taking a picture of. I could send her the photo. She'd probably enjoy it, too.

But if I send it, she'll ask where I am and what I'm doing, and I don't know how to explain any of this.

"Abby, come on!" Ida waves at me. She and Delia and Skye are already heading back to the elevator.

I shove my phone back in my pocket and jog after them.

TWELVE

LEO

OLIVER THROWS ONE long arm around me and the other around Dylan, and propels us both out of the elevator. We speed through the bookstore after Gabi, who is already way ahead of us. I glance over my shoulder, trying to see where Abby's going, but her team has disappeared into the rows of shelves.

"Where to first?" Dylan's as bad a nail biter as I am. They look like a wreck.

"Fantasy," Gabi says over her shoulder. "There's a book I want to grab before Team Loser does."

Well, this got competitive fast.

"Maybe we should split up," Dylan says, in between nails. "Like, all of us look for different stuff?"

Gabi turns down an aisle, and Oliver steers us after her. "Hang on," she says, "I want to make sure I can find this book first . . ."

She drags her fingers along the book spines, eyes narrowed. She looks disturbingly like a velociraptor on the hunt. "Aha!" She pounces, pulling her prey off the shelf, and turns around to share her victory. "Bam. Sapphic girls with swords."

The book she's holding does indeed feature two girls with swords on the cover.

"You're sure it's sapphic?" Dylan looks ready to have a heart attack.

"Yes, I'm sure." Gabi rolls her eyes. "I read it. I mean, come on. *Sapphics* with *swords*."

"On brand for you," Oliver agrees. "What next?"

"Let's split up," Gabi says. She waves the book again. "I've got our queer rep covered, so if we split up, we can cover more ground, like Dylan suggested."

We should definitely do something, or Dylan is going to pass out from stress. How can anyone get this worked up over a scavenger hunt?

"I'll take historical," Oliver says.

Gabi laughs. "Saw that coming a mile away." I guess I must make a face without realizing it, because she looks at me and says, "Oliver's obsessed with world wars and weird shipwrecks."

"I am not," Oliver says irritably.

"You kind of are," says Dylan.

Oliver removes his arms from around our shoulders and folds them across his chest. "So what if I happen to enjoy reading about the past so that I can better understand forces at work in the present? Anyway, whatever. Shipwrecks are cool."

Is he for real?

"*Obsessed*," says Gabi.

Oliver grimaces and stalks away. To the historical section, I assume.

Leaving me with Dylan and Gabi.

"So we've got science fiction and romance," Gabi says. Clearly a take-charge type.

"I don't know anything about romance," Dylan says, and looks at Gabi.

Gabi frowns at them. "What, and I do because I'm a girl?"

Dylan blushes. "No, that's not what I meant."

"I'm only sometimes a girl, you know. And what do you mean, you don't know anything about romance? You're dating Ida!"

Dylan gives me a slightly pleading look, like I'm somehow supposed to get them out of this. I shrug. "I don't know any romance books, either."

(Well, except for that *Clara Jane* book that Abby loves. But I'm not going to tell them about that.)

"Romance will be easy," Gabi says. "Every other cover has a shirtless guy, right? So let's all go look at science fiction first. Get more eyes on it."

Footsteps pound toward us and Delia skids into view. For a second, we all eye each other like this is some kind of tense standoff. I half expect Gabi to let out a battle cry and tell us to charge.

Instead, she barks, "Sci-fi time," and leads the way past Delia, who immediately begins scouring the fantasy shelves.

Gabi sets a fast pace across the bookstore; Dylan and I power walk to keep up, which feels ridiculous when a laid-back acoustic guitar version of "Jingle Bells" is playing on the store's sound system.

"So, um." Dylan twists their fingers together. "You read a lot of books?"

I dodge around a display of holiday stationery. "Uh, I read graphic novels sometimes."

Dylan's eyebrows shoot up and their eyes widen. "Oh, that's cool. Me, too. Do you ever read webcomics? Have you read *The Adventures of Trans Boy and the Electric Enby*?"

This is going too fast for me. "No, I . . . That doesn't sound familiar."

"Oh, man, it's *so good*. It's about this trans guy who discovers he can read minds, and his best friend—who's nonbinary—has this superpower where they can make electricity with their fingers, and they have adventures and save the world and stuff. If you like comics, you should check it out." Dylan suddenly flushes. "It's not as silly as it sounds."

Who says it sounds silly? It's a webcomic featuring a trans super-hero. That sounds awesome.

And it's just . . . out there. In the world. I kind of can't believe I didn't know about it.

Then again, why would I? Evan's the only other person I know who reads graphic novels and comics as much as I do, but he mostly sticks to stuff in the Marvel or DC Universes. Which makes it really ironic that he doesn't see his own resemblance to Captain America.

I've looked for books with trans characters at the library. In school and in town. I haven't found any. Maybe that's not surprising. Parents were probably *concerned*.

But a webcomic . . . Well, those are just out there online, right? For everyone?

"Is it free?" I ask.

Dylan grins. "Yeah. They have a Patreon, though, and it's really cheap, and then you get their podcast with extra audio stories and stuff."

Huh. I wonder if Evan would read a trans webcomic, if I started reading it. "Cool. I'll look it up."

"Stop talking, you slowpokes!" It's Gabi, way ahead of us now. "Let's get browsing!"

The science fiction section is dense. Partly because it's packed with fat books, and partly because the books themselves look dense. Every single one has tiny type and the plots all seem super confusing.

They're also mostly written by men. Or people who only use initials instead of a first name. And that could be a nonbinary person, or a woman, or a man. It could be anybody.

"This is such a pain," Gabi groans. "I'm both angry these people all seem to be dudes and angry that I have to try to figure out author genders at all!"

"This one might be a woman?" Dylan holds up a book written by

someone named R. K. Englort. If my last name was *Englort,* I don't
think I'd stop with *R. K.*; I'd go for a whole new pen name. "There's
no bio, but the main character is a woman . . ."

"Keep looking," Gabi says.

We spread out through the science fiction section, pulling books
out at random.

I wonder if Abby would read a trans webcomic. I don't know if
she reads webcomics, or graphic novels, but she likes books, so . . .

It would be fun to have someone to read something with. Someone to discuss things with, or just geek out with. That's kind of what
I do with Evan already. But it would be different to read something
queer, and talk to a queer person about it . . .

I wonder what section Abby is browsing right now, and I suddenly feel sort of sad I'm not on her team.

I glance at Dylan, farther down the row of shelves. They're currently frowning over an extremely fat book, balancing it awkwardly
in one hand and biting the nail of their other thumb.

I stick my current book back on the shelf (definitely no spaceships or robots in that one) and browse my way closer to Dylan.
"Hey," I say. Quietly, because I don't want Gabi to hear and yell at
us that we're not browsing fast enough. "Can I ask you something?"

Dylan looks up, eyebrows raised. "Oh. Um. Sure?"

"You and Ida are . . . dating, right?"

Dylan blinks at me. "Yeah."

"Did . . . did you just ask her out? Or, I mean . . ." Ugh, why this
so hard? "Did she already know, or . . . did she think you were weird?"

Dylan looks thoughtful. "Well, I *am* kind of weird . . ."

Man, I really wish Dylan could read minds like that trans boy superhero. "No, I mean, did she ever get weirded out because you're . . .
trans."

Dylan looks genuinely confused. "No? Ida asked *me* out, so . . ."

"She asked *you* out?"

"Yeah. Why?"

"No reason." I shrug, trying to be casual. "I was just wondering. I haven't, like, dated before. And I'm trans."

Dylan looks at me for a long moment. "Are you maybe kind of asking because of Abby?"

A tiny part of me wants to punch Dylan in the face simply so I don't have to answer the question. "No. I was asking because I wanted to ask."

"Well, obviously Abby knows you're trans, since you just said so upstairs . . ."

Why did I start this conversation? "Yeah . . ."

Dylan shrugs. "So."

So? What's that mean?

Dylan pulls down another book, like that "so" was some kind of answer that actually finished the conversation.

I turn back to the row of science fiction books in front of me. I'm not quite sure what just happened.

Up until right now, I've been about ninety-nine percent sure that there is nobody in Springfield who would date me. Up until right now, even though I did my best to ignore it and deny it, I figured nobody would date me because I'm trans.

Because I'm weird.

Because I'm a Logistical Headache.

I know I'm not the only trans guy in existence. I know other trans guys in other places seem to date people. I know how to google. But everything I found—pictures on Instagram, videos on TikTok, even posts on Tumblr—it all seemed so far away from Springfield. Too far away to feel—I don't know—real?

Except now here I am, standing next to Dylan, in the middle of a scavenger hunt with a bunch of queers. None of it's far away anymore.

And I'm not any different. I'm the same Leo I was in Springfield—a Logistical Headache, maybe sometimes even a menace—but Dylan just looked at me and said "So."

Like I'm so shrug-worthy I don't even need a complete sentence.

I don't know what to do with any of this. I feel like I'm one person and two separate people at the same time. One version of me confuses the Mrs. Waggoners of the world, makes parents *concerned,* while the other version barely gets a second glance from Dylan.

I open my mouth, because I feel like I have to say something back to Dylan, though I'm not sure what.

It doesn't matter anyway, because Gabi appears so suddenly that Dylan jumps.

"We should split up," she says. "Oliver isn't back yet, so he must be stuck in historical. I'll go help him out."

"I'll stay with sci-fi." Dylan is now trying to balance three books at once.

"Cool." Gabi slaps my shoulder. "Looks like you've got romance, Grinch."

And she jogs away.

Oh, *come on.* "Is she serious?"

Dylan glances up. "Yeah."

"I don't know anything about romance books."

"I mean, I don't really know anything about sci-fi, either, but that's the fun part." Dylan gives me a grin that looks so stressed it makes me question whether they're having any fun at all.

I scrub at my hair with one hand. "Okay, fine. Where's romance?"

Dylan jerks their chin. "Over by the table with all the journals."

Here goes nothing. I leave Dylan browsing the shelves and head for the romance section, skirting around a table full of blank journals with flowery covers. I wonder if the store put this table by the romance section on purpose. Pastel, flowery journals are obviously for lady people, and only lady people want to read romance novels, right?

I don't particularly want to read a romance novel, but also fuck that.

I slip into the romance section and start tilting books backward off the shelf, just enough to see their covers. All I need is a shirtless dude. Just one, and I'm done.

Nope, that guy's fully clothed.

That one's dressed and on a horse.

That one's shirt is see-through, but I don't think that counts.

A middle-aged woman edges past me in the aisle, shooting me a concerned look. Probably assuming I'm a butch lesbian looking at romance novels, or a teenage boy trying to find a sexy read. I don't know which is worse.

Okay, seriously. How hard can it be to find one shirtless dude? Aren't shirtless men the romance novel stereotype?

The middle-aged woman looks at me again. She's farther down the aisle now. I try to give her my best harmless grin and move down to the next row of books.

You have got to be kidding me.

I reach forward, tugging the book off the shelf. Not a shirtless dude cover, but a very familiar title. The edges of the pages are yellowed and soft from being turned dozens of times. The spine has faded. This is definitely a very used copy.

But it's a hardcover. Of Abby's favorite book. *The Hundred Romances of Clara Jane.*

I open the cover. There's a scrawled signature on the title page, the ink faded to brown. This is a signed copy. Just like the one Abby lost.

Wait. This isn't the one Abby lost, right? There's no way she could have lost it just this morning, and it's already turning up in a random bookstore.

I flip through the pages—no handwritten notes. So it's another signed, used copy that just happens to be here. In this store. On this shelf.

I close the book. The cover is the Empire State Building against a starry night, the black silhouette of a woman in a dress cut into the bottom. On the back corner is a Strand price sticker that originally said *$10.99*, but someone's crossed through it with a red pen and written *$5*.

What are you doing, Leo?

I should put this book back on the shelf. Put it back, forget I saw it, and leave it at that. Abby's team will have to look for a romance book, too, if they haven't already. Maybe Abby will find it herself.

But if she finds it herself, she might get it for Kat. Or text me, asking if she should get it for Kat.

I could hide it. Turn it around, pages out, or shove it back farther so she won't see it. Suddenly the last thing I want is for her to find this book, think the Universe is throwing her a miracle, and rush back to Kat.

Because if she does that . . .

Then this day will be over. I'll go back to my band and she'll go back to hers.

And so what? Why would that be so bad?

If Abby found this book, it would probably make her happy. So why am I considering hiding it? I mean, what kind of a jerk move would that be?

But I can't seem to put the book back on the shelf, because something else is niggling at the back of my mind.

Maybe the Universe isn't throwing Abby a miracle. Maybe it's throwing *me* one.

Ugh. *Come on, Leo.* I know my history with the Universe. Any time anything good happens, I turn around and get walloped. Won a band competition? Cool, time to get misgendered by a waiter at the celebration dinner. Coming out to parents went well? Just kidding, they're never gonna tell the rest of the family.

Fuck it. I don't care.

I tuck the book under my arm. I have to find a shirtless dude cover really fast now, because I need time to buy this copy of *The Hundred Romances of Clara Jane,* before I talk myself out of it. Before I spend any more time trying to figure out why all I want right now is to give this book to Abby. Not so she can give it to Kat, not because I still feel guilty (I don't), but because . . .

I pull out another book. Shirtless dude. *Yes.*

I check my phone. I've got time. I can buy this book for Abby and still find my team before anybody gets suspicious.

Okay, Universe. I see you.

I tuck *The Hundred Romances of Clara Jane* against my chest, between my hoodie and the shirtless dude book, in case Abby's lurking somewhere, and try to walk as fast and nonchalantly as I can toward the register at the front of the store.

There's no line. And the woman who winked at me is gone, replaced by a younger guy with gauged ears and a ponytail.

I slide the *Clara Jane* book onto the counter. "Could I buy this?"

"Yeah, sure." Ponytail Guy jerks his chin. "That one, too?"

Oh, god. I'm holding the shirtless dude book front-cover-out. "No, this one is just . . . It's just for a book club thing. Here, at the store. I'm not going to . . . I wasn't going to steal it or something."

Ponytail Guy gives me a weird look. "Okay, no worries." He scans the *Clara Jane* book. "Five dollars and forty-four cents. You want it gift wrapped?"

Gift wrapped? Are people seriously starting their Christmas shopping already? "No, just a bag, if you have one." I fish a ten-dollar bill out of my pocket and hold it out.

Ponytail Guy hands over my change and slips the book into a slim brown paper bag. "There you go," he says, like he's bored. "Happy Thanksgiving."

"Yeah, you, too." I'd honestly forgotten tomorrow is Thanksgiving. How did that happen? If you'd asked me yesterday, *So, think you'll forget about Thanksgiving coming up?*, I would have laughed. And then had a panic spiral.

I grab the paper bag. Maybe I should try to sneak back up to the second floor. See if I can stick it in my backpack before anybody asks me what's inside. I'm a little afraid of what will happen if the members of QYBC Triple-A think I was shirking the scavenger hunt to buy a book.

But halfway to the elevator, Dylan comes barreling out of the science fiction section. "Hey, Leo! I got one!"

Shit. Do I hide the bag behind my back? But that would be really obvious now. I do my best to hold it casually. "Cool. I found a romance." I wave the shirtless dude book.

Dylan glances at it, and then at the paper bag. "Nice. You seen Gabi and Oliver?"

"No. Maybe the history books ate them."

Dylan goes back to biting their nails. "Let's go find them."

They don't ask what's in the bag. Neither do Gabi and Oliver, when we bump into them halfway to the historical section. They're too preoccupied with the book they found.

"War *and* forbidden romance," Oliver says proudly. "I knew I could find something."

Gabi rolls her eyes. "You could've found it faster."

Oliver looks hurt. "I wanted to make sure I was right. The descriptions on book covers aren't always accurate."

"You don't need to go through the whole book to make sure it's right."

"I got pulled in."

Dylan glances at Gabi. "Was he sitting there reading again?"

Gabi gives a long-suffering sigh. "Yep. Come on, we're almost out of time."

We jog to the elevator. Gabi punches the button, and as soon as the doors open, the other team comes pounding up behind us.

I slip the paper bag behind my back.

But Abby doesn't seem to notice. Her pale face is flushed. Her eyes practically sparkle. She's grinning with a kind of abandon.

"Find good stuff?" she asks me as we all pile into the elevator.

Her smile drills a hole straight through me. "Yeah," I say. "I found good stuff."

THIRTEEN

ABBY

COMPLETELY PREDICTABLY, BOTH teams end up tied.

"You both found queer books!" Rae says, when Gabi and Delia protest. "What was I supposed to do?"

"Design a harder scavenger hunt," Gabi grumbles.

Dylan's eyes practically bug out of their head. "No, thank you, this was stressful enough!"

I pull my phone out and glance again at the text from Kat.

KAT

Got to intermission. Can't believe you're not here.

The show must be ending soon, right? It's after four thirty. And she's been covering for me for hours. I'm not even sure we'll have time to fit in another *THRoCJ* location now. Or another souvenir.

Why did I waste all this time? I'm supposed to be finding gifts for Kat, not doing selfish things for myself.

But a half hour seemed so short. And I don't regret it. Somehow, I can't quite make myself regret it.

The scavenger hunt is clearly over now, though, even if Gabi is still arguing with Rae about the tied results. So, I guess, even though I don't really want to . . .

I walk over to Leo, who's crouched behind one of the armchairs, trying to stuff a slim paper bag into his backpack. It doesn't seem to be going very well. "Should we go?"

Leo jumps, knocking his backpack over. "Oh. Hey."

"Hey." Is it just me, or does he look a little pink? "We should probably go, right? It's four thirty-five, and we have to get uptown . . ."

"Yeah. Right." Leo gives up trying to get the paper bag into his backpack. He picks his jacket up off the armchair.

I pick up my jacket, too. It's mostly dry now, at least. But that just makes me feel worse. My jacket is dry because we stayed too long. What was I thinking?

"What are you guys doing?" Dylan asks.

I turn around. Everyone is staring at us, even Gabi and Rae.

"Sorry. We should go." I shrug my jacket on and pick up my backpack.

"We don't get kicked out until five," Ida says. "You guys can keep hanging out if you want. We usually just talk about books or movies or—"

"Favorite queer ships, in any media, canon or not," Rae says enthusiastically.

"Yeah," Ida says, less enthusiastically. "Or that."

God, I want to. I want to stay in this queer bubble, with people who actually want to talk about queer ships. Maybe they'd even listen if I told them about that one gay *Clara Jane* fanfic. Maybe they read fanfic, too.

I can almost picture it. All of us sitting around, talking and laughing, and Leo occasionally looking grumpy, which would make us laugh more . . .

It's a bubble I didn't even know existed, and I'm not sure I've ever wanted anything more.

But I need to focus on what I'm really supposed to be doing. I need to focus on Kat, in case there's a chance for something to happen, because . . . that's what I've wanted for months. And if she says yes—well, that's something I'll still have when I go back to Westvale. That's something I can take with me.

So why do I feel so torn up about this?

"We should really go," Leo says. "Thanks, though."

Rae looks hurt. "Where do you have to rush off to?"

I open my mouth, with no idea what I'm going to say. I catch Ida looking at me, a tiny smile on her face. She's probably thinking about Kat, and everything I told her about Kat, and also about Leo . . .

"We gotta get back to our marching bands," Leo says. "We're in the parade tomorrow, so we've got . . . practice and stuff."

Kind of a lie but also kind of the truth. It's the obvious thing to say, anyway. But I suddenly find myself wishing I could tell Ida the whole truth—my whole plan—and see what she says.

"Wait, you're in the *Macy's* Parade?" Oliver says.

"Like, playing instruments?" says Delia.

Skye claps her hands together. "Queers in the parade!"

Now they all want to know what instruments we play and what music we're going to perform and what it's like to be in a marching band and how much we practice—and by the time we tear ourselves away for real, we've lost another fifteen minutes.

But before I can head for the elevator, Ida pulls me aside. "Give me your phone."

I hold it out.

She types and hands it back. "My phone number. Use it."

I blink. It takes a second for my brain to catch up. "But I thought you were with Dylan."

She laughs and quickly hides it with her hand. "No, silly, I'm not *hitting* on you. I'm trying to be your friend."

I stare at her. "I live in Missouri."

She smiles. "Yeah, I know. Ever heard of texting? Besides, maybe you'll find your way back to New York sometime. Or I'll find my way to Missouri."

I look down at my phone.

"Is that cool?" Ida says.

"Yeah. Of course." I glance up. "Sorry, I just haven't had a—"

"Very-definitely-absolutely-queer friend?"

Now I *know* she's thinking about Kat. "I was going to say 'long-distance friend,' but yeah."

"Abby, come on." Leo's at the elevator, holding the doors open.

But I hesitate a second longer. "Hey, Ida?" I pull up the picture I snapped earlier of the flyer on the store's notice board. "Where's this address?"

Ida squints at my phone. "Kind of near Times Square. It says the closest intersection right there, see? Thirty-Ninth and Eighth. That means West Thirty-Ninth Street and Eighth Avenue."

"Oh. Okay, thanks." I stuff my phone back in my pocket.

"I'll watch the parade tomorrow and keep an eye out for you." Ida punches my arm lightly. "Let me know who you pick."

"What?"

But instead of answering, she gives me a push toward the elevator, and yeah, I should really go. I run to the elevator, backpack bouncing awkwardly, and Leo lets the doors close behind us.

The elevator creaks slowly toward the first floor.

"What was that about?" Leo asks.

"Ida gave me her phone number. Like, to be friends."

"That's cool."

I can't quite bring myself to tell him about the flyer. Not because he wouldn't care, or because I'm afraid he'd laugh at me. I'm worried he *would* care. And the possibility of that somehow feels worse. "They were a cool group."

"Yeah." He scrubs at his hair. He's not even frowning. "They were."

We wind our way back through the bookstore to the entrance. When we reach the street, the rain has stopped. The clouds are disappearing, too. Weak afternoon sunlight glints on the pavement.

Leo pulls his beanie back on. "Now what?"

My mind goes to Kat's text message again. "Maybe we should go back."

"Go back where?"

Isn't that obvious? "Our bands! Maybe we should just go to Broadway now. I mean, the shows must be almost over."

"Yeah, I guess." Leo glances down at the paper bag he's still holding.

"You were right, we shouldn't have done that whole scavenger hunt thing." I feel bad, as soon as it's out of my mouth, because I don't even know if I'm mad about it, or if I just feel like I *should* be mad. And now it sounds like I'm blaming him, when I know I'm the one that pushed to stay.

"You just said they were a cool group," Leo says.

"Well, they were. Are. But I was supposed to be finding souvenirs for Kat." My stomach is tying itself in knots again. I can practically feel each minute slipping away from me. "And I just spent hours ignoring her and hunting for books."

Leo frowns. "It wasn't hours."

"You know what I mean. I was supposed to be doing something for Kat—otherwise it wouldn't be fair to ask her to cover for me—and instead I was doing something else."

He raises an eyebrow. "Right, so it's not fair I asked Evan to cover for me because I'm not planning to confess my undying love to him with a whole bunch of gifts?"

"No, that's not what I meant." I shake my head. This is coming out all wrong. "I just . . . The plan was to do something for Kat."

"Kind of seems like you spend a lot of time doing something for Kat."

What's that supposed to mean? "No, I don't."

"You take pictures for her blog—"

"It's not a blog, it's a Tumblr."

"You write her love letters—"

"They weren't love letters."

"And now you're looking for these souvenirs, and taking it out on yourself if you do anything else that's just, like, something *you* want to do."

That catches me off guard. "Looking for souvenirs was your idea."

Leo frowns. "Yeah, and yet somehow everything you just said was completely about you."

"What are you talking about? This whole thing we're doing is supposed to be about me telling Kat how I feel. So . . . yeah, I'm talking about me. Who else would I be talking about?"

He frowns harder. But all he says, in a low voice, is "Never mind." He slings his backpack down from his shoulder and goes back to wedging the paper bag into it.

I have no idea what he's suddenly so upset about. And I also don't want to fight with him. I swallow. Try to be friendly. "What's in that bag?"

Leo looks up at me. The frown is gone from his face. His eyes are wider than I've ever seen them. Wide and deep and almost vulnerable.

He shrugs and looks away again, back down at his backpack. "It's nothing." The paper bag crunches into his backpack, and he pulls the zipper. "We can head to Broadway if you want."

He doesn't sound angry. But he doesn't sound happy, either. He sounds kind of sad.

I open my mouth, wondering how terrible an idea it would be to ask him what's wrong. But my phone buzzes in my pocket before I can make up my mind what to say.

It's another text from Kat. This one on the group chain with Leo and Evan.

KAT

Show finished. Dismantling Fake Abby now.

Crap. We're too late. I really did waste too much time. "The show's over," I say to Leo.

"Yeah, I know." He's looking at his phone, too.

EVAN

Sweet, did it work?

KAT

Yeah. Chaperone tried to check in during intermission but I told her Abby was fine and then faked a coughing fit to distract her. Everybody's getting up now.

EVAN

Yesss, use that chaos to hide our fake friends!

I look up at Leo. What do we do? Run to the subway and hope a train shows up immediately?

It's what we *should* do. It's obviously what we should do.

And all I want is for Leo to say we don't have to. Because I don't want this to be over.

What is *this*? Looking for souvenirs? Running around New York like I get to make up my own adventure?

Being with Leo?

Leo looks at me, chewing his lip. I'm too afraid to ask what he's thinking, but I really, really want to know. Does he think we should go back? Does he want to?

God, I feel pulled in so many directions at once. I have no idea what to do.

KAT

This has been fun, guys.

Abby are you here

EVAN

Same. Go, team. Leo, we're heading to dinner in Times Square, where are you?

If I don't say something now, my heart is going to hammer straight out of my chest. "I don't want to go back yet." It tumbles out of my mouth. "I want to find something else . . . for Kat."

"Yeah." Leo swallows. "Yeah, me neither. Or . . . me too."

My knees turn to jelly, and for a second, I think my heart has actually exited my body. I drop my backpack on the sidewalk and bend down to pull out my folder full of information. "I'm pretty sure my band is also going to dinner in Times Square." I open the folder. "And then to Rockefeller Center and some place called Top of the Rock. What about you?"

Leo fumbles out the sheet of paper with his itinerary printed on it. "Um . . . some boat tour to see the lights of the Manhattan skyline. After dinner."

I close the folder and try to slip it back in my backpack. My hands are shaky, like I just jogged five laps around the football field. "What if we went to one more location from the book, and found one more thing for Kat, and then we meet our groups for the last evening stops?"

"You mean, like, meet up after dinner?"

"Yeah." I hold my breath. *Please say yes.*

EVAN

Guys??

Where r u???

"Okay," Leo says. Abruptly. "Let's do it."

He's smiling. Just barely. So small that most people would probably miss it. I would have, this morning. But I see it now.

Ida's voice pops back into my head. Her low mutter before I ran for the elevator. *Let me know who you pick.*

My heart hiccups.

No, it does more than that. It leaps straight into my throat.

I cough and focus on my phone. "Okay."

ME

Would you guys possibly be able to cover for us through dinner?

KAT

Seriously?

EVAN

Wtf Leo are u choosing to hang out with some girl over me?? 😣

LEO

Evan this is a group chat

I don't know what to text back. I suddenly want to explain to Kat—just Kat—without anyone else seeing what I write. I open our own text chain.

ME

I'm sorry. I know I said I would be back, but I'll explain when I see you. Promise.

Can you and Morgan and Amira please keep covering?

I stare at my phone. Three little dots pop up. Kat is typing. I wait for what feels like an eternity, watching those dots.

KAT

You better be up to something really good.

My breath rushes out of my chest.

ME

Thank you, you're the best, really

I switch back to the group chat.

EVAN

Mr Corbin is 100% having an epic migraine so I think we got u.
Plus Josh F tried to buy a beer from concessions so chaperones
got their hands full.

LEO

Thanks Ev I owe you

See you after dinner

Kat doesn't text anything else. To me, or to the group.

Why is this all so weird? Why do I feel so relieved and so freaked out all at the same time? This is what I wanted—to put off going back for a little bit longer. I'm going to do the big epic scene tomorrow, and I want to make sure it's perfect. I want to make sure I have enough souvenirs. I want to make sure I'm ready.

Because right now, I don't feel ready at all.

FOURTEEN

WEDNESDAY, NOVEMBER 22—5:04 P.M.

LEO

WHY DID I get this book for Abby?

What did I think was going to happen? I'd pull it out in some dramatic reveal and then she'd fling her arms around me like we're in a sappy Lifetime movie? Like I'd be the one getting the big, epic love scene?

I feel like a fool, but that's exactly what I hoped for. And I don't even know when I started hoping for it.

Get a grip, Leo. Abby loves Kat. She just made that really obvious, freaking out that she hasn't made this day about Kat *enough*. Focusing on *I* and *me* and *my*, as though I'm not even here, as though this whole plan wasn't my idea in the first place.

And now I feel selfish. And guilty. Abby's in love with Kat. Who did I expect her to focus on?

Besides, I've known her all of—I try to make my brain work— five hours? Six, tops? People don't fall for other people in six hours. People don't even make friends in six hours.

Or, at least, I don't.

I'm crushing on Abby. That's all this is. A totally ridiculous crush, which I probably only have because Dylan shrugged and said "so," like maybe Abby (or someone) could like me. Dylan put the possibility in my head and now here I am. Being ridiculous.

Thanks, Dylan.

So, I could give her the book anyway. What else am I going to do with it? Lug it around in my backpack for the rest of the trip? I should hand it over, out of guilt if nothing else. *Hey, sorry I lost your book, here's a replacement.*

Except I can't make myself do it.

We're walking down Fourteenth Street, heading west toward Chelsea Market, finally. We decided to skip the subway, now that it's not raining anymore. According to Abby's phone, taking a train wouldn't really save us that much time, and it's probably better to make sure we have enough fare to get back to our bands later.

So, I have time. Plenty of time. But if I give Abby the book, she might call it quits right now. Decide we don't need to go to Chelsea Market, because she has a signed copy of the book, and even though it doesn't have all her notes, it'll still mean a lot to Kat, and that's enough.

And if she decides that, this day will be over.

Not literally. I'll still go see the lights of Manhattan by boat, which I'm sure will be spectacular. I'll still spend tonight rehearsing in front of Macy's. I'll still march in the parade tomorrow.

But the thing I really want, more than any of that, is another hour with Abby.

Stop overthinking. Just be here.

If I only get one more hour, I might as well be present.

I try to push my guilty feelings aside and squint at Abby. The sun is going down ahead of us, turning our shadows long and lean, but even with all these buildings, it's still stabbing me right in the eyes. "So, what's Chelsea Market? A grocery store?"

Abby grins a little, but it looks tight. Strained. And she's walking really fast. "No, it's this, like, indoor place with lots of stores and food and stuff. I think."

"So . . . a mall."

"No. I don't know. It sounds cuter in the book. Clara Jane meets this guy at a candy store there."

"She has one of her hundred romances in a candy store?"

"She doesn't really have a hundred romances. Just eight."

"That seems like false advertising." I mean it as a light joke, but it comes out sounding bitter. What's wrong with me?

Abby just shrugs, biting her lip.

Stop trying to say something smart. Say something real. "You never really told me about this book. I mean . . . why you love it so much. What it's about."

Abby shoots me a puzzled look. "Yes, I did. Magical romance, Empire State Building, New York City. And you think all those things are silly."

"No, I don't."

She raises her eyebrows.

"No, really. I don't hate . . ." I rub the back of my neck. Does she really think that? "I don't hate magic or romance."

A small smile tugs at Abby's mouth. "Okay." She takes a slow breath. "It's about this girl named Clara Jane. She lives in New York, and she's stuck in a time loop. Like, she keeps living the same day over and over, but each time she meets a different guy and has a different whirlwind romance. At the end of the day, she realizes she's not really in love with the guy, and then the day starts over again."

"She has to keep dating guys forever?"

"She meets the right guy at the end of the book, and really falls in love, and then she escapes the time loop. Or that's the implication, anyway."

I think about this for a minute. "Hang on. So, coupledom is the only way to escape literal, actual purgatory?"

Abby blinks. "Um. I hadn't thought of that." Even in the fading light, I can see she's blushing. Unless that's the biting cold. "I never said it was an *amazing* book, but I like reading stories where people fall in love. I like believing that can happen, that *could* happen, especially for—"

She stops talking abruptly and looks down at the sidewalk.

Was she going to say for people like me? *Was she going to say* for people like us?

I want to know, so badly, but I'm too scared to ask. Too scared of hearing the answer, if the answer is *yes*.

She clears her throat. "Anyway"—she's clearly trying to make a save—"it's got some good fanfic."

That was not the save I was expecting. "Fanfic?"

"Yeah." She looks at me sideways. Like she thinks I might bite. "And?"

I hold up my hands. "I'm not judging. Really. I've just never read fanfic of anything."

Her face softens. "Maybe you should. A lot of it's queer."

Oh.

"Plus you get to keep living in your favorite universe, in, like, five hundred different ways."

I grin. "Seems like you're kind of obsessed with living things over and over again."

She mirrors my smile, and then she looks away. A chilly breeze spirals down the street and blows her hair into her face. Now that it's dry, her curls have bounced back, somehow wilder than before.

She brushes them away absently. "I don't know. I think it's more like . . . I want things to work out, and if they don't, then I want another chance."

We're walking slower now. I don't know if I slowed down, or if she did. "Like, if you had to step in dog shit and get on the wrong train, then you should be able to rewind and get the chance to *not* step in dog shit?"

Another smile slips across her face. "Well, I'm not getting a rewind, but it's kind of still a second chance, right?"

My stomach sinks, right down to my knees. "Yeah. Right."

*   *   *

It doesn't take us that long to get to Chelsea Market, but it's still dark by the time we do. It seems like the sun went from sinking slowly to tumbling past the horizon in a matter of minutes. The temperature drops and the streetlights flicker to life overhead. The cars rumbling past us have their headlights on.

Not that there are all that many cars out now. Or people, for that matter. I wonder if everyone left work early to get a head start on cooking, or traveling, or staking out their spots for the parade tomorrow.

Or maybe—I think as soon as we heave open the door—they all went to Chelsea Market.

Outside, Chelsea Market is a giant red brick of a building. Inside, it's a mishmash of exposed-brick walls, high industrial ceilings, and sleek modern glass. And it's all decked out for Christmas. Twinkling white lights hang from the ceiling like hundreds of tiny icicles. Holly jolly Christmas music hits us as soon as we're through the door, along with the echoing hum of a whole lot of voices. There are people everywhere, bundled up in coats, with shopping bags or backpacks over their shoulders, picking out bottles of wine and long loaves of crusty bread. And probably fancy turkeys and fancy cheese, too. I guess New Yorkers do their Thanksgiving shopping at the most artisan-looking shops I've ever seen, all lined up in a row like this is an old European street, instead of the inside of a warehouse.

Abby stares around as we wander under a brick arch, complete with an old-fashioned clock that's wreathed in gold and silver ornaments. "I almost feel like we're locals," she says.

I get what she means. This definitely isn't a crowd of tourists. Everyone's moving too fast for that. I wonder if she's trying to imagine that she's a local, too. Pretending, for a minute, that she lives here and can disappear into this anonymous city, far away from the kind of town where everybody *knows* when you come out.

Where everybody will have opinions, even if they don't tell you what they are. Where sooner or later, you'll end up as a Logistical Headache.

I look up at the steel beams high overhead, wrapped in more twinkling lights. Down at the knobby brick of some of the storefronts. "What should we look for?"

Abby's shoulders hunch up to her ears. She looks tense again. "How about food first? Dinner?"

Maybe that's why my stomach feels weird. I'm just hungry—again. It has nothing to do with how anxious Abby looks, or how desperately I want her to not look anxious. But I can't figure out how to say anything comforting. All I manage is "Good idea."

Neither of us seems to feel that adventurous, because we head for another pizza-by-the-slice place without even discussing it. It's not as cheap here as it was at that hole-in-the-wall where we ate lunch. I'm getting down to my last few dollar bills.

We sit at a little table with our slices, watching people hustle through the market.

"Do you think New Yorkers ever walk slow?" Abby says.

"No," I say, around a bite of pizza. "They've all got important places to be."

Someone power walks past us, so fast they actually generate a gust of wind.

Abby grins at me. "Where do you think he's going?"

"Really important business meeting?"

"The night before Thanksgiving?"

Good point. "Really important turkey?"

She almost chokes on her pizza. "Now I'm just picturing a turkey in a suit."

We finish our pizza and chug some soda, and then Abby says she needs to find the bathroom, so we join the hustle and bustle again until we see a restroom sign pointing down a narrow hallway.

"You can leave your backpack, if you want," I say.

"Oh. Thanks." Abby shrugs it off and leans it carefully against the wall.

I stand next to it, fidgeting with the straps of my own backpack, while she disappears into the ladies' room. I look back and forth between the two bathrooms on either side of a drinking fountain. LADIES and GENTLEMEN. The gender binary in all its glory, once again.

I also need to pee. But there's no gender-neutral bathroom here.

I have used the men's room before. Several times. At a high school in Atlanta when we were there for a competition, at the movie theater, even at Springfield High, once, before an early band practice on a Saturday morning when no one else was around.

But Evan went with me, each of those times. It felt humiliating and comforting all at once. Nobody's going to mess with you when your friend looks like an Avenger. Even if he does wear a T-shirt featuring a tuba-playing scuba diver under the words *Terrible Underwater Breathing Apparatus* a little too often.

Evan really loves corny jokes.

I lean my head back against the wall and squint up at the fluorescent lights overhead. This is New York. Maybe nobody would care. If that men's room is anything like the rest of the city, maybe nobody would even look at me.

"Hey!" Abby reappears, rubbing her hands on her jeans. "Do you want to go?"

"Uh, no, that's okay."

"You sure?"

"This . . . isn't the best place."

She blinks at me. And then her mouth forms a little *o*.

She got it. I wish I could sink into the ground right now.

"I'll hang out and wait." She points to the bathroom. "It's up to you, but . . ."

Is she offering to guard the men's room for me?

That's not really going to stop anything from . . . happening. If anything is going to happen.

But there's nobody else around right now. "You sure you don't mind?"

She smiles. "You waited for me!"

It's not remotely the same thing, but I can tell she knows it, in the way her eyes are focused on mine, in the way she's really *looking*. She's being casual on purpose. She's pretending it's the same thing, because that would mean it's no big deal.

It's just a fucking trip to the bathroom, but . . .

"Okay. Thanks." I drop my backpack next to her and head into the bathroom. It's empty, but I still try to be fast. Into the stall, out of the stall, wash my hands, dry my hands. Even though I know I don't belong in any other bathroom, I still feel like I'm getting away with something. Or at least being a nuisance.

A Logistical Headache, yet again.

Abby's waiting for me outside, swaying gently from side to side like she's dancing to some music in her head. Or maybe practicing some formation for tomorrow.

Ugh. I don't want to think about tomorrow. Not yet.

Abby grins when she sees me and holds up her hand. "Victory is yours. High five."

Is she serious?

"If you want to," she adds.

I give her a high five. It's kind of embarrassing. And also matters more than I want to admit. It's something else she offers with reckless abandon. Like spinning in the rain. Who cares what anyone thinks. "Thanks."

She looks at me for a long moment, and then she looks away, while I pick up my backpack. "Sorry, I hope I didn't put you on the spot." She says it to the floor.

"You didn't." We walk back down the hallway to the bustling corridor of the market. And maybe I should leave it at that, but something draws the rest out of me—the things I usually think, but don't say. "I wish it didn't have to be such a *thing*. I sort of wish nothing had to be a *thing*. Like, I wish I could just be invisible, but only because I look like an ordinary guy and nobody gives me a second glance." I hunch my shoulders under my jacket. "Probably not very loud-and-proud of me."

Abby shrugs. "I'm not exactly loud-and-proud, either. I mean, I know I'm not even out. I think I want to be out, eventually, but mostly . . . I just want to exist."

"You exist to me."

Abby pauses, right there in the middle of the hustle and bustle, and looks up at me. People dodge around us like we're two rocks in the middle of a river. Several of them definitely swear, and plenty more give us really dirty looks.

And I suddenly hear myself. "God. Sorry." I pull off my hat and scrub at my hair. Is it a million degrees in here? "That was super cheesy."

She smiles. Not a laughing-at-me smile. Just . . . a smile. A little shy, maybe a little hopeful. "Yeah. But . . . I'm cheesy. It's cool."

"I just meant that I get what you mean. About wanting to exist. You know, like other people exist, without proving anything or whatever." I try to shrug casually, but all I manage is a shoulder twitch. "So . . . you exist to me. I see you as queer, if that's what you want, whatever other people see or don't see."

That's not any better. But I mean it, and I don't want to take it back.

She watches me. "You exist to me, too."

These things don't happen in real life, but I could still swear the echoing din of footsteps and voices disappears. The people rushing past us blur into the background. All I see are the pinpricks of light in her eyes, from all the twinkling strands overhead.

It might be the first moment, in my entire life, that I want to last forever.

"Thanks," I say.

I wish I could say something else. But it's all I can think of. Just *thanks*. Again.

Someone bumps into Abby, trying to get around her. A quick, annoyed "Watch it" and then the woman is past us. But it still breaks the moment.

"I guess we should keep going," Abby says.

"Yeah."

But we hesitate. Like we're both waiting for the other one to move.

She's the one who finally starts walking. "I was thinking we could look for some candy. You know, like the scene in *The Hundred Romances of Clara Jane*. The guy at the sweets shop is the owner, and he teaches her how to make caramels."

"Sure, that sounds good." I drum my fingers against my leg as we walk. I feel like we're both saying stuff just to say stuff. Looking for the next souvenir because, well, that was the plan.

But I don't know what else to do. I don't know how to get that magical moment back, or what I would say if I had the chance to.

"Hey, look!" Abby points to a storefront with CARLY'S CARAMELS painted on the window.

It's perfect. Just like her book. But all I can manage is a shrug.

The shop smells overwhelmingly of sugar. It's full of chocolates and tea and brightly colored taffy. Blocks of fudge sit on parchment paper in a glass display case. The whole place is a sea of pastels and swoopy fonts.

Abby goes straight for the table of caramels. She picks up a bag and her face falls. "These are kind of pricey," she says quietly.

I look over her shoulder. Eighteen dollars for the smallest bag. Ouch.

"We have some single caramels, too." High heels click across the floor. A woman with cotton candy–pink hair and a light blue apron smiles at us. Everything about her matches the shop so closely that

I wonder if this is Carly. "These are two dollars each." She points to a glass jar on the counter, filled with soft candies, each individually wrapped in pastel paper.

"Oh. That's perfect, actually. Thanks." Abby drifts to the counter.

I hang back while she picks out a caramel and pays for it. I somehow can't bring myself to be any more involved. I study my shoes, scuffing my toe against the floor.

"Here." It's Abby, appearing suddenly at my shoulder. She holds out a little candy in a slightly waxy blue wrapper.

I take it automatically.

We stare at each other.

"Are you going to eat it?" Abby asks.

What? "Isn't this for Kat?"

She smiles, her eyes crinkling. "No, I got another one for Kat." She holds it up and unzips her backpack. "That one's for you."

I look at the caramel. "You didn't have to."

She tucks the candy for Kat into her backpack. "I know, but . . ." Her eyes meet mine again. "I wanted to."

My stomach twists with guilt. The book in my backpack suddenly weighs fifty pounds. "Thanks."

Why do I keep saying *thanks*?

"You're welcome." She ducks her head and pulls out her phone. "We should probably go."

I let my breath out. I had my hour. And then some, I realize, looking at my phone. It's almost six thirty.

"Yeah," I say. "We should go."

FIFTEEN

ABBY

IT'S COLD WHEN we head back outside. Cold and windy. My eyes immediately tear up and my ears ache. I pull my hood up and tuck my hair inside it.

"So . . . Times Square, right?" I try to say it lightly, even though none of this feels light.

"Yeah," Leo says. "Times Square."

I glance up at him, but he's squinting at the bright sign beaming CHELSEA MARKET into the darkness above our heads. So I look back at the map on my phone. My fingers are so cold it's hard to type. And I can't seem to make the map make sense. My mind is too full. Too full of twinkling lights and caramels and the way everything seemed to pause when Leo said *You exist to me*. "So . . . I guess if we want to go to Times Square, we should . . . um . . ."

"You can take the High Line."

I jump, and so does Leo. A young woman in a black apron and a puffy parka is leaning against the wall of the building, her phone in her hands. The glow from the screen lights up her face. I wonder if she works inside.

"Sorry." She grins. "Didn't mean to scare you."

"What's the High Line?" I ask.

"Elevated park. You can walk all the way to the 7 train at Thirty-Fourth Street, and then take that to Times Square." She points down the street. "See those stairs going up, past the bridge? Take those up and when you get to the High Line, go right."

"Is that fastest, do you think?"

The woman shrugs. "The A's normally way faster, but the construction right now is pretty terrible. I was twenty minutes late for my shift because the train took so long to show up." She pulls a face. "Walking will take a while, but at least it's predictable."

I would personally be okay with never laying eyes on another A train in my life, and based on Leo's face, I think he might feel the same way.

I could still look at my phone, just to check if there's a faster way. Another train, or maybe even a bus. New York City has buses. I've seen them rumbling down the streets several times today.

But I don't want to look. If I don't look, then I won't know, and if I don't know . . .

I'm arguing myself in circles. I know I am. I said we should get back—and we *should* . . .

"Let's try it," I say to Leo.

He just shrugs. So I thank the woman in the apron and we dash across the narrow street in the direction she pointed. Sure enough, there's a railing and set of concrete stairs, right where she said they would be. We climb up, Leo taking the steps two at a time with his long legs, and me pounding behind him. The stairs bend around several tight corners, along a brick wall, and then we walk back out into the open air, onto a bridge over the street. When the woman said *park,* I pictured big, sweeping spaces like Central Park, but this isn't any wider than the street below us. Bare, skeletal trees clack their branches gently, and tall, browning grasses rustle in the breeze. The paved path almost seems to glow with a soft yellow light; I can't even see where the lightbulbs are. Maybe they're hidden among the plants?

"Hey, look." I point to two rusted metal rails, overgrown with plants, disappearing ahead of us into the darkness. "Train tracks."

"Yeah." Leo's looking at his phone. "Wikipedia says it used to be an elevated train track. And now it's a park."

"That's so cool." A little shiver runs up my back. "It's another liminal space."

It slips out before I realize what I'm saying. Leo looks at me. "A what?"

"Um . . . it means a space between. Someplace that feels out of time, or disconnected, or between where you came from and where you're going."

We've started walking, automatically, or maybe because standing still is too cold.

It is really cold.

"Maybe that's what I am," Leo says. "A liminal person." He grins, a little wry, or a little sarcastic. A little *something,* anyway, that isn't quite a real smile. I'm starting to think he's convinced himself very few things are worth a real smile. "Liminal person occupying a liminal space. Not a girl, not really a guy."

"You *are* a guy, though." But I mouth his words to myself, silently. *Liminal person.*

"You seem to have a really easy time saying that."

"Saying what?"

"That I'm a guy."

I study his worn-out Adidas as he walks next to me. He walks like a guy, even though I'm not sure I'd know how to explain what that means. Who knew boys and girls walked differently, anyway? I certainly never thought about it before.

But they do. And he does. I wonder if he does it on purpose, or if this is just how he's always walked. If anyone does it naturally, or if it's something else we learn without realizing we're learning it.

"You told me you're a guy," I say to Leo. "So I believe you."

Leo frowns down at the pavement. "I guess I should be grateful somebody does," he mumbles.

Happy to be here, grateful for the opportunity. It suddenly comes back to me, what he said this morning. Muttering it under his breath. I thought it wasn't fair, when he said it. I thought he was rolling his eyes at me, judging me, but now . . .

"You don't need to be grateful." It comes out louder than I mean it to.

Leo looks at me in surprise.

"Sorry." I lower my voice. "But . . . you don't need to be grateful to people just because they aren't *dicks*. You're not asking too much. Of anybody. Definitely not your family. And I . . ." I'm talking too fast. "I'm sorry, I don't mean it's not a big, complicated mess, because I know it is. I just . . . I don't think you need to be grateful."

The corner of his mouth turns up. "Maybe *you* should talk to my parents."

Even in the cold, my face grows warm. "Yeah, right. Me, who hasn't come out to anybody."

He laughs a little, breath puffing in clouds. "You came out to me."

Oh.

I guess that's true.

I stop walking, next to an empty wooden bench illuminated by small, round lights set into the pavement underneath it.

"We should scream," I say.

Leo stops, a few steps ahead of me. "What?"

"Just, like, an angry, pissed-off scream. For the hell of it. No-body's here."

Leo looks at me like I've lost it. "Now?"

"Yeah." And maybe I have lost it. "Now."

But he stays frozen in place. So I jump up on the wooden bench, look up at the purple sky between the skyscrapers, and yell.

It tears out of my lungs. A raw howl. A sound that's every frustration, every mixed-up, turned-around, anxious and awful feeling I've had. A sound that's everything I haven't figured out how to say, everything I barely understand, every fear I've kept to myself.

I scream it all into the sky until I run out of air and the echoes bounce away into the city.

I look back down at Leo, still standing on the walkway. I wait.

And then he steps up on the bench beside me. He leans his head back. And he yells, too.

A bubble wells in my chest. I take another breath, and yell with him.

"Shut up!" someone shouts back at us, from somewhere in the distance.

"What the hell's wrong with you?" Another shout, from somewhere else.

"Fucking kids."

That last one comes from farther down the High Line—a woman walking her dog ahead of us.

I run out of breath again and bite my lip. I didn't see her before. She probably thinks we're super weird.

But I don't really care as much as I thought I would. Maybe because I did it for Leo. And a little bit for me. And right now, that feels like everything.

Leo's out of breath, too. We glance at each other, and he snorts, and I start laughing. Wind whistles into my face again. I wipe my watering eyes.

"That felt kind of great," Leo says.

My laughter runs out, and we lapse into silence, standing on this bench and looking around at the lights of the city—the glow from lit windows, the ambient grayness in the sky, because it probably never gets truly dark in New York.

"Do you think maybe all queer people feel like that?" I ask.

"Like what?"

"Like a liminal person." I ball my hands into fists inside my pockets and jump down from the bench. It's freezing. "I mean, I don't know what I am except *not straight*."

Leo jumps down next to me. "That's still knowing something."

I start walking again, quickly, because if I don't, I feel like I might turn into a Popsicle. Leo falls into step beside me. "It feels like I'm just . . . waiting. Waiting until I figure something out, except I don't even know what the thing is. And in the meantime, that whole waiting part of me is invisible to everyone else." I glance at Leo. "See? I'm even weirder than you."

"Yes," he says, with a perfectly straight face.

I punch him lightly on the arm.

He cracks a smile and holds out a fist. "Liminal queers?"

The glow from the lights along the path catches in his eyes.

I bump his fist with mine. "Liminal queers."

The wind picks up, bending the tree branches around us, and my nose is numb by the time Leo's phone tells us we're coming up on Thirty-Fourth Street. We didn't talk much for the rest of the walk, but it was a comfortable silence, even if we were kind of hustling because of the cold. We stuck so close to each other that our jacket sleeves touched. I wondered if Leo noticed. But I didn't want to point it out, in case that made him pull away.

The High Line slowly slopes downward and the skyscrapers fall away on one side, into a dark stretch of nothingness across the highway. Water, I realize. The Hudson River again, just like this morning.

This morning feels so far away now. Almost like another lifetime.

The path in front of us bends away from the highway, back into the city. The slant is steeper now, and we follow it all the way down to the sidewalk. At least it's not as windy down here. The buildings around us are tall glass needles reaching into the sky, and it takes us a while to find the subway station between all of them. We have to backtrack a couple times, trying to follow ourselves on the map on Leo's phone. Maybe I should find it stressful, but instead it just makes me laugh. Even Leo shakes his head with a crooked grin as we dodge around a few people walking on the street, and then pass them again when we turn around and go back the way we came.

It turns out the reason we can't find the entrance to the subway is because it's down a narrow side street, on the edge of a little park that kind of reminds me of Union Square, except without all the Christmas. Also, this entrance looks nothing like the subway entrances we've seen so far. No sign of a green railing or a green-and-white lamp. Here, there's a soaring canopy of metal and glass, with rows of escalators leading down underground.

We step onto an escalator, and Leo says, "Whoa."

The whole ceiling above us is a tiled mosaic. One side is whites, yellows, oranges, and reds, and the other is deep purples and blues.

"Kind of looks like the sky," I say. "Day and night."

Leo nods and pulls off his hat, stuffing it into his jacket pocket. Even though he's been wearing a hat for most of the day, his hair still sticks straight up on one side of his head. It makes me happy—the ridiculousness of it. The way he doesn't seem to notice.

The station is just as fancy when we get underground. The floors are white tile, and there's another mosaic in a dome in the ceiling. It doesn't look anything like a bathroom. It's not even that grimy.

"I think we should have subway fare left." I fish my yellow Metro-Card out of my pocket. "I hope."

Leo grimaces. "I haven't been keeping track."

Nothing to do but try, then. There are more people here than we've seen since leaving Chelsea Market, but there are also loads of turnstiles, so we don't have to wait in line. I swipe my card and *yes*. There goes the last of my fare. I push through the turnstile.

Leo swipes his card behind me. "Crap. It says 'insufficient fare.'"

Wait, what? "But we've taken the same number of trips."

Leo shoots his MetroCard an irritated look. "Yeah, but we probably didn't have the same amount of fare to begin with."

Oh. Because we're from two different bands with completely different itineraries that just happened to line up for a few stops. Duh.

"Could you put more money on the card?" I fumble with my backpack to look for my wallet. "How much does a single ride cost?"

Leo fishes around in his pockets, pulling out a couple crumpled bills. "Um . . . I don't know, but I've only got two dollars left." He looks back at the turnstile. "I'm gonna jump it."

What? "No, no, you can use my debit card . . ." I fumble it out of my wallet.

"Save that for another souvenir." Leo glances at the people pushing their way through turnstiles around us. "It's fine. Nobody's gonna notice."

"There are probably cameras! Or sensors!"

Leo plants his hands on either side of the turnstile.

"What if somebody comes after us? We could get fined, or arrested, or—"

Leo vaults himself over the turnstile. His shoes hit the ground. I freeze, wallet in one hand, debit card in the other, waiting for a blaring alarm, for someone to shout at us, or police to appear out of nowhere . . .

"Come on!" Leo grabs my hand and pulls me into a run with him. Somehow I stuff my card and wallet into my jacket pocket and we go racing down the tunnel, dodging around people with briefcases and shopping bags, following the signs pointing us to the 7 train. We thunder down the stairs to the platform, backpacks bouncing awkwardly.

A few people waiting on the platform turn to look at us as we finally slow down, staggering and out of breath. But they all turn away after a few seconds, going back to their phones, or leaning out into the tunnel, looking for a headlight.

Leo drops my hand to grab a stitch in his side. "Told you."

"Told me what?" I curl my fingers into my palm. My hand suddenly feels cold, without his fingers wrapping around mine.

He grins. "Nobody noticed."

I try to look disapproving, but I know it's not working. I don't feel disapproving. I feel elated. "I still can't believe you just jumped a turnstile." I start for the map in the middle of the platform.

Leo follows me. "Hey, I might need those two extra dollars. What if there's an emergency?"

"An emergency that needs two dollars?"

"Could be a pizza emergency."

I snort. I can't help it. "That's true. You could get an emergency slice of pizza."

He smiles. "Are we in the right place, at least?"

I swear I can feel that smile radiating through me to my fingertips. I look back at the map. "Yeah, I think so. We're all the way at the end of the line." I point to the black dot that marks the 7 train's last stop, before (I guess) it turns around and goes back the other way. Which means we can only go one direction from this station—no chance of getting on the wrong train.

The platform vibrates underneath us, practically familiar now. A headlight glows in the distance, and a minute later, a train rumbles into the station, slower than the other trains we've seen. It barely generates any wind at all.

It doesn't look like the other trains, either. These train cars all look old. Really old. Their sides are dark green metal instead of shiny silver, and they're wide and boxy. The lead car has two lit-up signs above the front window, but they're not digital. They look like they're backlit with a plain old lightbulb. One sign has a big s with the word SPE-CIAL stamped underneath. The other says HOUSTON and 2ND AVE. Underneath the window is a Christmas wreath.

The other subway trains all had more cars than I could easily count. But this train only has four.

"Um," says Leo.

I'm confused, too. Maybe the 7 trains just look . . . like this? Or maybe we're somehow in the wrong place and this is some other special train. I look up, but the sign above our heads says *7*. With an arrow, pointing right to this track.

The train's doors creak open. A man wearing a conductor's uniform, complete with white gloves and a cap, leans out of one of the cars and bellows, "Times Square, Forty-Second Street is next!"

Leo and I look at each other.

"He said *Times Square*," I say. "This must be right."

Leo shrugs.

So we step onto the train. The doors creak closed behind us.

I feel like we've stepped back in time. The seats are upholstered in pin-striped vinyl. The floors are the color of red brick and the walls are minty grin, stamped with CITY OF NEW YORK in bold, brassy letters that just . . . look old. It's something about the font.

The other people who have boarded the train seem excited. One guy is holding a small kid, pointing around the train car while the kid stares, mouth open.

"Hey, look." Leo knocks a knuckle against a poster framed on the wall of the train car.

New York Transit Museum
Holiday Nostalgia Train
This train car is from 1936

"Whoa." I look around, at the giant rivets in the train car's body, at the old advertisements lining the walls up near the ceiling. "I didn't even know there were subways in 1936."

"So I guess they just have these cars in, like, a museum?" Leo's still squinting at the sign, like maybe it will tell him something else.

"Yep, and they run them as a train for a few weeks around the holidays," says another voice.

We both turn around. It's the dad carrying his toddler, who's currently pointing at a particularly bright advertisement near the ceiling—luncheons at some diner for seventy-five cents.

"These are actually real train cars?" I ask.

The man nods. "They're at the Transit Museum the rest of the year."

"That's so cool." I watch him wander away down the length of the subway car, pausing to look at each of the advertisements with his kid. "Kat would love this. She sews all these vintage-inspired dresses. This would be such an amazing place to take pictures."

Next to me, Leo shoves his hands into his pockets and turns away. "Yeah," he says, but he doesn't sound that excited. "It's cool."

The train jerks into motion. We stagger over to a small bench seat next to a window and perpendicular to the wall. The vinyl cushion is stiff and weirdly bouncy, but there's something sort of nice about being crowded up against the window, with Leo next to me.

Outside, the station slowly blurs, and then everything turns dark as we pull into the tunnel. This is my last train ride with Leo. Next stop is the last one—literally. For us, anyway.

I wish I hadn't yelled at him so much, when we first met. I wish the Universe could have found some way to tell me that underneath the glowering and grumping, he's the kind of person who puts on ridiculous sunglasses. The kind of person who smiles, if you wait long enough. The kind of person who will spend a whole day getting lost in New York City, staring at pig buttons and yelling into the sky.

But I guess that's not really how the Universe works. You never know what you're missing until you've already missed it, and time always seems to go too slow when you want it to go faster, and too fast when you wish it would slow down.

I glance at Leo's hand, resting on his knee, fingers idly tapping another rhythm. All I want to do is hold his hand again. Tightly, the way he held mine when we ran down the tunnel after he jumped the turnstile.

You love Kat.

My stomach twists. I do.

I did.

I know I did. So why does it suddenly feel like something I have to tell myself, instead of something that just *is*?

I can't reach out and wrap my hand around Leo's now. It would be weird. It's not something that guys and girls do, without it *meaning something*. Of course he grabbed my hand after he jumped the turnstile. He did it to pull me along, because we were running, because we were actually worried someone might chase us.

But now . . .

I've thought, dozens of times, about that moment at the bonfire, holding hands with Kat. Whether it Meant Something. Or whether she thought we were doing it as friends, because it's something girls can do, without it meaning anything at all.

What a weird, gendery thing. I wanted it to mean something, to hold hands with Kat, but I have no idea if it does. And I have no idea if I could hold Leo's hand, as friends.

Do the rules change, if we're both queer?

Do I want them to?

The train slows down and my window brightens. I look up. We're pulling into Forty-Second Street.

How did that go so fast?

The doors open. Farther down the train, the conductor yells, "Times Square, Forty-Second Street! Next stop, Fifth Avenue!"

But Leo doesn't get up. And since I'm stuck between him and the wall, I can't really get to the door if he doesn't get out of my way. And I guess I *could* just stand up, and push at him, and make him move . . . but I don't want to.

We sit there, frozen in place.

The doors creak closed again. The train jerks forward.

We missed our stop.

"What are we doing?" My voice comes out a whisper.

"I don't know," Leo says.

"We were supposed to get off there."

For a moment, Leo is quiet. Then he says, "Oops."

I can't decide whether to laugh or freak out. "Oops?"

He taps his fingers on his knees. "We can get off at the next stop."

But when the train pulls into Fifth Avenue, we still don't get up. What am I doing? I need to go back. We both do.

It's too late now, though. The train doors close again, and we rumble back into the tunnels.

Should I text Kat? What if we miss our bands, *again,* and this time Kat tells one of the chaperones what's going on? After all this, I could still end up being the Girl Who Got Lost In New York.

The train pulls into the next stop. The conductor bellows, "Grand Central!"

That snaps me out of my thoughts. "Wait, Grand Central?"

Leo glances at me. "What?"

"Get up." I push at Leo. "We're getting off."

"Ow." He rubs his arm, but he slides off the seat. I grab his jacket sleeve and drag him off the train and onto the platform. The doors creak closed a second later, and we watch the old-fashioned train rattle away into the tunnel. "What was that about?"

"Grand Central," I say. "It's another location from the book."

"Uh . . . Weren't we heading back, though?"

"You weren't exactly getting up, either."

He rubs a hand at his hair, which is still stubbornly sticking up on one side. But he doesn't argue.

So I keep talking. "Grand Central is supposed to have this amazing ceiling with, like, all these constellations painted on it. That's what the book says, anyway." Who am I trying to convince here? Leo or myself? "I just thought . . . maybe we could look. Really quick."

Leo hesitates, but only for a second, and then . . . "Yeah. We'll be quick."

He offers his arm, like some old-fashioned gentleman, and I grin. Loop my arm through his, like I did in Union Square.

We walk arm in arm all the way up the stairs. I guess we could run. Or at least jog. We both just said we'd be quick. But I don't want to move any faster, and I don't want to be any farther away from Leo.

I have to let go when we get to the turnstiles, because there's only room for one of us to go through at a time. But Leo waits for me on the other side, and offers me his arm again.

This subway station is definitely more crowded than the Thirty-Fourth Street one we just left. People weave around each other, all heading for different stairs leading to different trains. We zigzag our way to the escalators and ride up to the next level.

Wow.

Grand Central is more than grand. It's beautiful. And enormous. It must be, because we seem to be in a massive hallway of polished, beige stone, but I don't even see any train platforms, so there's no way this is the whole station. There are plenty of people, carrying backpacks, wheeling suitcases, jogging down the hall with briefcases, their footsteps turning to bouncing echoes around us. And there are a lot of stores, too, which is not exactly what I expected to find in a train station. Do people . . . shop here? I mean, there's a pharmacy, which I totally get. Maybe you're catching a train and realize you forgot your toothpaste.

But there's also a jewelry store. And an eye doctor. And a store with fancy letter-writing supplies.

The whole place is also a maze, passageways branching off around us, with words like VANDERBILT HALL and LEXINGTON PAS-SAGE carved into their stone arches.

"Any idea where we're going?" Leo asks.

I jump out of the way of several people with duffel bags who rush past us. Of course. It's the day before Thanksgiving. A lot of people are probably running to catch trains, off to see their families or friends for the weekend.

"Well . . ." I look around. "I just wanted to see the ceiling, and the big clock. They're in the book and I guess I figured they must really exist . . ."

"Main Concourse, maybe?" Leo points to the words engraved in the stone arch above our heads.

It seems like as good a guess as any. "Sure, let's try that?"

But in the middle of another passageway—this one has huge, glimmering chandeliers hanging from the ceiling—something else catches my eye.

It's a little model train, sitting in a store window that's stamped with NEW YORK TRANSIT MUSEUM in frosted white letters. And the model train looks exactly like the old subway train we were just riding.

Wait, isn't that what the guy with the toddler said? Those old train cars live at the New York Transit Museum, except when they run on the track during the holidays.

"Hey, Leo?" I grab at his sleeve. "Can we look here for a second?"

Leo seems to have gotten distracted by a map of Grand Central, stuck on a giant pillar in the middle of the passageway. He turns around. "Okay."

The place turns out to be a gift shop for the New York Transit Museum, as far as I can tell. I guess there probably isn't room for a whole museum inside a train station, even if that would have been cool.

Clearly everyone else is off catching actual trains instead of shopping, because the store is empty. We wander past books about trains, T-shirts and sweatshirts with trains on them, little model train sets for kids. There's even a mini Christmas tree, turning slowly around on a tabletop, decorated with train ornaments.

Near the back, I spot a collection of magnets, all stuck on a whiteboard hanging from the wall. Some of them just say NEW YORK TRANSIT MUSEUM, but several are 3D renderings of subway cars.

And up near the corner is an old-fashioned one. In little cursive letters underneath the car itself, the magnet says MTA 1936. Just like the train we were on.

I pluck the magnet off the whiteboard and flip it over in my fingers. The price tag on the back says $5.99.

Leo comes up next to me. He points one narrow finger at the subway magnet. "That's a good souvenir."

I glance at him, but he's staring at the magnet in my hand. I can't read his expression. "Yeah." I run my thumb over the old-fashioned car. It *is* a good souvenir. "Maybe it's too expensive."

Leo raises an eyebrow. "It's six bucks."

"Yeah, I know . . ." What's wrong with me? This would be perfect. Nothing represents New York City like a subway car.

"Hang on." Leo reaches into his pocket and pulls out two crumpled dollar bills. "Here. A contribution to the train magnet fund."

My face heats up. "Oh, you don't need to—"

"I've got two dollars for an emergency, remember?"

I look up. Leo's looking back at me, close enough that I could count the freckles smattered across his nose, if I wanted to. There's a tiny hint of a smile on his face.

I look away. "I have a debit card. It's fine. I'm just being silly."

He shrugs one shoulder and stuffs the bills back in his jacket pocket. "Okay. If you're sure."

"Yeah." I wish I felt sure. I wish I felt sure of anything. "Thanks, though."

"Anytime." He rubs the back of his neck, looking awkward. "Just . . . trying to help with the epic scene, right?"

I manage a grin, and turn for the checkout counter. I try to imagine giving Kat this little magnet, describing the old-fashioned train to her . . . but all I see is Leo, tapping his fingers on his knee, next to me on that bouncy vinyl seat.

I can't picture the epic scene at all.

SIXTEEN

WEDNESDAY, NOVEMBER 22—8:00 P.M.

LEO

MY PHONE BUZZES while Abby's at the cash register.

EVAN

Leo

Where are you

Well, I kind of knew this was coming. I mean, we skipped our subway stop and now we're just wandering around Grand Central. What did I think was going to happen?

Buzz.

EVAN

Are you blowing us off?

Buzz.

GINA

Wtf Leo

They're pissed. Of course they are. I'm being a selfish dick. And they're stuck covering for me.

I glance at Abby, over by the cash register.

> Sorry. Still with Abby. Might not make it to next thing. I know you guys are mad but plz can you keep covering

I send it and wait, thumbs hovering over the screen. Do I say anything else? Try to invent an excuse?

Or, worse, tell them the truth: that I'm still with Abby because I could listen to her talk forever, because something about the way she talks leaves me all the room I need to just exist, without saying anything.

Because the way she smiles and laughs with abandon makes me think I could learn to do the same thing.

Because even though I didn't mean to, I think I might be falling for her.

"All set!"

I jump, and accidentally enter a string of gibberish into the chat box. Abby's coming toward me, holding up the magnet.

Backspace, backspace, backspace. "Great!" It comes out falsely bright. Abby doesn't seem to notice.

"So I've got a button, a flute ornament, a caramel, and a subway car magnet," she says, ticking each souvenir off on her fingers.

"Okay. That's . . . that's good." I glance at my phone, but Evan and Gina haven't responded to my text. "Listen, Abby . . ."

She's got her backpack open, sticking the subway magnet in an inside pocket. "Yeah?"

God, I really don't want to tell her this. "We should . . . we should go back."

She glances up, and I swear her face falls. "Yeah." She looks away. "Yeah, we should."

"I guess we're both gonna be jumping turnstiles this time."

Abby doesn't seem to hear me. She's tugging absently on one of her hoodie ties, looking out at the passageway and all the people rushing past us. "Can we do one more thing?"

Yes. We can do ten more things, as long as I get to do them with you. "Um, sure."

She glances back at me. "Can we go see the big room? You know, the one in all the pictures, if you google *Grand Central*." This is clearly something she's done. "I just want to see if it really looks like the book described it. I mean, we're already here and everything..."

"Yeah." What else do we have to lose at this point, really? "Let's do it."

Abby flashes me a grin, grabs my hand, and pulls me back into the passageway. Her grip is tight and warm as she tugs me through the crowd, under an archway with MAIN CONCOURSE etched into it. We turn a corner, pass under an evergreen garland studded with red bows, and there it is. An absolute cavern of a space, dotted with Christmas wreaths and lit by huge, glittering chandeliers set into mirrored alcoves along the walls. Hundreds, or maybe thousands, of lightbulbs run around the edges of the ceiling, giving it a warm glow.

And the ceiling is...

"Holy shit," Abby whispers next to me.

It arches over our heads like a massive cathedral. And it's teal. Not exactly what I was expecting for a building that otherwise looks like a weird cross between a church and something out of Ancient Rome. Across the teal surface are drawings—outlines in gold of a flying horse, two fish, a crab, some dude holding a club—all of them pinpricked here and there by round yellow lights...

"They're constellations," Abby says.

"What are?"

"The designs. See?" She points. "That's Orion, that's Pisces..."

Now I get it. The little pricks of light up there—lightbulbs, I guess, set into the ceiling—are where the stars would be in the constellations. The dude with the club is Orion. The two fish are Pisces.

I'm not sure what the flying horse is about, though.

For several minutes, we stand there, fingers twined together, looking up at this celestial ceiling, while a cacophony of footsteps and voices echoes around us.

"So what happens here?" I ask. "I mean, in the book?"

"Clara Jane runs after this guy she likes," Abby says. "He's leaving on a train, and she runs through Grand Central to try and catch the train, but she's too late."

Sounds on-brand for this book. "Where's he going?"

"Connecticut." She glances at me sideways. "And I know that's not very far away, but it's a big deal in the book."

"Does she get the next train?"

"No, she ends up realizing she wasn't in love with that guy anyway, and then the day starts over." She looks thoughtful. "That's actually the only romance that doesn't get to the Empire State Building."

"I thought you said the book *ended* at the Empire State Building."

"It does. But all the guys she dates ask her to meet them at the top of the Empire State Building, and partway up, she realizes she doesn't love them, and the day starts over. But at the end, she realizes she *does* love the guy."

Okay. I think I get it. "And that breaks the time loop."

"Yeah. I mean . . . it seems like it does. She gets to the top of the building and the elevator doors open."

My phone buzzes in my pocket. Evan or Gina, finally texting back. "How'd we do?" I know I'm delaying the inevitable, but I don't want to look away from the ceiling yet. I don't want to let go of Abby's hand. "Any book locations we didn't get to?"

Abby chews her lip, thinking. "Um, there's this café, but it's supposed to be in Brooklyn, and anyway I'm pretty sure it's made up. I googled it once and the only café I found with that name is in Vermont. And there's a bit in Central Park, but the only souvenir I got there was dog shit."

I grin.

"And there are scenes at Clara Jane's apartment and stuff, but otherwise . . ." She pauses. "Just the Empire State Building."

Oh.

This just makes me feel worse. What's the matter with me? I don't care about this book—even though Abby makes it kind of sound like fun. And maybe also super confusing.

But still, the idea of ending our day now, short of that final stop—the stop that's literally the grand finale of the book . . .

It's like, *close, but no cigar.*

I let go of her hand and pull out my phone. Text from Evan, like I suspected. But he's on the group chat.

EVAN

Benefit of getting on a boat when it's dark: totally convinced Mr. Corbin that Noah Lowry-Smith was actually Leo.

I stare at the message. *Noah Lowry-Smith?* Seriously? We look *nothing* alike. Noah's got a pierced eyebrow. He uses a gallon of Axe body spray a day. Mr. Corbin should be able to recognize him from the eye-watering aroma if nothing else.

Hang on. Why is Evan on the group chat, acting like still covering for me is no big deal? Why haven't he and Gina replied to *my* text?

My phone buzzes again.

KAT

Ha our chaperone didn't even take attendance before this Rockefeller Center tour so we're good

Winning.

Why are they acting like us missing the last stop of the night was the plan all along?

"We're off the hook."

I look up. Abby has her phone out, too. Right—group text. Duh. *Off the hook?*

"Rockefeller Center isn't all that interesting." I try to say it lightly, to make her feel better. To make her feel like she's not really missing anything.

But she said *off the hook*. Almost like this is where she'd rather be.

My heart hammers, loud enough that I'm halfway convinced it's echoing around us, just like all these footsteps and voices. "Hey, Abby?"

She's still frowning at her phone. "Yeah?"

I look around the concourse. At the kiosk in the middle of the floor and the big, round, antique clock rising above it. The clock Abby wanted to see, probably. At the ticket counters. At the digital board above them, listing the arriving and departing trains.

Anywhere but Abby's face. "What do you think it means? To believe in the Universe?"

She looks at me quickly. I can see it from the corner of my eye. But I focus on the people around us—parkas and boots and bobbing pom-poms on hats, all rushing from A to B.

She slips her phone into her pocket and tilts her head back to stare up at the ceiling. "I guess . . . I think it means believing that sometimes things line up perfectly. You find that perfect moment, or you get that epic scene that you thought only happens in the movies." A smile creeps across her face, and somehow I'm looking at her again. I can't help it. "Or your friends manage to keep covering for you, even when it seems like you should be busted."

"You don't think sometimes stuff just happens?"

"Like what?"

She's going to hear my heartbeat. I'm sure of it. "Like maybe somebody gets on the wrong train, and it's not because of some will of the Universe, it just . . . happens."

"You mean chance," she says.

"Yeah. Chance."

Her gaze tips back down, skimming over the people around us. "I guess some things are just chance. I don't . . . I don't think every single thing happens for a big cosmic reason or something. It's just that . . . the world sucks. A lot." She shrugs, but it looks carefully casual. "Sometimes I want to think that things can magically line up and work out. That it's not all a shit show, and every once in a while . . ."

But she doesn't finish the sentence.

She doesn't need to. "That's why you love that book so much. Because Clara Jane gets to keep trying until things magically line up—"

"—and she gets to the top of the Empire State Building." Abby smiles. A little shy. A little self-conscious. "Yeah, I guess so."

I take a deep breath. Here goes everything. I drop her hand and pull out my phone.

Abby eyes it. "What are you doing?"

"Just looking something up . . ." I pull up Google Maps. Carefully type. Wait approximately forever. *Yes.* I turn my phone to Abby. "The Empire State Building is a fifteen-minute walk from here."

Abby stares at the map on my phone, her face blank.

"We've hit all the other book locations." Did I misread this moment? Does she want to try to catch up with her band? I mean, I may have missed the boat—literally—but Abby could still get to Rockefeller Center.

"Is it even open now?" she asks.

"Who cares?" My breath catches. "We can just look at it."

She hesitates. Glances at the antique clock, poking up like a sentry in the middle of the concourse.

8:20.

And then she grins at me. "One last stop?"

I could fly. "One last stop."

I'm beginning to think everything is huge in New York. Grand Central was enormous, but the Empire State Building is massive. I figured it would be tall, but I had no idea it was also wide. It takes up an entire block and hurtles so far into the sky that I can't even tell where it ends. There's a faint glow up there—probably from the lights near the top. It gets lit up at night, doesn't it? Of course, then again, the night sky here just generally glows.

What is a building this big even used for?

"Do you think it's still open?" Abby says.

We're standing on the street across from the Empire State Building, and the city lights make her eyes sparkle. Her nose is pink from the cold.

"This is supposed to be the city that never sleeps, right? Let's go see."

I don't wait for an answer, just jog across the empty street to the revolving doors on the opposite sidewalk. Abby follows me. The building hours are printed in gold lettering right next to the doors. Seasonal hours, weekday hours, weekend hours . . .

It takes me a while to skim through it all, but finally:

Doors Close 10 P.M.

Last Elevator to Observation Deck 9:15 P.M.

I pull out my phone. It's only 8:33. "We've still got time. The last elevator doesn't go up for another forty-five minutes, and my band isn't supposed to be back at the hotel until ten."

"Same for us. I think." She hesitates, still staring at the doors. "But we probably can't go up, right? I mean, there must be tickets."

Oh. Right. And tickets cost money. And for a real tourist attraction like this, they can't be cheap.

"Let's just go in," I say. "We're here. Might as well."

She looks almost nervous. I wonder, for a second, if I made the wrong call. If I thought I was trying to grab hold of the Universe, but once again, the Universe is saying *just kidding*.

Then Abby takes a deep breath. "Yeah," she says. "Might as well."

And she grabs my hand and pulls me through the revolving doors.

SEVENTEEN

ABBY

THE LOBBY IS almost as grand as Grand Central. Polished stone floors and walls, a soaring high ceiling, and a mural of the Empire State Building itself, against an art deco–style sunburst. It's all so *big*. Even the Christmas trees on either side of the mural, covered in gold tinsel, dwarf the information desk between them. The whole lobby glows like the sun really is shining in here.

And it's full of band nerds.

I definitely knew that our bands were not the only ones currently in New York City for the parade tomorrow. And I guess I knew, somewhere in the back of my mind, that those other bands must be doing their own sightseeing today. But it never occurred to me that we might actually run into them somewhere.

But here they are—another marching band, all in matching green-and-white varsity jackets, pointing and talking loudly and trying to form some sort of line to go up the escalators.

Leo elbows me. "Take off your jacket."

I wish I could see around all these people. I just want a peek up the escalator. "Why?"

"Just do it." Leo's already shrugging out of his jacket and slinging it over his arm, practically inside out, so the black-and-gold colors aren't visible.

Oh. Is he really thinking what I think he's thinking?

I slide my backpack off my shoulder and pull off my jacket, holding it over my arm the way Leo's holding his. Trying to be casual, like we just got too hot.

Leo shoots me a grin, and then he joins the edge of the marching band blob.

This isn't going to work. We're going to get in so much trouble.

But I follow him.

We stick to one side of the group, inching forward, ducking and looking away any time we see one of the chaperones. They're pretty easy to spot, since they're all adults and they all look as frazzled as I remember Mrs. Gunnerson looking. At the bottom of the escalator is a Black woman in a gray suit with bright blue lapels, complete with an old-fashioned gray-and-blue cap. She's talking to one of the adults and scanning some sort of pass on their phone.

And then we're on the escalator, riding up.

And then we're stepping off.

We fall back, a few steps behind the rest of the group as all of us do that slow museum-walk across the stone floor. Which I guess is appropriate, since this area seems to actually be some kind of museum, full of big black-and-white photographs, models of the Empire State Building, and informational plaques saying things like WON-DER OF THE MODERN WORLD and OPENING DAY.

Leo jerks his head at a sign. ELEVATORS TO OBSERVATION DECK THIS WAY.

I glance around, but nobody's watching us. The marching band is spreading out through the exhibit, chaperones wandering after them.

I pull my band jacket back on, and so does Leo—so none of the chaperones will run after us, thinking we belong to their band.

And then Leo grasps my hand and we slip away through the museum, following the signs for the elevators. There's no one else here, except the marching band, so we jog along a pathway marked by red velvet ropes—there must be incredible lines on busy days—until we round a corner into a hallway of elevators. A man in a gray-and-blue suit and cap is standing in the center of the hallway. My heart leaps into my throat, but he simply extends a hand to an open elevator.

Leo grips my hand tighter. "Which floor is the observation deck?" he asks. "The one outside?"

"Eighty-six," the man in the uniform says. "But this elevator just takes you to the eightieth floor. Then you gotta go to another elevator. That'll take you the rest of the way."

"Okay, thanks." Leo does his best to smile casually, but it looks a little tense.

And then we're in the elevator. The doors close in front of us. Inside, the walls are gray-toned marble with a black silhouette of the Empire State Building.

It looks like the black silhouette on the cover of *THRoCJ*.

Leo punches the button that says 80. The elevator lurches up, leaving my stomach on the floor.

I'm taking the elevator to the top of the Empire State Building. Just like Clara Jane.

The author of *THRoCJ* likes to use phrases like *she wanted to pinch herself* or *she felt like she was dreaming,* and I always thought that was a little unrealistic. Nobody ever pinches themselves in real life. Nobody ever confuses real life for a dream.

Except right now, I do want to pinch myself. Right now, I do feel like I'm dreaming.

Forget that flyer. The one I took a picture of at the Strand and asked Ida about. Forget the event the flyer was advertising, the one that's going on right now. The reason I hesitated, just for a moment, when Leo said we should see the Empire State Building.

I squeeze Leo's hand. This is where I want to be.

The digital numbers above the door rush by. How fast are we going? It must be fast. My head feels stuffy. I make myself yawn, and my ears pop.

Ding. The elevator stops, and the doors open onto another hallway that looks almost like the one we were just in. More velvet ropes. We pass a few people this time, going the other direction, taking the elevators back down from the top.

Another man in a suit and cap. And again, he waves us to an empty elevator.

Leo punches the button for 86.

The ride is much shorter this time. Only a few seconds, and then the doors open onto a smaller, darker hallway. Strips of white lights illuminate the edges of a set of stairs. We climb our way up, fingers on the railing for guidance. Leo leans his back against a door, pushing it open . . .

A blast of icy air rushes in as we step out onto the open-air observation deck. It whistles painfully in my ears and blows my hair into my face for the five hundredth time today. But I don't care.

Laid out in front of us is the whole city, like a galaxy. A bright blanket of stars. Some near—the lights of skyscrapers close by—and some farther away. Lights from thousands of windows. From hundreds of cars. From streetlights and subway stops and big, digital billboards. All receding away into the dark horizon.

"Well?" Leo, next to me. "What do you think?"

He's watching me, with the barest hint of a smile. No frown in sight.

"Will you make fun of me if I say it's magical?" I ask.

"No," he says, and I know he means it.

I slowly let my breath out. It clouds in front of my face. "It's magical."

His smile widens, and he wanders over to the row of binoculars on stands that make them look like parking meters, lined up along the edge of the observation deck. He leans down and sticks his face against one.

"Can't see anything," he says. He straightens up. "I guess they need quarters."

I lean my elbows on the concrete half wall of the deck, staring through the crisscrossing lines of the steel bars rising in a diamond pattern above us. The wind is making my eyes water and my teeth chatter. From somewhere else on the deck, I hear the faint murmur of a few voices. But right here, at least, we seem to be alone.

Leo leans beside me. "What do you think you're gonna say to Kat?"

A jolt of anxiety goes through me. "You mean tomorrow?" I say, even though I know the answer. "I don't know."

Another gust of wind ruffles Leo's hair. He shivers and pulls his beanie back on. "You'll figure it out."

How can he sound so sure? I don't have anything figured out. I have four souvenirs and no words to say. "I didn't think it would be this hard."

Leo looks down at the streets below us. "Yeah. Kind of unfair, right? Straight people have it so much easier than they realize."

That makes me smile. "I guess I'll have to focus on the objects, like you said." I take a breath. "Give her the button and tell her how much I love her sewing."

"Give her the flute ornament and tell her how much you love her playing." He looks thoughtful. "What about the candy?"

"I think she's sweet?" I laugh, because it sounds silly.

Leo grins. "The subway magnet?"

"Um . . . an apology for getting on the wrong train?" But the words stick in my throat. Because even though I got all these things for Kat, my memories of finding them are all tangled up in Leo. Leo wearing ridiculous sunglasses, Leo laughing in the rain, Leo holding my hand in the middle of Grand Central.

Leo just . . . being here. As his whole, rough-edged, honest self.

"Hey, look." Leo reaches across the half wall we're leaning on. At the very edge, an inch away from plummeting off the side of the building, is a penny. A little glimmer of copper against the stone. Leo picks it up and lays it in front of me. "Souvenir."

I pick up the penny. It's frigid—so cold it turns my fingertips numb. But otherwise, it's completely ordinary. Not very shiny, or very grimy; minted three years ago. "A lucky penny from the Empire State Building," I say.

"Exactly." Leo nudges my shoulder with his. "That seems like a sign from the Universe, right?"

I glance at him, but for once, he doesn't sound teasing. He's just looking back at me, his nose pink from the cold, so close that if I leaned forward a few inches, I could bump it with mine.

It takes me a minute to find my voice. "A sign of what?"

He says quietly, "That you'll get a happy ending."

I swear I stop breathing. I swear my heart stops beating.

All I want to tell him right now is that even though we've spent the whole day together, I feel like I could spend tomorrow together too, and the day after, and the day after, and . . .

He's so close.

I think I'm leaning toward him, and I think he might be leaning toward me . . .

Someone lets out a loud peal of laughter. Sudden footsteps, coming closer.

I pull back, or Leo pulls back. We both pull back, and I turn around, in the direction of the footsteps. A small knot of people has rounded the corner of the observation deck, laughing together as they make their way toward us. They stop a few yards away, peering down at the city and pointing things out to each other.

What did I almost do?

I look down at the penny in my hand. I'm in love with Kat. I've been in love with Kat for months. One day can't possibly undo all of that.

"We should go," Leo mumbles behind me.

I close my fingers around the penny and stuff my hands into my pockets. "Yeah."

We're silent on the ride down. First to the eightieth floor, past the man in white gloves, and then down to the second floor. The other marching band is still there, wandering around. But nobody gives us a second glance as we dodge around them to the escalator.

"Have a nice night," the ticket taker says when we reach the lobby.

I know I should say something polite back to her. Even just *thanks*. But I can't. She feels like part of the dream, and I'm waking up.

EIGHTEEN

LEO

WE HEAD FOR Times Square without even discussing it. We both know the day is over, for real this time. It's obvious in the way there's more space between us than there's been all day. You could fit three sousaphones in this gap. And that would still be less awkward than whatever is hanging in this silence.

I don't have it in me to suggest jumping the subway turnstiles, and what's the rush now anyway? We have time before our bands arrive back at the hotel. So we walk up Fifth Avenue, each of us on either side of this chasm, while a hundred *why*s crash around in my head.

Why did I almost kiss her?

Why *didn't* I kiss her?

Why didn't she kiss me?

And what does this mean, anyway? What does it mean that I thought—I really thought—she wanted to kiss me?

Fifth Avenue is practically empty now. There are barriers blocking every single intersection we pass. Down one street I see blue and red flashing lights—a police car. Maybe they're blocking off the streets to get ready for the parade tomorrow.

Panic knots in my stomach.

But now, it's not just about the cameras. Not just about the Ex Family.

I'm panicking because I'm running out of time. To do what, I don't even know, but tomorrow is roaring down on us and the rest of today, and whatever it means, is getting pushed out of the way.

We pass a wide, unexpectedly regal stairway, guarded by two stone lions, leading up to a building that's all columns. Another piece of architecture that looks like it belongs in Ancient Rome or Washington, D.C. Carved into the stone over the columns are letters that spell out THE NEW YORK PUBLIC LIBRARY.

Damn. The library in Springfield looks like a squat toaster compared to this.

I should have just given Abby that book instead of almost kissing her. We were at the top of the Empire State Building. Giving her the book would have been plenty epic. Giving her the book would have left us room to be friends.

Ugh. Why am I always screwing things up?

We hit Forty-Second Street, and I look back at the map on my phone. "This way." I turn us around the corner.

We follow the hulking shape of the library along Forty-Second Street, until it ends abruptly in . . . light.

It's a park, or something. Rows and rows of trees, but they're all wrapped in white, twinkling lights. The open space between them is filled with what look like tiny glass houses. Or greenhouses. Does New York City have a park full of greenhouses?

Behind all the greenhouses is a much larger structure that's half tent, half glass, and has to be at least two stories tall. There's also an enormous Christmas tree, decked out in colorful lights with a big white star on top.

I stop. Did we take a wrong turn somewhere and end up back at

Rockefeller Center? There was a big unlit Christmas tree there that I saw this morning.

But that tree had to be at least fifty feet tall. This one isn't nearly that big.

Abby has stopped, too, staring at all the lights and the little greenhouses. Her face glows, round and warm and soft, and her hair is a curly mess around her shoulders, and her shoulders are hunched up because it's freezing.

And she's so beautiful, I don't know how I ever looked at her, yesterday afternoon in the hotel lobby, and thought she looked ordinary.

"Want to walk through?" It tumbles out of my mouth. I'm desperate to close the chasm.

She glances at me and smiles, small and shy. "Sure."

The greenhouses aren't greenhouses at all. They're tiny shops—pop-ups like the holiday market we left back in Union Square. Just . . . teeny-tiny houses made of clear plastic on metal frames instead of white tents. Most of them are closed up and dark, but a few still have their doors open and some lights on. The people inside are clearly closing up for the night, packing away ornaments, candles, knitted scarves and hats. A lot of the same stuff I saw in Union Square.

Past the pop-up shops, spread out in front of the Christmas tree, is an ice-skating rink. An outdoor one, right in the middle of the park, just like the one at Rockefeller Center.

I guess New Yorkers like ice-skating. Even at night. There are still people out there. Couples hold hands and groups of friends skate around each other and laugh, while projections of big blue snowflakes whirl across the surface of the ice. Around the rink, pillars lit in purple and blue and pink stand like beacons in the dark, and between them are more people, sitting at café tables, talking or pulling off their skates.

There's music, too. For a second, I think it must be piped in, coming from speakers somewhere. Until I spot the band busking at the end of one row of tiny shops, right next to the Christmas tree. It's a small band, just four people. A lady singing and playing the tambourine. A guy on guitar next to her, another guy on banjo, and a person wearing an enormous puffy coat who might be a man or a woman or neither playing a piano keyboard on a stand. The guitar case is open in front of them, full of dollar bills and loose change. The people closing up their shops nearby are dancing a little to the music: some upbeat, vaguely folkish song that I don't know. I wonder if the band wrote it. They sound good, and they look like they're having fun.

They finish the song with a flourish. The shopkeepers clap. The banjo guy waves at them. The guy with the guitar kneels down and starts collecting the dollar bills out of the guitar case. I guess they're packing up, too.

Makes sense. It's been cold, but now it's starting to approach frigid.

Abby wanders over to the band. "That was so great," she says. "Have you been playing here all day?"

I trail after her, because apparently I want to be close to her more than I want to avoid making small talk with random strangers.

The singer laughs. "Just for a couple hours while the Winter Village was open." She waves a hand at the rows of little plastic houses.

"Well, you sounded amazing."

She raises her eyebrows. "You guys musicians?"

"Oh. Um . . ." Abby glances at me. "Yeah, actually. We're in marching band. Or . . . bands. Different bands."

"Hey," says the banjo player, "you're not playing in the parade tomorrow, are you?"

Abby looks suddenly shy. "Yeah. We are."

"Nice!" says the keyboard player. "If you had your instruments, I'd say we should jam before we head out."

Abby lights up. "I do have my instrument!" She slings her backpack down from her shoulder. "I have my clarinet with me. I actually accidentally left it in my backpack this morning, because I was kind of rushing off, but . . ." She looks at me again. "We don't have to. I mean, you don't have—"

"I have my sticks." Wait. Why did I say that? I don't have drums. I don't want to play in front of these people. I've been stubbornly ignoring any thought of playing tomorrow for as long as possible.

Plus, the last time I played, there was that whole losing-my-place-and-ruining-an-entire-dress-rehearsal-in-front-of-the-whole-town thing.

"You a drummer?" says the keyboard player.

Part of me wants to say no. "Yeah."

"Oh, man." The keyboard player turns around and rummages through a suitcase behind them. "I brought this to play when we did 'Little Drummer Boy' earlier . . ." They reach into a cardboard box and pull out a single small tom-tom.

It is not a nice drum. It looks like it cost twenty bucks. It's scratched and scuffed and probably only eight or ten inches across—the smallest sizes toms come in. But it is a drum. And I've got sticks. And I'd look like a real jerk if I refused to play now.

I shrug, push down the knot of panic, and say, "Sure, I can use that."

Abby crouches down on the pavement and starts unpacking her clarinet. So I take the drum from the keyboard player, sit on the edge of the amp, and wedge the drum between my knees.

Abby sticks her clarinet reed in her mouth while she carefully fits the instrument together. It's sort of funny to see her as a musician. I knew she played clarinet, obviously. We're only here because we're both in band. But it's still different, watching her fasten the reed onto her mouthpiece. Like somehow it hasn't really hit me until now that we have music—and marching band—in common.

Abby asks the keyboard player for a B-flat and tunes her clarinet, wincing a little bit, laughing at how cold it is, warming the instrument in her hands before she runs up and down a few scales, her fingers moving with an almost careless grace.

I think every instrument sort of has a personality type. The kind of person it seems to attract. Drummers are chaotic. Low brass players are all some combination of laid-back and weird. Trumpeters are the jocks of band, all convinced they're badasses.

Abby fits the clarinet—happy not to be the star of the show, sort of anxious, constantly getting drowned out by louder voices. Like, say, those trumpets.

Or the flutes.

But Abby makes the clarinet sound beautiful, even just running up and down scales. I've never really paid attention to a lone clarinet before. It's a mellow, steady voice, singing gently to itself.

Abby takes the clarinet out of her mouth, blowing on her fingers. "I'm ready."

The keyboard player launches into an intro, and the guitarist and the banjo guy quickly join in. I don't know the song, but it lurches and sways like some piratey sea shanty, and the good thing about being a drummer is you almost don't really *have* to know the song. As long as you find the beat and know the tempo, you can play along. It's all about finding the right pattern and then putting your own spin on it.

So . . . here goes.

I twirl my sticks and lay down a beat underneath the other instruments. Simple at first, and then filling in around the downbeats as I get more comfortable.

The singer starts in on a lilting melody, and it's definitely some kind of sea shanty because the lyrics are all about waves and true loves and honestly, it sounds depressing as shit, but I don't care. The rest of the song is upbeat, and now Abby's joining in, improvising harmonies and little clarinet comments in between the verses. I catch her gaze, and her eyes crinkle at the edges, like she's smiling at me around her clarinet.

The chasm closes with a slam.

This tom is kind of wimpy. It sounds plasticky. But the singer set her tambourine on the amp next to me, so I loop that in, too, adding an extra clang on the offbeats, where I'd put a hi-hat if I was playing a real drum set.

Slowly, just like in band, I feel the whole group coalescing around my rhythm. I'm by myself this time, no drumline around me, but I'm still the glue holding everything together. The anchor as our energy rises, all of us finding each other in the chords, in the rhythm, in the soaring melodies . . .

I throw in a wild fill as we hurtle into the chorus. The keyboard player lets out a whoop.

There's this feeling that happens, when you're on the field with your whole band, and you reach the climax of whatever you're playing, and you just *know,* deep in your core, that everyone around you is absolutely nailing this drill. It's hard to explain, but you forget about your legs burning. The air catching in your lungs. The sweat running down your back.

All you are is the music. Not just whatever piece of it you yourself are playing. Not just the rhythm, the beat, the drive. Not just your sticks against your own drum.

You're part of the whole thing. Your rhythm is part of the harmony, and that's part of the melody, and all of it together is what makes it music.

I don't know what that feeling is. Maybe it's joy. Maybe it's freedom. Maybe it's having *space*—space to create something with your body and your energy and your intention that doesn't exist for any reason other than being beautiful.

But *that's* the feeling I've been missing. That's the feeling I forgot. The feeling that's been erased by panic, bit by bit, as this trip got closer. That feeling of being part of something bigger than myself.

That's why I love marching band. Not just because our formations look cool, even though they do. Not just because I feel like a badass when I play drums, even though I do. Not just because we win competitions, even though that's pretty great, too.

I love band because when I'm on the field and everything around me is working perfectly, I am fully *me*. But also, at the same time, I don't matter at all, because none of it is really about me. None of it is about my name or my gender or my pronouns or what clothes I wear or what small existential crisis I'm having today.

It's kind of like being in New York City. Sure, it's crowded, but somehow, I still feel like I've had more space today than I've had in months. Space to breathe, space to exist, space to disappear and become anonymous.

Fuck. I want that back—this kind of freedom. No matter what happens with my family, I'm not letting go of this again. Even when it's something like "Seventy-Six Trombones" that we've practiced to death, I'm not letting go of this space. I'm done contracting, making myself smaller so I'm less inconvenient to everyone else. It's not just about being angry and screaming my head off into the Manhattan sky. It's about taking up space with everything. With *me*.

I drum loud and wild through the chorus. Back off to gently underpin the verses. And then rise up and crash us into the chorus again.

We wail and thunder our way through this song until the keyboard player lifts a hand and we hit the last chord together. And then we all start laughing, breath clouding in front of our faces. The last of the vendors are gone now, but a few people at the café tables clap.

"That was so fun!" Abby is grinning, so wide it looks like it hurts. "Thanks for letting us play."

"Hey, you guys are great," the singer says. "Thanks for jamming."

"I think I better pack it in, though," says the guitar guy. "My fingers are freezing up."

The band members nod in agreement, and soon they're all packing up. I help the keyboard player load the tom drum back into its cardboard box, and then into a wheeled cart, along with their keyboard.

"Good luck tomorrow," the singer says, picking up the amp. "Have fun in the parade!"

"Thanks!" Abby looks up from where she's kneeling on the sidewalk, stowing her clarinet back in her backpack.

The band waves and they all trudge off into the night. The wheels of the cart squeak. The murmur of their voices slowly fades.

I glance at the ice-skating rink. It's so close. And there's no line. The only staff people I see are some guys wearing neon yellow vests. And they're busy disassembling the ropes strung between those poles they use for crowd control. What are they called? Stanchions?

On an impulse, I grab Abby's hand and pull her toward the rink.

"Leo, what are you—"

I let go of her hand, drop my backpack on the sidewalk, and jump the railing.

"Leo!" Abby shouts after me. "What are you doing?"

Flailing around like an awkward bird is the answer. My sneakers slide across the ice and I have to wave my arms frantically to avoid falling right on my ass. Several skaters swerve to avoid me.

Behind me, Abby laughs. "Get off, you're gonna get us in trouble!"

I somehow manage to waddle around in a circle until I'm facing her. "Only if you keep yelling about it."

She looks around, but the neon-vest guys are still working on the stanchions. I'm not even sure they've seen me through all the skaters gliding around the rink.

"Come on!" I wave at Abby and almost overbalance again. "Nobody's looking. It's fine."

"Fine? You look like you're two steps away from a concussion!" She chews her lip, glances once more toward the guys in vests, and then she drops her backpack. She climbs awkwardly over the railing and shuffles slowly toward me, arms outstretched for balance.

I bite back a grin. "I mean, take your time."

She gives me the finger. "Excuse me for trying to get over there in one piece!"

I laugh, in a way I'm not sure I have all day, or even all week, and it doesn't even have that much to do with her flipping me off while also trying not to fall over.

It's just that I feel like I can breathe. Like I'm still riding the adrenaline rush of drumming my heart out.

Abby flaps a hand at me, making little grabby motions with her fingers. I hold my hand out and she grasps it, and we spin around awkwardly on the ice together, both giggling like we're five, while people wearing actual ice skates zoom past us.

"This is so much harder than I remember!" she says.

"What, you've slid around a rink in your shoes before?"

"No! I mean, ice-skating!" She yelps as her feet almost go out from under her.

"Yeah, I think this is easier with skates on." My feet slide apart and for a terrifying second, I'm dangerously close to doing the splits.

"Hey, this was your idea!" Abby tries to pull me back up and almost falls over again.

"And you followed me." I manage to get my feet back under me—with a lot more flailing, which makes Abby laugh. And that makes her wobble again. So I grab her, which makes me wobble, and that makes her laugh harder, and pretty soon we're holding on to each other, laughing and spinning around in circles.

Until we run out of momentum and our laughter fades. And then we're just looking at each other, still grasping each other's jacket sleeves.

Her eyes are so bright, and she's smiling so big. And I realize it's not just the wild drumming that felt like freedom. It's not just music that gives me space to breathe. It's not just the anonymity of New York that lets me feel more than angry and small . . .

The day's almost over, but I refuse to run out of time.

I lean forward, and I kiss her.

NINETEEN

ABBY

EVERY THOUGHT FLIES right out of my head. My mind goes completely blank. I have no idea what I was just doing, or what I was planning to do next. The world condenses down into this moment—Leo's mouth against mine, his jacket gripped in my hands, my feet slipping, barely, against the ice.

This is the kind of kiss I've read about in books, in fanfiction, the kind of kiss I wasn't even sure was real. But I'm here now, and it *is* real, and I'm going to melt, or catch fire, or explode.

It's so much more than any kiss I ever imagined. Even the ones I imagined with Kat.

Wait. *Kat.*

No. No, no, no. What am I doing? This isn't supposed to be happening...

I pull away, or maybe Leo pulls away, or maybe we both pull away. All I know is I'm sliding on the ice, too fast and too clumsily to keep my balance. I knock into Leo, and suddenly we're both falling...

Ouch.

"Oh my god, are you okay?"

Skates scrape against ice. People are stopping, changing direction, coming over to us.

"Do you need help?"

"Where are your skates?"

"Are you guys okay?"

Oh, god. Everyone's staring. We got through this whole day being practically invisible, shouting at each other in a subway station, jumping turnstiles, but now, *of course,* everyone's looking at us. Even people all the way across the rink. And I'm all tangled up with Leo, both of us flat on the ice, and I can't seem to figure out how to *untangle* myself . . .

"I'm fine." I get an arm out. And then a leg. "We're okay. Nothing happened." Somehow, I manage to get myself back on my feet. Leo's getting up next to me—I think. I don't look at him. I can't manage to look at him, because my face is on fire and my eyes are prickling and that kiss was . . .

That kiss was everything.

And now I'm spinning into crisis. Because my tailbone hurts and my elbow is sore and everyone's staring at us . . .

. . . and I'm not gay. Or, I'm not *just* gay, because that kiss . . . that kiss means I'm complicated, and even if Ida said labels don't matter, they're still a way to know who you are. And now I have no idea who I am, or what I want, or what I'm doing.

All I know is that I need to get out of here.

"I'm fine." I say it again, but it comes out mumbled. I start shuffling back toward the edge of the rink. People part to let me through. I try to smile, to look okay, but my chin is trembling and my hands are shaking and I feel like I'm coming undone.

This is so much worse than stepping in dog shit.

I reach the railing and blindly clamber back over it. And I guess I must have convinced people I'm really okay, because nobody's following me. Everyone's going back to skating. Going back to their friends. Going back to their night. Moving on.

The only person left staring at me from the ice is Leo.

I turn around and grab my backpack from the sidewalk, because if I keep looking at him, I'm going to crumble. I pull my phone out of my pocket. I should text Kat. I should tell her I'm coming back, right now.

But instead, I start scrolling backward through my texts with Kat. Further and further, until I get to our texts from before this trip. I don't know what I'm looking for. Something to tell me what to do, I guess. Something to remind me how much I love Kat. To make me feel those butterflies again, like I did at the bonfire. To remind me what today was for in the first place.

Instead, I feel like someone reached into my chest and squeezed the air out of my lungs. *This isn't how love is supposed to work.* Clara Jane didn't scroll through her phone, looking for a text message to prove which guy was her true love.

Clara Jane had magical moments. Clara Jane just *knew.*

Because you're supposed to *know.*

Everyone always knows. In books, in movies, in fanfiction. Or at least, *you* know, when you read. When you watch.

Something clunks, and I jump. It's Leo, climbing back over the railing next to me, picking up his backpack and slinging it over his shoulder. He doesn't look at me. Just pulls out his phone and frowns over it, punching at it with his thumbs.

My own phone buzzes in my hand. A message in the group chat.

LEO

We're coming back now. Thx for covering.

My eyes prickle again. I can't tell if I want to cry or explode. "I guess that's it then." It snaps out of me, but I don't care.

He looks up with a scowl. "You didn't seem interested in hanging around."

My throat tightens. "People were staring!"

He frowns harder. "Right."

What's that supposed to mean? "You're the one who made me go out on the ice. What are you so pissed about?"

For a second, his glare vanishes and he just stares at me, eyes wide. Then he juts out his jaw. "Nothing. We should go."

He turns on his heel and stalks away, through the empty chairs and tables, heading for the edge of the park.

My vision swims. I jog after him, my heart pounding in my ears. "Nothing? That's all you've got to say?"

He glowers ahead like I'm not even here. "It doesn't matter."

Something inside me breaks. Forget crying. Now I'm ready to explode. "You kissed me! After I *told* you I was in love with Kat. After I told you about the book, and the notes, and everything I wanted today to be. You *kissed* me. How does that not matter?"

His shoulders hunch higher. "Forget it."

"Oh, sure. Okay." We're weaving through the dark, empty shops now. An abandoned village of tiny glass houses. Or another liminal space. "It was *your* idea to go out on the ice. *Your* idea to go to the Empire State Building. This whole thing was your idea! I didn't ask you to hang out with me all day!"

He reaches the edge of the park and starts across the street without waiting for the walk signal. There's no traffic now anyway. "Wow. Thanks." His voice is thick. "Glad to know I was just a deadweight forcing you to do a bunch of stuff you can't stand."

A gust of cold wind hits my face. My eyes water. "I didn't mean—"

"You know, if you hate spending time with me so much, maybe we should just find our own ways back to the hotel, since there's clearly no reason for us to spend any more time together." He walks faster. "You got what you wanted. Leave me alone."

But I run even faster to catch up. I can't seem to breathe. My lungs won't expand. "Fine!" What am I saying? "I guess I should since you're still determined to be a grumpy asshole!"

"Now I'm a grumpy asshole?" Leo whirls around to face me, silhouetted against a distant, colorful glow radiating into the sky from farther down the street. "I spent the whole day helping you patch up this completely ridiculous fairy-tale plan of yours because you're too much of a coward to tell your best friend you like her. How does that make me an asshole?"

He blurs in front of me. I blink and tears run down my face in hot streaks. "Oh, right, you're a *real hero,* helping me out because you lost my book."

"At least I have one foot in the real fucking world!" he shouts. "Instead of pretending I live in a romance book where everything is perfect and magical and I never have to do a damn thing myself because the Universe will set it all up for me!"

It lands like a slap. "I'd rather believe in a little magic than just hate everything because I'm an angry and spiteful person!"

"You have no idea what it's like for me!" Leo yells. "You have no idea what it's like to be trans where I'm from!"

"I know I don't!" I'm yelling, too. My throat is raw and my voice is shaking, and I can't make it stop. "But it wouldn't matter if I did, because you're determined to be an asshole and make yourself miserable!"

"If I'm such an asshole, then why'd you spend the whole day with me?" Leo's eyes look too bright. "Why'd you keep blowing off your big crush to hang out with me?"

"I wasn't blowing off—"

"Right, you just used me to fix your grand romantic plans."

"You *wanted* to help! Because you felt guilty!"

"Well, I'm *done* feeling guilty!" Leo swings his backpack around in front of him and yanks open the zipper with shaking fingers. "So here. You might as well have this." He shoves a small brown paper bag at me. "Now we're even."

And he turns and storms away.

I take a step after him, but the bag is heavy and I don't have a grip on it. It tips and a book slides out, landing on the sidewalk so hard that the front cover flies open.

The title page is yellowed and dog-eared, but I recognize it right away, because I've looked at that font and those letters dozens and dozens of times.

The Hundred Romances of Clara Jane.

And underneath the title, in a familiar scrawl, is the author's signature.

I crouch down. For a second, I wonder if Leo somehow found it—the copy I lost—but as soon as I pick up the book, I know that's not true. This book feels different, worn in different ways. The signature is even in a different place on the title page.

I look at the paper bag in my hands. Leo had a paper bag when we left the bookstore. The one he stuffed into his backpack.

He must have found this book during the scavenger hunt. And he got it for me.

Wait. Leo . . .

I straighten up, clutching the book and the bag, and run to the end of the block, my backpack bouncing against my back, my throat burning. There are more people here. More taxis. A digital billboard across the street flashes so brightly that for a second, I can barely see. I blink spots out of my eyes, squinting, turning in a circle.

But Leo's gone.

TWENTY

LEO

I CAN'T WALK fast enough. I can't get out of there fast enough.

I want to storm off and leave Abby behind, and I want her to catch up and stop me. I want her to call out to me, and I'm scared of what will happen if she does. So I walk faster, heading right into the massive neon explosion of Times Square. Even this late it's crowded, full of taxis and buses and people on the sidewalks.

I stumble into a jog, crossing another street ahead of a slowly cruising taxi. I'm on the next block now, with a whole building between me and Abby, but I keep going. The jog turns into a run. Faster and faster, until I'm barreling down the streets of Manhattan in the dark, which isn't remotely what I thought I'd be doing on this trip, but I don't care. None of this is what I thought would happen.

Getting lost.

Spending the whole day with a girl I just met.

Falling face-first in love with that girl like . . . like . . .

Like someone who believes in the Universe.

Like someone who isn't a Logistical Headache.

My hat slips back on my head and the wind spirals into my ears.

Cold air burns my throat. My feet hurt each time they hit the side-walk, which makes perfect sense, because I've been on my feet all day. And I'll be on them for a good chunk of tomorrow. Great.

The hotel is in sight now, and I'm going to look like I've completely lost it if I run up to the sliding doors at top speed. So I slow down. What am I running from anyway?

The hotel doors whoosh open, and I walk into the lobby at a perfectly reasonable pace, trying to catch my breath.

Not that there's anyone to notice. The woman behind the front desk is leaning back in her chair, watching something on her phone. An older couple in nice clothes walks out of the restaurant in the lobby and passes me on their way out to the sidewalk.

I head for the elevators and ride up to the eleventh floor with the weatherman on the little TV all to myself. Sunshine tomorrow. Highs in the upper fifties. Should be a lovely Thanksgiving. Blah-blah.

The doors open on the eleventh floor, interrupting speculation about whether it will rain this weekend. I walk out into the hallway.

And I stop, staring at those little rectangular signs, with that Hotel Font, on the wall in front of me. This way to these rooms. That way to those rooms.

Boys' rooms on one side of the elevators. Girls' rooms on the other.

I start to cry.

This fucking hallway is the straw that breaks my back. Sobs tear out of me. I can't breathe and I can't see straight and my knees go weak. I crumple up on the floor in front of the elevators, pulling my knees up. Pressing my fists into my eyes.

I don't know what I'll do if someone wakes up and hears me. I don't know what I'll do if one of those doors opens and some adult chaperone sticks their head out. Or, worse, someone else in band does.

But nobody wakes up. Or maybe they do, and they don't open the door. Either way, it's just me, on this beige carpet, crying my eyes out. Because for a brief moment, I felt free tonight. For a brief moment, I felt like a version of me that wasn't dragging around all this extra shit. A version of me that could just exist—fuck what anyone else thinks—because I could drum my heart out, because I could fall in love, because I could kiss someone, because I could spend a day with a person who didn't seem to care what was under my shirt or in my pants, who didn't know me "before," whatever that even means.

But now I've landed back in reality, where boys stay on one side of the hallway, and girls on the other, and somehow that's clear and fine and acceptable to everybody but me.

Worse, I managed to fuck everything up with the one person who made me feel . . .

Well, the most like *me* I've ever felt.

Good job, Leo.

I cry until I have a pounding headache. Until my nose is so stuffed up I can barely breathe through it. Until my whole face feels puffy and my mouth tastes like salt.

And then my phone buzzes.

I fumble it out of my pocket, pulse racing, because maybe it's Abby . . .

It's my mom. She's calling me.

My head spins. "Hello?"

"Oh. Leo. Hi." My mom sounds confused.

Did she butt-dial me? Who even does that anymore? "Mom? Are you . . . Is everything okay?"

"Yes! Sorry. I thought you'd be asleep and I'd get your voicemail."

I wipe my eyes on my sleeve. "Why were you calling my voicemail?"

"Um. Well. Because . . ." She clears her throat. "I wanted to tell you something. *We* wanted to tell you something—your dad and me—but I wanted to make sure you knew before the parade tomorrow . . ."

"Knew what?"

She hesitates. "That I'm sorry. We're both sorry. We . . . we talked to Casey."

What? "Casey? Why?"

"She called us, this afternoon. She was . . . um . . . She was upset, because she talked to you this morning . . ."

Oh, lord. "Mom, it's fine, I told Casey why you and Dad didn't want to—"

"No, it's not fine. Honey, listen. We were already thinking about our fight on Monday, and then Casey called because she felt guilty, after she talked to you, and we had a long talk and . . . we're going to tell everyone." She lets her breath out, a quiet sigh. "Our families. Your families. We're going to tell them tomorrow. And . . . and if they're not okay with you—with *us*—then we're going to ask them to leave."

The silence of the hallway is suddenly deafening. "You're going to . . . what?"

"We realized, talking to Casey, that . . ." I hear her swallow. "We can't ask you to hide parts of yourself forever. We . . . we didn't *want* to do that, Leo, but it's just . . . our relationships with our families are complicated and . . ." She hesitates, like she's catching herself. "We were scared, and I know that's not fair to you, but that's what it is. Was. And I know Casey thinks none of this is a big deal . . ."

I rub my forehead. My head is throbbing. "Mom—"

"Leo, I need to get this out. I love you, and I love Casey, and you both make decisions that don't make any sense to me, but . . . I love you. And if I love you, then I support you, and that means I can't get picky about what parts of you I support, just because the rest of the family is around. I mean, maybe I didn't want to see it at first, but now I do. You'll be who you are with or without us. And when Casey said she told you that you should tell the extended family yourself . . ."

Oh, boy.

"I thought that wasn't very fair of her, because that's an awful lot to expect you to do. It's not your responsibility to deal with whatever they might feel just because you want to be yourself around them. And then your dad and I realized that—well—if it's not fair of Casey to expect you to take on the burden of telling them, then it's not fair of us to expect you to hide who you are because we've been too scared to tell them."

Oh.

That's . . .

"Leo?"

I stare at the neutral beige wallpaper across from me. That's it. That's what I've been waiting for. A piece of it, anyway.

And I . . .

God, I feel so tired.

"Leo?" Mom says again.

"Yeah." My voice is hoarse in my ears. "I'm here."

"Are you okay?"

Yes.

No.

No, I'm not. I've spent months trying to fit myself into a role my parents kept telling me would somehow make my life easier. Months smiling along so they didn't have to be uncomfortable. Weeks shrugging like my sense of belonging mattered less than everyone else's, so my school wouldn't have to be uncomfortable.

As much as part of me wishes I lived in that romance novel of Abby's, I can't just magically start the last year over again. Even though I'm hearing everything I desperately wanted, and the apology that goes with it—none of that's going to magically fix the holes that exist in me now. The holes that are there because little pieces of me that trusted, that felt safe, have been carved away.

No, I'm not okay.

But all I say is, "Yeah," because I can't say anything else to my mom. Not right now.

Maybe someday.

But not right now.

"I'm really sorry we didn't tell them sooner, Leo," Mom says quietly. "Maybe we got too used to hiding ourselves. We've hid bits of ourselves from our families for years. But, you know, this isn't the same as"—she chokes out a laugh—"hiding that you snuck out to go to a rock show as a teenager, or that you had a fling with a girl in college . . ."

I'm sorry—*what*?

"This is who you are. And that's . . . that's different. I want you to know that we know—it's different."

Clearly Casey and I need to do some digging into our mother's past. But right now, I just say, "What are you going to tell them?"

Mom is silent. Finally, she says, "Well, Dad and I did some research, but I guess . . . maybe we should ask you. What do you want us to tell them?"

It's such a simple question. And, in a way, it's the question I've been thinking about for months. But now that I'm here, the answer doesn't feel simple at all.

Was I always a boy?

Was everyone just wrong about me for sixteen years?

Or do things shift, and change, and maybe someone can be many things at once, or many things at different times?

And at the end of the day, does it even matter?

I don't know. All I'm sure about is the me of right now—this month, this week, today. All I know is that this version of me—the version that spent today feeling free—is real. Because if it wasn't, I wouldn't have felt that free. If it wasn't, I wouldn't hurt like this.

"Tell them I'm a trans boy," I say.

"Okay," my mom says.

"Tell them my name is Leo."

"Okay."

"My pronouns are he, him, his. Those aren't preferred, they just *are.*"

"Okay."

"And . . . and that's how I want to be talked about—even in the past."

She hesitates this time, but still, she says, "Okay."

Now I hesitate.

"Anything else?" she asks.

"I don't know. Can that be all for now? And maybe . . . maybe something else later?"

"Yes," she says.

I almost want to ask what Dad will do if Grandma Brewer demands to know how my parents could have let this happen. Or what Mom will do if Nonna Cesari says this is a fad. Or what either of them will do if anyone in the Ex Family just refuses to go along.

Well. I guess Mom and Dad will ask them to leave. I wonder if they'll actually do it, if it comes to that. Casey will. I'm pretty sure.

I hope it doesn't come to that. But even if it does . . .

I don't care. For the first time, I don't care, because I don't need to. Even though she's fumbling, even though there are still holes inside me, my mom decided to listen. My dad decided to listen. Hell, even Casey seems to be listening.

To them, I am not a Logistical Headache anymore. And for tonight, that's a step. It's enough.

"I love you, Leo," Mom says.

My vision swims. "I love you, too, Mom." It feels rusty, in my mouth, like it's going to take some time before I can use it without also adding, to myself, *and you hurt me.*

"Good luck in the parade tomorrow," she says.

"Thanks. Good luck . . . telling everyone."

"Don't worry about it, sweetheart. Who knows? They might be fine, but we're ready if they're not."

And there's the other weird thing about being trans. Maybe my family *will* be fine, but that almost hasn't occurred to me. It seeps in through your skin, the idea that nobody's going to be fine. That you're asking too much of them if you expect them to be fine. And that idea eats away at you until you assume it's fact.

Which, now that I think about it, I've been doing for a long time.

"Call us after the parade, okay, Leo?"

"Yeah. I will."

"Good night."

"'Night, Mom." I lower my phone. Glance at the time. Less than two hours of Wednesday left. It's almost tomorrow.

I open a new text message to Evan.

ME

I have a lot to tell you.

TWENTY-ONE

WEDNESDAY, NOVEMBER 22—10:05 P.M.

ABBY

I HOLD THE *Hundred Romances of Clara Jane* against my chest and look around me, at the lights of Times Square. A digital display running around the edge of a building, above its doors, tells me it's a little after ten.

God, I am such a failure. I've ruined everything now.

Why can't I ever figure out what I want at the right time?

Why can't I ever figure out what I want to begin with?

I can't believe I thought I could be Fearless Abby. Fearless Abby who's adventurous and spontaneous. Who decides what she wants and goes for it. Who could actually, for once, be the heroine, the main character who gets those perfect, magical moments.

The thing is, when Leo kissed me, for a moment, I felt like I was. I felt like *everything*.

But now, here I am, at the end of this day where I thought—maybe—the Universe was making something happen for me . . . and I'm still Old Abby.

Afraid and indecisive and confused and small.

And alone. Just me and *THRoCJ*. Again.

I missed a whole day I could have been with Kat, with my friends—the people who know Old Abby. What did I throw that away for?

What's wrong with me?

I can't keep standing here. Leo told the group chat we were coming back, and anyway, our band is going to be running through everything in front of Macy's in five hours. Which means I've got less than five hours to sleep.

I blink my eyes clear and pull out my phone, because I'm freezing and I should figure out how to get back to the hotel. But I'm shivering and trying not to cry, holding a book and a bag and a phone, and instead of hitting the Google Maps icon, my thumb slips and taps on my photos.

And the first one that pops up is the flyer I photographed at the bookstore. Because of course. It's the last picture I took.

Thirty-Ninth and Eighth, Ida said.

That's not very far away from here. And it's only just after ten.

And the flyer says that the author of *The Hundred Romances of Clara Jane* will be reading a short work of fiction—as part of something called Waterside Writers Presents—at a café on West Thirty-Ninth Street at Eighth Avenue, from 8:00 to 10:00 P.M. Tonight.

I look down at the book in my hands. I should go back to the hotel. Whatever today was, it's over, and . . .

And I can't go back. Not yet.

I pull up Google Maps, and before I can think better of it, I start walking. Away from Times Square. Toward Thirty-Ninth Street.

I walk faster and faster, slowing down only for a second to toss the crumpled paper bag into a trash can.

It's ten minutes after ten when I reach the corner of West Thirty-Ninth and Eighth Avenue. I slow down, glancing between the photo on my phone and the storefronts.

There. The venue is a teeny tiny café, stuffed in between a deli and an upscale clothing boutique. MOREAU'S COFFEE.

My heart is thumping so hard it's practically moving me, back and forth, on the sidewalk. I reach out and tug on the door.

It doesn't budge.

My eyes skip to the café windows. The lights are still on, but they're dim, and the café is empty, except for one person behind the counter. A person who's now dodging around the edge of the counter and coming toward me.

She turns a bolt on the other side of the door and opens it a crack. "Can I help you?"

"Sorry, I was just . . ." I hold my phone up, because my eyes are filling up and I'm not sure I can keep talking.

The woman squints at my phone and then gives me a sympathetic look. "You're kind of late. That event already finished. There'll be another one next month, but . . . we're closing up now."

"I know." It chokes in my throat. "Or, I mean, I know I'm really late, I was . . . I was really hoping to meet one of the authors. She wrote my favorite book . . ."

"*The Hundred Romances of Clara Jane?*"

"Um. Yeah. How did you know?"

She raises her eyebrows. "Well, you're . . . holding the book."

Oh. Right. I grip it tighter and wish, a little, that I could sink into the ground.

The woman leans around me and points across the street. "She went over there. See that restaurant? She might still be there; we finished kind of early, but she only left, like, ten minutes ago."

I turn, searching the storefronts across the street. My eyes catch on a little red awning. GINO'S BAR & RESTAURANT. "Thanks."

"No problem." The woman closes the door.

I glance both ways, but the street is empty, so I walk across it. My fingers are numb, clasping *THRoCJ* against my chest, so close that my heartbeat vibrates it.

I stop outside the door to the restaurant and look in the window. And there she is.

I turn to the back cover of the book, to the author photo, just to make sure.

The woman at the restaurant bar is wearing glasses that the woman in the picture doesn't have, and her hair is shorter, and she's wearing a peacoat instead of a fluttery blouse . . . but it's definitely her. The sandy hair, the pale skin, the long, straight nose, the dimple in her chin.

She's here. I actually found her.

I rub my sleeve across my face, trying to get rid of the tear streaks. And then I take a deep breath and walk in.

The restaurant is warm and candlelit, with faint jazz playing in the background. The bartender doesn't seem to notice me, too busy putting glasses back on shelves. A few people are still tucked into tables in the corners, but their plates are empty and their conversations are a murmur.

I feel completely out of place in my band jacket, my wrinkled jeans, my dirty sneakers. I can tell this is a nice restaurant. It has those pristine white tablecloths—the kind I thought all restaurants would have in New York, because they do in *The Hundred Romances of Clara Jane.*

I adjust my grip on the book, venture up to the bar, and say to the book's author, "Hi, I'm really sorry to interrupt you, but I love your book."

The Author jerks a little, looking up from her pad of paper. She blinks at me and her eyebrows go up. "Sorry?"

"I love your book. *The Hundred Romances of Clara Jane?*" I hold it out, like she might need reminding. "I'm Abby. I'm here with my marching band. Well, not *here* here, just . . . in New York, because we're playing in the Macy's Parade tomorrow, and . . ." And I'm babbling. "Sorry, I don't mean to be creepy or anything. I saw this flyer in a bookstore that you were doing a reading, but I missed it, and the person closing up said you might be here, and I wanted to tell you I love your book."

The Author smiles, and now (except for the glasses and the

shorter hair) she looks just like her picture, even down to the shock-ingly dark lipstick and dramatic eyeshadow. "Thank you. I haven't heard anyone mention that book in a while."

"Oh," I say. "Really?"

I mean, I know it's not a Great Book, and it came out kind of a long time ago, but I've read fanfics about it, which means people wrote fanfics about it. And she's an author. In New York City. I guess I thought she probably ran into people every day who knew who she was and had read her book.

"So you're playing in the parade tomorrow?" The Author asks.

She's trying to be nice. I swallow. "Um, yeah. Our marching band. We drove all the way from Missouri."

Her perfectly shaped eyebrows jump. "Oh, wow! That's a long way. You must be really excited."

"Yeah." Or I was, before today messed everything up. But I can't tell her that. "We practiced a lot."

"I'm sure you did." The Author gives me another smile and turns, almost imperceptibly, back to the bar counter.

That's my cue to leave, but I can't. I have to ask, now that I'm here; I have to ask her that question. The one I emailed her about, care of her publisher. The email she never replied to.

Maybe it's silly, but I need an answer. Something to hang on to.

"Sorry." I wish my heart would slow down. "I was just wonder-ing . . . I sent you a question, a few months ago?" (It was over a year ago, but I don't want to make her feel guilty.) "Well, actually, I sent it to your publisher, because that's what your website said to do, but I never heard back, and I wondered if I could ask you now . . ."

She turns, just slightly, back to me.

"I know the book is called *The Hundred Romances of Clara Jane* . . ." My mouth has gone dry. "But in the book, Clara Jane only has eight romances."

The Author nods.

"Well, I read this theory on Tumblr that maybe Clara Jane had already been in the time loop before the story started, so she'd had lots of romances already, and only the last eight were in the book." I swallow again, trying to make myself slow down. "But I've read the book almost twenty-five times now, and I feel like the first romance in it is actually, really her first one. And she just has eight romances, even though the book title refers to a hundred. I wondered if you could clarify?"

My voice squeaks at the end. I really hope The Author doesn't notice.

If she does, she doesn't let on. She just smiles. "That's a good question. I didn't have any other romances in mind besides the ones that are actually in the book."

"Oh. So why . . . ?"

She laughs. "My publisher liked the sound of *The Hundred Romances of Clara Jane*. It was a little more epic and magical than my original title."

Epic and magical. Sounds like something I would say.

And also seems a little misleading. False advertising, like Leo said.

I wait, but she doesn't say anything else. I desperately want to ask what the original title was, but I force myself not to. Maybe it's private. Something she wants to keep, just for herself. I guess I can understand that, even though it would have been cool to go back to Tumblr and post that The Author herself told me what was correct. And here was the original title to prove it.

Of course, maybe nobody would believe me. When would I have met The Author anyway? I keep checking the Events page on her website, but it hasn't been updated in three years. That flyer in the bookstore was the first time I've heard of her doing anything public, and how many people would have seen that flyer? It wasn't even an event just for her.

So instead I ask, "It didn't bother you that the title wasn't really accurate?"

The Author gives a tiny shrug. "You know . . ." She looks at me almost sadly. "I've kind of moved on from that book. I don't really think about it much anymore."

Wait, what? How can she not think about it? She created it. She *wrote* it. The characters, the romance, the story, everything. Not that I expected her to reread her own book as much as I reread it, but somehow, the idea that she's moved on, that she doesn't even really think about my favorite book, or seem to care about it much anymore . . .

I feel kind of abandoned.

Maybe I look disappointed, even though I don't mean to, because The Author's expression turns anxious and she says, "Would you like me to sign your book for you?"

I look down at the copy that Leo threw at me—the one I'm still clutching to my chest. "It's already signed, actually."

Now The Author looks really anxious. "I'm sorry, did we meet earlier tonight?"

"No!" I wave my hand. "Someone just found a signed copy for me—at this bookstore, the Strand. It was already signed when he got it." I know I shouldn't keep talking, but I can't seem to stop myself. "He got it for me because I had this other signed copy that I found at a bookstore in Missouri, and I was going to give it to my best friend, but I lost it on this trip. Earlier today, actually . . ." I'm babbling again, and even worse, my eyes are filling up and *I can't cry.* Not in front of The Author.

"It's nice that you were going to give my book to your best friend." The Author sounds like she's reaching for something to say.

And it makes me feel worse. "Thanks." It's what I'm supposed to say. "I was actually going to tell her that I . . . I had a crush on her. I mean, I was in love with her. Or . . . I am. And we both love *The Hundred Romances of Clara Jane,* so I got her this special signed copy, and I wrote these notes in it for her. Sorry, I know some people feel like writing in books is bad . . ."

The Author shakes her head.

"Anyway, I was going to tell her how I felt on this trip, but then I lost the book, and this guy I was with helped me come up with this whole other plan, and then he found me this other book, and he gave it to me before I came over here, and anyway . . ." I'm saying *anyway* too many times. I shouldn't be telling this story to complete strangers, and The Author *is* a complete stranger, even if I've read her book almost twenty-five times. That doesn't mean I know *her*.

And yet I still thought she'd be exactly the same person she was when she wrote this book. Because I showed up here and asked her questions like all she does every day is think about this story that she wrote years ago.

Which is so silly. After all, I'm not the same person I was when I first read this book.

I'm not even the same person I was this morning.

I met Leo, and now everything's different.

"Can I ask you one more question?" I say.

The Author smiles and pulls her wallet out of a chic leather bag hanging over her chair. "Sure."

"Is anything in the book based on real life?"

The Author takes several bills out of her wallet and lays them on the counter next to her empty glass. "Not really. It's a book—a work of fiction." She looks apologetic. "It's really completely made up."

I nod. Makes perfect sense. I mean, there's a *time loop*.

But all the same, I was hoping a tiny piece of it was true.

"Do you think the Universe can ever be magical, like it is in your book?" The question tumbles out of me, before I can stop myself. Even though I know I shouldn't ask her another question. But I can't *not* ask.

Because if the book is all fiction, if it's not even based—just a little—on some special moment in which the Universe *worked out* . . .

Well, then everything I've been telling myself is untrue. There's no guarantee anything will work out for me. There's no guarantee I won't just be the weird queer girl in a suburb of Missouri, the queer girl no one will ever fall in love with or even really understand.

The Author tucks her wallet away. "I think the Universe can be magical, sometimes." She smiles, and this one looks more genuine than even the smile in her picture on the back flap of *THRoCJ*. "That's why I wrote that book, in the beginning. Because I do think that, and I wanted to write about it. Sometimes the Universe can throw a little magic your way. But at the end of the day, I think it matters just as much what you decide to do with it. If it didn't, then . . ." She shrugs. "We wouldn't have a say in anything. The Universe can't decide everything for us."

My mind goes back to the skating rink, to scrambling over the railing to join Leo on the ice. To the way Leo leaned forward and kissed me, grasping my arms so tightly.

Those moments felt like magic, and also like . . .

Like moments we chose.

My eyes fill up again. "Yeah, I guess." I try to shrug lightly. "I mean . . . it's kind of magical to me that you're here. Or . . . that I got to meet you." I look around. "Maybe you're here all the time."

She laughs. "I like this place. Sometimes I come here to people watch after work, even when I'm not reading silly poems with my writing group across the street." She picks up her pad of paper, waving it vaguely before putting it in her bag. "I like to write down things I notice when I people watch. Bars and restaurants are great places for that."

I feel suddenly hopeful. "Inspiration for a new book?"

Her smile fades. She shrugs. "Maybe."

"Do you think you'll ever write a sequel to *Clara Jane*?"

She shakes her head. "No. I'm sorry."

It stings, but not as much as I thought it would. "That's okay. I guess Clara Jane's story kind of wrapped up at the end."

The Author nods and slips off her barstool, shouldering her chic bag. "I'm sorry, I should really go. It's getting late."

She's right. And I need to get back to the hotel. "Yeah, of course." I take a step backward, even though I'm not blocking her way.

She looks at me, and then she says, "How about I sign that book anyway? So it's really for you?"

"Oh." I hold it out. "Okay."

She fishes a pen out of her bag and lays the book on the bar counter, opening the cover and scribbling on the title page. "Nice to meet you, Abby," she says, and hands the book back to me.

"Thanks." She remembered my name. "Nice to meet you, too."

She gives me a last smile and walks away, her heeled boots clicking on the polished restaurant floor. I watch her slip out the door onto the sidewalk, wrapping a plaid scarf around her neck. In a few steps, she's out of sight.

"Excuse me?" The bartender gently taps on the counter to get my attention. "I'm afraid we're closing."

"Oh." I realize the few people remaining at tables are starting to get up, too. Gathering their coats while a waitress picks up their dishes and napkins. "Sorry. I'll . . . I'll leave."

I duck out of the restaurant to the sidewalk. I'm alone; The Author must have rounded a corner, or gotten in a cab, or something. I jump out of the way as the last few patrons leave the restaurant behind me, laughing with each other and walking away down the street.

I know I should start walking, too. I've got to get all the way back to the hotel, and the longer I put it off, the less sleep I'm going to get before the big run-through in front of Macy's.

But I can't stop myself from opening the cover of the book in my hands. On the title page, underneath the old, fading signature, The Author has written:

To Abby—the Universe is what you make it.

TWENTY-TWO

LEO

I DON'T KNOW how I'm awake right now. But I also don't know how I slept.

I did, though. I snuck into my hotel room without waking Gina or Zuri or Rebekah. Splashed cold water on my face, brushed my teeth, and then completely ran out of steam. I just sank down on the bed I was sharing with Gina, still in my clothes, face-planted into my pillow, and passed out.

The next thing I knew, Gina's phone alarm was blaring.

Even though I'm terrible at mornings, I snapped awake. Completely awake. Maybe because it's not like this really counts as a *morning*. It's still dark. This is the middle of the night, no matter what the little A.M. on my phone tries to tell me.

My phone that's almost out of battery. Because I fell asleep before I could plug it in.

I'm currently in the lobby of the hotel, in my black-and-gold marching band uniform, black shako hiding my hair, which is sticking up even worse than before, if that's possible. The lobby is buzzing now, gold plumes bobbing everywhere. Ms. Rinaldi, in a black jacket with *Springfield* on the back in shiny gold letters, is working her way toward Mr. Corbin, who's standing near the elevators with a tray of four coffee cups, looking like death.

Next to me, Evan says, "You threw a *book* at her?"

I've just finished telling Evan and Gina everything. Every part of yesterday that they didn't see. Every event that happened while they were on the trip we were all *supposed* to be on.

"You *kissed* her?" says Gina.

It all came tumbling out the minute Gina and I ran into Evan at the elevators. He just pointed to the last text message I'd sent him, from the hotel hallway after I talked to my parents, and I spilled. I talked while we took the elevator down to the first floor. I talked while we trooped into a back storage room to unpack our instruments. I talked while we walked back out of the storage room to stand awkwardly in the lobby, waiting for the signal to head out for our last rehearsal—the run-through for the camera crews in front of Macy's.

I'm not sure I've ever talked more in my life.

I try to shrug casually while I settle my snare harness on my shoulders. And try to keep an eye out (in a very not-obvious way) for Abby. If we're heading out for our last run-through, maybe her band is, too.

"*Leo.*"

I jump. Evan is giving me a very disapproving look, made all the more intimidating by the giant sousaphone looped around his torso, its enormous silver bell pointed right at me.

"You kissed a girl," Evan says, "and you threw a book at her—literally—which means you have feelings for her, so what are you going to do?"

I glare at him. "I don't have feelings for her." It's a lie, but I say it anyway. Because all I told them were the events. Like, that I kissed Abby. I didn't tell them about the avalanche of feelings that came with it.

Evan groans. "Yes, you do. And she has feelings for *you*."

"No, she doesn't. I threw a book at her."

"Yup," says Gina.

"And we yelled at each other."

"Yup," Gina says again.

I turn and glare at her. "What point do you think you're making?"

Gina gives me a very bored look. "You don't throw a book and yell at someone you don't like."

Is she nuts? "Yeah, actually. That's exactly what you do if you don't like someone."

"No." Gina jabs a petite finger into my chest. "*You* don't. If *you* don't like someone, you just refuse to talk to them. The silent treatment. The Face. Now you're telling us you spent that much energy *arguing* with someone? You're in love with her."

"So what if I am? It doesn't matter."

"I can't believe you didn't just tell us yesterday," Evan says, pouting.

"I didn't tell you for exactly this reason! Because I knew you'd make a big deal out of it, and it doesn't matter. I fucked it up because everything around me is always fucked up, and she clearly doesn't feel the same way, so whatever."

"Everything around you is not fucked up," Evan says. "I mean, based on the phone call you described, your parents are actively working to unfuck themselves."

I wince. "Please don't ever put the f-word and my parents in the same sentence again."

"I didn't." He looks offended. "It's the *un*-f-word."

Ms. Rinaldi blows a few short blasts on her whistle, like we're outside on a football field. "Let's go! Let's go!" She waves her arms toward the lobby doors. "Follow me, please!"

Our band amoeba slowly begins to move, all of us funneling through the doors and out onto the sidewalk. I'm really glad I'm wearing long johns under my band uniform, because it's *cold*. I can see my breath.

Ms. Rinaldi waves a flashlight so we can see her, and off we go. Down the sidewalk, chaperones on either side to contain us, one long train of marching band.

"So what are you going to do?" Evan says.

I blow on my hands. "What do you mean?"

Gina shakes her head. "God, he's useless."

"So useless," Evan agrees.

I have the distinct feeling they've spent a good chunk of the last twelve hours discussing me while I was off with Abby and couldn't defend myself.

I also know they're baiting me, but I can't help myself. "Why am I useless?"

Evan looks delighted that I fell for it. "Because you're head over heels and Abby obviously feels the same way. And yet you're still standing here like, *What do you mean?*"

I resist the urge to drop my sticks and strangle him. "Didn't you hear anything I said? Abby's in love with Kat. Remember Kat? That other person in the group chat? Abby flipped out when I kissed her, because she likes *Kat.* And even if she did like me, maybe a tiny bit, I yelled at her. And then I threw a book! You really think she likes me after that?"

"See, this is what I mean." Evan wipes away an imaginary tear as we turn a corner. "This is how I know you love me. You don't argue like this with just anybody."

The urge to strangle him increases. "*Evan.*"

He sighs. "Leo. You're in love with Abby."

"No, I'm not."

"You literally just admitted it."

"Doesn't matter."

"It *does* matter."

"Evan, it's too late to—"

"It's not too late if you just admit it—"

"Okay, fine!" I yell. "I'm in love with Abby!"

Approximately half the band stops dead and turns to look at me. So do some of the chaperones. And a couple people with badges and reflective orange vests who seem to be directing traffic around the parade route.

If the Universe really felt like looking out for me, this street grate I'm standing on would give way so I could disappear down that hole and escape all the stares. But the Universe hates me, so the grate stays put.

"What's the holdup?" Ms. Rinaldi blows her whistle again. "Let's go, Springfield!"

People turn away, one by one, and the band amoeba starts moving again. With all these barriers at every intersection, we don't even have to wait for walk signals. We can keep moving, right through the crosswalks, the whole place cleared and ready for tomorrow. Or . . . today. *Ugh,* why am I not sleeping right now.

"Fine, I'm in love with Abby," I say, quieter. "She's funny and nice and beautiful and I really don't understand her obsession with romance novels but she makes me want to read them anyway. Are you happy now?"

"So happy," Gina says, but Evan solemnly shakes his head.

"You still haven't said what you're going to do about it," he says.

I open my mouth, even though I have no idea what to say, because I wasn't planning to do anything about it—but Gina saves me the trouble of thinking of a reply.

"Holy shit," she says, and points.

Up ahead, lit up by spotlights and streetlights and a bunch of giant lamps on tripods in the street, is Macy's. A tall, old beige building, just like half the buildings I've seen in New York so far, but you can't miss that it's Macy's. I mean, yeah, it *says* MACY'S, right there, in gold letters on the side of the building, but there's also a giant inflatable turkey resting on the awning over the store's entrance, not to mention the huge BELIEVE sign, suspended several stories above the street. Every letter sparkles.

On either side of the entrance are rows of empty bleachers. And across the street, in among all the lights, are cameras. Cameras on tripods. Cameras on dollies. There's even a camera on a freaking crane. And right now, they're all pointed at—I stand on my toes to see over everybody's heads—another marching band. For a second, my heart leaps, but this band is all decked out in red-and-white uniforms. They practically look like candy canes.

Abby's jacket was purple and white. It's not her band.

"Run it again!" a voice barks over a bullhorn. Sharp and professional.

Three hundred candy canes rush for their places. A whistle blows, the drumline counts off, and a second later, the band starts playing "Rudolph the Red-Nosed Reindeer." Bright and peppy.

Just like Abby said about her band's Christmas medley. *If it can be pepped up, we've pepped it.*

God, is everything going to make me think of Abby?

The cameras move smoothly around the band. I guess this is a final run-through for everybody, camera crew included.

After a minute, I realize Evan and Gina are staring at me.

"What?" I say.

"Nothing." Evan quickly looks away.

It hits me that they're waiting for me to panic, like I have every time I've seen a camera recently. They're waiting to see if I'm going to freak out, like I did on Monday.

But instead, all I'm thinking about is Abby.

The band ahead of us finishes, and the echoes barely die away before the voice on the bullhorn barks, "Great, moving on, everyone."

Ms. Rinaldi blows her whistle. "Set!" she yells.

That's our cue to get into formation, all of us piling in behind the banner with *Springfield High School* on it. Gina disappears into the trombone section. Evan joins the sousaphones. And I take up my spot on the outside of the snare line. Ready to march right past those cameras.

I twirl my sticks in my fingers, while a slow B-flat starts up around me. The droning sound of everyone tuning. It's loud and diffuse at the same time, the cold air eating up the sound, even as it also bounces chaotically off the buildings and sidewalks around us.

Two whistle blasts from Lindsay Waggoner. The drum major signaling *Horns up.*

"Springfield High," says the bullhorn voice. "Let's go."

Another whistle blast from Lindsay. The snare section leader taps his sticks to set the tempo, and we start marking time. Marching in place. Eight counts and then the drumline picks up.

Muscle memory takes over, everything I forgot on Monday coming right back, as the drumline drives everybody forward. I glance down at my feet. The street really is green, underneath us. The big green rectangle, just like I've seen on TV.

Has Abby already seen all this? Is her band ahead of us? Or behind us?

She'll love this. Thundering into the night this way, in front of empty bleachers, under lights so bright that this whole block looks like the middle of the day.

It's a liminal space. A dress rehearsal. A run-through. All in a city that's not quite awake and not quite asleep. Another transition moment. Another in-between.

We make it all the way through "Seventy-Six Trombones," and I do fine. I think. I don't even really know. I'm on autopilot; that's better than forgetting where the hell I was supposed to go, at least. Goes to show I really have practiced this thing to death.

But I don't exactly feel present, either. Not the way I did when I was drumming wildly on that shitty tom with those buskers, with Abby smiling at me around her clarinet.

We freeze in our final positions, the last note echoing down the street.

"Moving on," says the bullhorn voice.

And we turn, just like we practiced at home, and march off,

playing our little coda, just like we will for real in . . . six hours? Five? What time is it, anyway?

The coda falters and the rhythm breaks as soon as we're off the green rectangle, the whistle from Lindsay signaling that we can fall out of formation and quit playing. Chaperones and people in vests are waving us off down a side street. Ms. Rinaldi applauds, hands raised so we can see them. For the real parade, we'll end with a little more grace, but for now . . .

We're saving our energy. Nobody's here to watch anyway. I wonder, for a second, about slipping away again. Using the dark and the chaos of camera crews to ditch my band and go looking for Abby. She must be here somewhere, right? Her band has to do a run-through, too.

But I give that idea up almost as soon as it crosses my mind. I have no idea where Abby is. She could have already finished her run-through and left the parade route for all I know. And anyway, I can't exactly be stealthy wearing a snare harness, with a gold plume waving around on my head.

It's too late. The most I could do is text her, whenever we get the chance to actually sit down. That would be the sane thing to do— even though I don't know what I'd say. *Sorry for being a dick* doesn't even begin to cover it.

The sound of another marching band blares down the street. Some other school's run-through. I listen, because I can't help hoping, but they're playing "My Favorite Things" from *The Sound of Music*. Not a medley of jazzed-up Christmas tunes. Not Abby's band.

I shoulder my way through my band, heading for the low brass section, and Evan and Gina.

TWENTY-THREE

ABBY

IT'S STILL DARK outside when we shuffle into the restaurant for breakfast. It's not a Planet Hollywood this time, but it looks pretty similar, minus all the movie costumes. Big, dimly lit in purple and pink and blue, with large round tables draped in plain tablecloths. In the middle of the restaurant is a long buffet table with covered hot dishes and baskets of bagels and dispensers of orange juice and coffee.

This clearly isn't what this restaurant does most of the time. I wonder if Macy's contracts restaurants to feed everybody breakfast. Or maybe our school paid for it. I don't even know.

And right now, I don't really care, either. I'm so tired I could go to sleep right on one of these tables.

But instead, I line up with everybody else, yawning and picking up a paper plate. I don't even notice what I put on it. I only know I put orange juice in my cup because I stand for too long, trying to decide between orange juice and coffee, and Morgan nudges me with her elbow.

"Earth to Abby. You're holding up the line."

I sit at a table with Kat, Morgan, Amira, and Jared Nguyen, who seems to have recovered from his unfortunate sightseeing-boat barf. The table gradually fills up with more woodwind players, everyone kind of mumbling, all of us too tired to really raise our voices.

Maybe I should have gotten coffee. I feel like a zombie. My head hurts. I barely slept three hours, because even though I felt exhausted when I finally got back to the hotel, it still took me ages to fall asleep.

Kat woke up when I tried to sneak into the room. She came into the bathroom with me, squinting in the light, and asked if I was okay.

I thought about pulling out the copy of *THRoCJ*. I thought about trying to explain. About The Author, and what had just happened. But in the end, I just said *yeah,* and nothing else. I mean, what else could I say? Where would I even start? How could I explain about The Author without explaining about the book, about why I had the book, about why Leo had gotten me a copy of the book in the first place . . .

And then the whole thing would unravel. And I felt like I might unravel with it. So I tried to give her a smile, and then I turned around and picked up my toothbrush. Kat stood there for a few more seconds, and then, in the mirror, I saw her shake her head and let her breath out, and she left the bathroom.

By the time I finally climbed into bed next to her, she was asleep again. Or seemed like she was. Which left me to stare at the ceiling, out the window, and at my phone charging on the bedside table, hoping it would light up with a text from Leo.

It didn't.

Amira pokes my arm and points at my plate. "Abby, are you eating bacon again?"

"No." But when I look down—sure enough, there's a strip of bacon, sitting on my plate. I have absolutely no memory of putting it there.

And, of course, it makes me remember telling Leo about how I swore off eating pork. Babbling away in that sewing store in Chinatown. The way he just smiled at me, the corner of his mouth turning up, which I know now counts as a real smile. At least for him.

A real smile that he doesn't trust just anybody with. Which makes it mean so much more.

I glance at Kat, next to me, but she's not looking at my plate. She's scrolling on her phone, like she didn't hear Amira at all. She's looking at pictures of New York, I realize. Probably pictures she took yesterday, without me. Maybe Evan even sent her his pictures of the abandoned subway station.

I push the bacon to the edge of my plate. Kat's barely said three words to me since I woke her up last night. We're finally in the same place—she's even sitting right next to me—and it's like she doesn't want to talk to me at all.

I give Amira a shrug. "I guess I'm just wiped." I fake a yawn, which turns into a real one.

Morgan leans her head down on the table. "Seriously. I could go to sleep right now."

Amira is still watching me. "Are you really okay?"

"Yeah." I try to smile. "Totally fine." I stuff some hash browns in my mouth to show I mean it.

Amira looks doubtful, but she goes back to her food.

On the table next to me, Kat's phone buzzes. She snatches it up, hands cupped around the screen so I can't see what's on it. And she still doesn't look at me.

I eat through my scrambled eggs, but they taste like nothing. What is going on? The day has barely started. The sun isn't even up yet. And everything feels wrong.

For a split second, I wish I'd never gotten on the wrong train, because if I hadn't, maybe Kat would be the one asking if I'm okay, instead of Amira. Maybe I even would have taken that as my cue—the Universe telling me this was the Moment. If I'd never met Leo, maybe I'd be sitting here right now and I'd pull out my carefully annotated copy of *The Hundred Romances of Clara Jane* and hold it out to Kat. Or maybe I'd be sitting here holding her hand under the table, because I would have given her The Book yesterday.

Then again, if I'd never met Leo, Kat wouldn't have any reason to ask if I was okay right now. Nobody would, because I wouldn't be feeling like this. Who knows if I would have found the right moment to give Kat The Book, or tell her I loved her, or any of it.

I set my fork down.

Here I am, sitting next to Kat, fantasizing about what might have happened if yesterday had gone differently, except . . .

Except the only part of yesterday I really want to be different is the end. If I could do it again, like Clara Jane, I wouldn't pull away when Leo kissed me. I wouldn't fall on my butt on the ice. I wouldn't ruin everything. I'd kiss him back, and then . . .

Then I'd go back to the hotel and tell Kat all about it, because she's my best friend.

All I want her to be is my best friend. Not my girlfriend. Not my true love. Just my best friend.

Shit.

My eyes are filling up again. My throat is closing up. I couldn't get more food down now if I tried.

I have to get out of here or I'm going to start crying.

I push my chair back. It scrapes across the floor loudly. Kat and Amira and Morgan look up.

"Sorry." I grab my backpack up from the floor. "Just . . . uh . . . bathroom." I turn and walk as fast as I can toward the restroom sign in one corner of the restaurant.

The bathrooms are down a hallway, kind of like at Chelsea Market. This hallway is a lot smaller and narrower, but the bathrooms are still right next to each other. MEN and WOMEN. I think again of Leo, and a weird mix of rage and grief knots up my insides. I never spent much time thinking about bathrooms before, and now I'm mad I didn't.

I push my way through the door marked WOMEN. Push my way

into a stall and lock the door behind me and lean my back against it, clutching my backpack to my chest.

What am I doing in here?

I squeeze my eyes shut. I should be out there eating breakfast and complaining about how tired I am, while also getting antsy, waiting for the hours to pass until it's time to head back to the beginning of the parade route and do it all for real.

But instead, I'm in here, trying not to cry, because I miss Leo. I miss him bouncing his leg and tapping his fingers. I miss him putting on silly sunglasses. I miss him drumming his heart out like there's nothing else in the world, and all I want right now is to know if he's okay. If he's heard anything from his family, about what might happen today, about what will happen when he goes back home. All I want is to kiss him, and mean it with my whole self, and then tell him how that kiss was *everything*. Tell him it felt like magic, and laugh when he gets that uncomfortable frown on his face.

I want to tell him thank you for the book. Even if he did throw it at me.

The door to the bathroom squeaks open. "Abby?"

Crap. It's Kat. "Sorry. I'm coming. Um . . . just give me a minute."

I'm hoping she'll take that as a good enough response and leave, but she doesn't. She sighs, and her footsteps come closer. "Abby, what's going on?"

I press my fingers against my eyes. I can't keep hiding in here. It's Kat. And she's talking to me.

I should really start talking to her.

I take a deep breath and open the stall door.

She's waiting for me by the sinks, her arms crossed over her bibbers—our uniform pants that are basically just really low-cut purple overalls. Kat's ditched the top half of her uniform—the cropped purple-and-white jacket with its stiff collar and silver buttons down the front—and she's just wearing a plain long-sleeved T-shirt.

It's something I've always liked about Kat, and about being in band with Kat. Kat loves fashion and sewing and wearing the beautiful dresses she sews, but whenever we're in band together, she's dressed as plainly as me. It's all about being comfortable for the show. She doesn't try to stand out. Her hair is up in a messy bun that she can hide under her shako, and she's not even wearing any makeup, beyond a little eyeliner.

In other words, in band, she's not future fashion designer Kat. She's not Tumblr Kat. She's on the same level as me. She's just . . . Kat. Even if right now she looks annoyed.

I set my backpack on the bathroom counter and tug open the zipper. "I need to tell you something."

"Yeah," she says. A little sharply. "I think you do."

I know I deserve it, but it still stings. "I'm sorry I didn't come back when you expected me to. Last night. And I'm sorry I got on the wrong train—"

"Abby, this isn't about the train." Kat's face crumples. She suddenly looks more hurt than I've ever seen her. "This is about you ditching me. I kept covering for you, the whole day, and it kind of seemed like you didn't even care."

I stare at her. "I *did* care."

"This was supposed to be *our trip*. Together. In New York."

"I know."

"But you still blew me off." She blinks, like she's about to cry. "All day."

I open my mouth, but I don't know what to say. Because she's right. And I feel terrible. "I'm . . . I'm sorry. I know it was supposed be our trip. I know that was the plan, and I really, really cared about it. I was trying to do something for you. That's what was going on all day. I mean, I got on the wrong train by accident, but after that . . . Everything I did after that was for you. I just . . . couldn't tell you."

She frowns. "What's that mean?"

God, I really hope nobody comes into the bathroom right now.

"I had a plan for this trip. I found this signed, hardcover copy of *The Hundred Romances of Clara Jane* at the bookstore—"

Kat looks confused. "The bookstore?"

"Benny's Books in KC. You know, where we found the original?" I swallow. I can hear my pulse in my ears. "Anyway, I underlined my favorite parts of the book, and I wrote these notes to you in the margins on the pages, and I was going to give you the book, because we were in New York on this trip . . ." My voice wobbles. "But then I got on the wrong train yesterday, and a lot was going on, and I accidentally left the book on the train. So, the rest of the day . . . everything that I was doing . . . it was all trying to fix this plan. Leo came up with this idea that since I couldn't get the book back, maybe instead we could go to all the places that are in the book, like the Empire State Building . . ."

Kat looks surprised. "You went to the Empire State Building?"

"Yeah." I take the penny Leo found on the observation deck out of my backpack and lay it on the counter between us. "And then we could find a souvenir from each place, and that would still be related to the book, but also about you and me and this trip, and I could give you those things instead. So that's what we did. That's what we were doing, all of yesterday. We went to the Empire State Building, and we found this penny, on the observation deck. And I got this subway magnet at Grand Central." I pull out the magnet and set it next to the penny. "It's an old subway car. And we went to Chelsea Market, and I got you this caramel"—that goes next to the magnet—"because . . . you remember the scene with the caramels in the book?"

"Yeah . . ." She's looking down at the collection of things on the counter.

"We also went to this holiday market in Union Square—and Union Square doesn't really have souvenirs, but I found this ornament." I lay the tiny silver flute next to the caramel. "And we went to

Chinatown—you know, like that first date Clara Jane goes on—and we found this really small sewing store, and I got you this button." I pull it out, but I can't quite bring myself to lay it down next to everything else. "It's your zodiac sign, and I thought you could sew it on something that you make. You're so good at designing clothes . . ."

That's what I was going to say, right? Something about how talented I think she is, at designing clothes, at flute. How pretty she is. How much she means to me. All the things you're supposed to say to someone when you tell them you love them. And all things that are still true. She is so good at fashion and at flute. She is so pretty. She means so much to me.

"Kat . . ." I take a slow, shuddering breath. "I'm gay. Or . . . I thought I was. I'm queer anyway. And . . ." I swallow, to keep my voice from wobbling again. "I brought the book to give you, and then I spent all of yesterday finding these souvenirs because . . . I was hoping the Universe would give me a perfect, magical moment to tell you—to show you—that I was . . . I was in love with you."

I set the button down next to the flute ornament.

Kat reaches out and carefully picks it up, turning it over and over in her fingers, looking at the little tiny pig.

The moment drags on for so long that it feels like we have our own time loop. A few seconds, repeating over and over, until one of us figures out what to say.

Finally, Kat says quietly, "Was?"

My heart splinters. "I think I'm in love with Leo."

Something in Kat's face changes, barely, but I don't know what it means.

"I'm so sorry I ditched you. I know this trip was supposed to be, like, the two of us in New York, and that really is how it started for me. I'm sorry I didn't tell you any of this stuff before. I was so confused, when I got back to the hotel, because I'd just had this fight with Leo. He kissed me, and I think I knew I was starting to like him, but I'd spent months liking you, and . . . I'm sorry I didn't tell you that earlier, either. I . . . I couldn't figure out how to do it at home."

Kat looks up from the button. She opens her mouth, but nothing comes out.

Oh, god. She doesn't know what to say. Of course she doesn't. I've just laid all of this on her, and in a *bathroom*. Why am I so awkward?

Kat looks down at everything on the counter. "I love you, Abby," she says, but something about her voice tells me what's coming. "As a friend."

"That's okay!" I swallow again. "I mean, I had feelings for you before, but I don't want to fuck things up with us, and—"

"I'm not sure if I like anyone." Now Kat looks at me. Anxious.

Wait. What?

"I've never . . . I've never had a crush." Kat's voice is barely above a whisper. "Or . . . maybe I have, because sometimes I . . . I think people are beautiful. But I don't want to date them. I don't really . . . I don't really want to kiss anyone or . . . stuff." She shifts. One shoe squeaks on the floor tiles.

"Okay." My head spins, brain desperately trying to catch up. "So, you're saying—"

"I've been googling and I think maybe I'm ace," Kat says. "Like . . . asexual. And maybe . . . maybe aromantic. I mean, I love reading *THRoCJ*. And fanfics. And I really like talking about them with you. I'm just not sure if . . . if I want that kind of romance. For me."

Oh.

"I don't want you to be hurt." Kat's voice wavers. "You're my best friend. I don't want any of that to change . . ."

All I can think to say is, "You were googling?"

Kat blushes. "And . . . um . . . looking at Tumblr. I know that sounds weird, but I didn't know what else to do . . ."

I laugh. Which is completely the wrong thing to do, but I can't stop. I'm laughing—and also kind of crying—at the same time.

Kat looks hurt again. "Abby . . ."

"No, I'm sorry, I'm not laughing at you. Really." I make myself take a deep breath. "It's just that I thought it was just me. I thought I was the only one googling and looking at queer Tumblr. I even read this gay *Clara Jane* fanfic—"

"The one where Chris is Christina instead?"

"Yeah, that one."

Kat smiles a little. I do, too. We both look down at the small collection of souvenirs on the counter.

I rub my sleeve across my eyes. "So you're really not attracted to anyone?"

Kat shrugs one shoulder. "I don't know. Not so far? Sometimes I think I just want friends and . . . that's enough." She glances at me. "And you mean a lot to me. As a friend. And that's why I got pissed. I was really excited to do this whole trip with you, and ride the subway, and see *Wicked* . . ."

"I'm know. I'm really sorry. Especially about *Wicked*." I hesitate. "Was it good?"

She smiles a little. "It was amazing." Then she sighs, and her face turns anxious again. "So, you're queer and I'm ace . . . Is that queer, too? I don't know."

"I don't really know either, but I think you can be queer if you want." I reach out and gingerly poke her arm. "Thanks for telling me."

"I'm sorry I didn't tell you sooner," she says.

"I'm sorry I didn't tell *you* sooner."

Kat looks back down at the little pig button she's rolling between her fingers. "I'm glad you told me now. I mean . . . we can both go home and be—I don't know—some kind of queer together?"

"Yeah." The thought of going home twists a little. "I haven't told my parents yet."

"Me, neither." Kat glances up. "I'll be there when you do, if you want."

She says it casually, but I know by the look on her face that she doesn't mean it casually at all. My throat closes up again. I have to swallow a few times before I can manage to say, "Same."

"What are you going to do about Leo?"

I let my breath out. "I don't know. It's all . . . mixed up."

"Why?"

"Because we got in that fight, and anyway, I haven't even known him for that long, and then there's the whole thing where I thought I was gay and now . . ."

Her eyebrows go up. "Now what?"

"Well . . ." What's okay for me to say? What has Kat already figured out or guessed at or wondered about? "Leo's trans."

Kat just looks at me.

"Transgender," I say.

Now her look is A Look. "Okay. So?"

"I . . . didn't know if you knew."

"I didn't, but so what?"

I don't know what to say to that. I just told my best friend I was in love with her, and that I was queer. And now I know my best friend is ace, and Leo being trans isn't throwing her at all.

I suddenly think of Ida. Of my time in the Strand, surrounded by queer people. I wonder what she would think of this, if I told her. Somehow I suspect she'd probably say, *See? Told you we're everywhere.*

"I just . . . don't know what that makes me," I say, "if I'm in love with Leo. I mean, I had a crush on Blake Orlowski for a while—"

"Ew," Kat says.

My face heats up. "That's not the point. The point is, then I was in love with you, and I *know* I was, even if I don't feel that way anymore. But now I'm in love with Leo. So . . . what kind of queer does that make me? Bi? Pan? Something else?"

Kat stares at me. "Abs, who gives a shit?"

I blink.

"You don't really need a label in order to fall in love with someone, do you?" Kat gives me a lopsided grin. "I mean, you like Leo. Isn't that . . . enough?"

I stare at her.

I thought if I found the label—the thing I was that wasn't Straight—then I'd know *who* I was. What I was supposed to like. Who I was supposed to like. As though the label came with a kit: *Congratulations, here are the things you need to be a lesbian.* I mean, why else was I browsing queer clothing tags on Tumblr and analyzing why I'd been wearing plaid flannel shirts for years?

Until yesterday. Yesterday, I hung out with a bunch of queers who maybe had labels, but I didn't really know what they all were, and I didn't care, and neither did they. I mean, Ida told me she didn't even *like* labels. Which isn't to say that labels don't matter, or that I won't find one I want to use eventually, but . . .

I open my mouth, and the whole rest of the truth pours out. I tell Kat everything I didn't tell her last night. I tell her about almost kissing Leo at the top of the Empire State Building, and then *actually* kissing Leo at the ice-skating rink. I tell her about the horrible things I said to him, and about the book, and about The Author.

When I finally stop talking, Kat says, "Leo found you another copy of *Clara Jane*?"

"Yeah. We were at this bookstore—it's sort of a long story—but . . ." I can't figure out how to finish that sentence, so I just pull the book out of my backpack. I couldn't bring myself to touch it after I got back to the hotel, so it's been sitting in my backpack ever since. I hand the book to Kat.

She takes it with a kind of reverence, opening the cover and running her fingers over The Author's message, scribbled on the title page. "'The Universe is what you make it,'" she says. She looks up at me. "*Abby.*"

"What?"

Kat taps the message in the book. "You just told me you were waiting for the Universe to give you some magical moment, right?

I mean, when you wanted to give me the book. So, that didn't work out, but what if . . . what if you weren't wrong?"

I feel lost. "What do you mean?"

"What if the Universe *did* give you a magical moment, it just wasn't the one you were expecting? Maybe the magical moment was getting on the wrong train with Leo. Maybe the Universe stuck you and Leo together, and maybe . . . maybe you're right, and things really can be kind of epic and magical sometimes."

I stare at her, while yesterday replays in my mind. Stepping in dog shit. Running down the stairs. Flinging myself onto that train, right next to Leo. And everything after—all the near misses, the detours, the mix-ups . . .

Everything I thought was happening because the Universe didn't care, or maybe actively hated me . . . Everything I thought was ruining the perfect moment I was waiting for . . .

"But it's too late anyway," I say. "I missed the moment. We're gonna leave New York."

"In, like, twenty-four hours," Kat says. "But look what you did with the last twenty-four." She turns the book around and holds it out to me, still open to the title page. "Maybe the Universe can only do so much, Abs, and then you have to do the rest."

I look down at the scribble in the book.

To Abby—the Universe is what you make it.

What I make it. Me. The me who steps in dog shit, who scrambles over railings to get into an ice rink, who obsessively reads my favorite book twenty-four-and-a-half times, who has no idea what queer label fits but falls in love anyway.

The me who, right now, can't figure out what's the Universe, what's just plain chance, and what's a choice I'm making, and honestly doesn't care, because maybe it's all kind of magical.

"So what do I do now?" I say.

Kat sighs. "I mean, go back and finish breakfast, I think. We still have this whole parade thing to do."

Oh. That. "Yeah, I guess that's kind of important." I look back at the collection of souvenirs on the counter. "Those are still for you, if you want them."

Kat carefully scoops them all into her palm. "Of course I want them, you weirdo. You're my best friend."

TWENTY-FOUR

LEO

SOMEWHERE DOWN THE street, a siren blares and a massive cheer goes up, echoing off the skyscrapers and floating back toward us. It's the biggest cheer I've ever heard—even bigger than the crowd when we competed at regionals last spring. It ripples up the street like a wave, as everyone catches on and the crowds lining the sidewalks start yelling, too.

The parade is starting.

Here we go.

My stomach churns, and I'm not sure if it's nerves or the coffee I drank or the fact that I slept for approximately three hours.

Or the fact that my phone has about five percent battery remaining.

I should have texted Abby while we were at breakfast. But I couldn't figure out what to say, and then my phone was at ten percent, and then eight . . . and now I'm too afraid to use it for anything. Because what if Abby texts me?

Or what if my parents do?

I thought Evan and Gina would be bugging me to text Abby, after how much they bugged me about her during our last run-through. But they seemed distracted during breakfast. Evan kept looking at his phone and exchanging glances with Gina, and at one point, when she announced she was going to the bathroom, he said he'd go with her, which was just weird.

Ugh. We're going to start moving any minute now. I need to find Evan. He's not that far ahead of me. Maybe I can dodge through everybody, really quickly, and borrow his phone. Because even though I don't know what I'm going to say, I have to text Abby. I have to tell her I didn't mean it, or I *did* mean it, or . . .

Lindsay Waggoner blows her whistle. *Set.* The huge Pikachu float ahead of us starts to move. Double blast. *Horns up.*

Shit. It's too late.

I shove Abby out of my mind. Shove my family out, too. I can't do anything about any of it right now. I'm stuck here for the rest of the parade.

So I might as well really *be here.* I've worked my ass off for this, and I've lost too much time to panicking and stressing and ruining dress rehearsals on football fields already.

Not today.

We start marching, all of us in the drumline tapping our sticks against the rims of our drums to set the tempo for the rest of the band. The people filling the sidewalks cheer again as we launch into a drum cadence to drive everyone forward. The chaperones walking on either side of us wave to them. Mr. Corbin looks a little less like death this morning. He's carrying a backpack stuffed with water bottles and first aid kits just like all the other chaperones. I guess the coffee he had earlier helped him out, too—his smile looks pretty genuine as he waves, and I swear he's got an actual bounce in his step.

As far as I know, he still has no idea he lost track of me for most of yesterday.

I don't know how much time passes before we get to that big green rectangle—the end of the parade, the final big show for the bleachers full of people and the cameras in front of Macy's. I'm in the zone, completely focused in a way that makes me feel like time has ceased to matter.

I have to hand it to Ms. Rinaldi. She planned perfectly. Because even though I have no idea how long it takes us to reach Macy's, we play through "Seventy-Six Trombones" (sans choreography) three times, in three different locations, and each of our additional pieces—the ones we've played for other parades or competitions— twice, which is exactly what she told us she was aiming for. Plus, the wind players all get breaks in between, while the drumline fills up the space, and even the drumline gets a few breaks, where we back off to stick taps to keep our marching tempo. All of us gathering energy for the next number.

Everything goes quiet as we get close to Herald Square. None of the bands are supposed to play here—we're too close to the cameras. I can hear cheering in the distance. It gets louder as we turn the cor- ner onto Thirty-Fourth Street and march out in front of the cameras. I've watched this parade on TV so many times, I can imagine the NBC announcers, even if I can't see or hear them right now.

"And here comes the Springfield High School Marching Band, all the way from Springfield, North Carolina . . ."

The energy of the crowd pounds in my chest, through my veins, and thunders into the drum in front of me.

". . . These seventy-five kids ranging in age from fourteen to eighteen will be performing the classic 'Seventy-Six Trombones' from The Music Man . . ."

I hit my spot on the green rectangle. My mark. Tap my sticks in time with the drumline around me as the whole band turns as one to face the cameras.

". . . Under the direction of Jennifer Rinaldi, this marching band has swept competitions in the southern states recently, which no one ever expected them to do, but they've been beating the pants off bigger bands with their impressive skills . . ."

Okay, they probably won't say that last part, but that doesn't mean it's not true. And I'm proud of that. I'm proud of how hard we've worked to get here, and I'm not going to let anything get in the way of that again.

The cameras are barely three feet from my face, because I'm on the edge of this rectangle, right in front. The spot I was terrified of two days ago.

But now I raise my chin as the whistle blasts again and the sunlight slides off the brass bells rising around me, and I stare ahead just like I'm supposed to, because I'm here for my band—one piece in the whole—and I'm done being afraid of who sees me.

The line of sousaphones moves first, followed by the trombones. Now the drumline parts as the trumpets slice us down the middle. My feet follow the path they know by heart. My hands lead with the rhythm I could perform in my sleep, but I'm as awake as I've ever been.

Strident brass vibrates the pavement. Every drum strike sends a thrum through my body. The momentum of everyone around me drives me through our formations, but I'm also the momentum driving everyone else. We're all a kinetic force together, and I feel it—that *thing* I so desperately wanted back.

It's not just freedom. It's more than that.

It's infinity.

Pure energy that will never run out. Joy without limits. That feeling of touching something I'll never quite know or understand, but I don't need to. It's enough to know that it's there.

Even in something like "Seventy-Six Trombones."

We reach the last phrase. Sandy Dixon ducks next to me, and I duck after him, and Gavin Holtz after me. A wave runs through our whole band, everyone ducking in turn and then lifting back up. And now one final spin—the glittering BELIEVE sign goes flashing by—and *freeze.*

A split second of silence as the final note echoes down the street.

The crowd roars.

I keep my mouth clamped shut, like we're supposed to, even though I can't drag air through my nose fast enough. The whistle blows. The section leader counts us off again, and the drumline drops in with our marching rhythm. As one, my band turns in place and marches off the green rectangle.

It's over.

Whatever's waiting for me when I get home—I did it. I got through this performance. We got through this performance.

It wasn't the end of the world at all. It was glorious.

11:15 A.M.

Ending a parade is always weird. We've marched in parades before. There's the really unimpressive Springfield Fourth of July Parade, which features our band, the mayor, and, like, twenty other people, but we've also marched in state parades. And reaching the end is always a little bit . . . anticlimactic. It's not like crossing a finish line in a race or something, where people cheer you on right to the end. Sometimes it's not even super obvious where the parade really ends.

That feeling just gets amped up to a thousand when it's the Macy's Thanksgiving Day Parade. On TV, the parade ends with Santa arriving on a giant sleigh float in front of Macy's. There's confetti and fake snow. It's pretty climactic.

But for us . . . Well, I'm not sure how far ahead of Santa we are, but we just get to the end, and there are the people in reflective coats again. We're waved off onto a side street. The chaperones come through with water. Ms. Rinaldi comes through clapping and smiling. People start pulling out their phones for pictures.

Phone. I shrug out of my snare harness, setting it carefully on the ground, and fumble my phone out of my pocket. The screen is blank. I press the button to wake it up, and nothing happens.

Fuck.

Evan shoulders through the crowd, which is easy when you're an Avenger with a sousaphone, with Gina and her trombone following in his wake. "Leo!" He holds up his hand for a high five. "Up top!"

I ignore his hand. "Evan, give me your phone."

"Why?"

"I need to text Abby, and mine is dead." I hold it up.

Evan lowers his hand, and he and Gina glance at each other.

"What were you going to text her?" Evan says.

"That I was a jerk? That I'm totally in love with her?" I let my breath out. A frustrated grunt. "I don't know. Why do you care? Give me your phone!"

"No," Evan says.

Is he joking? "What do you mean, *no*?"

"I'm using my phone."

"No, you're not! It's in your pocket! How are you using it?"

Gina sighs. "Evan, just show him."

"Show me what?" I say.

Evan fishes his phone out of his pocket, turns it around, and holds it right in front of my face. On the screen is a text message.

KAT

Abby loves Leo!!!

I stare at it. My brain spins. I open my mouth, but nothing comes out.

"Great," Gina says. "You broke him."

Evan looks perplexed. "*You* told me to do it."

I finally find my voice. "When did you get this?"

Evan swipes so I can see the timestamp on the message.

6:45 A.M.

This morning.

I can't seem to wrap my mind around this. "Abby was going to tell Kat she loves her. I mean, that's why we got all these souvenirs from these locations in the book. We had this whole plan. Abby had this whole plan. Does this . . . Did Kat reject her?"

Evan sighs. "Leo—"

"Are you sure Kat isn't confused? Maybe Abby's still waiting for the right moment—"

"*Leo.*"

"—like after the parade. Maybe Abby just told Kat about me and Kat got confused—"

"Leo!" Gina yells.

I stop. They're both looking at me like I am the densest person on the planet.

"Kat texted me that because all three of us were texting about you guys yesterday," Evan says. "I mean, come on, y'all disappeared on us. Obviously we were going to start a new group chat and try to figure out what the hell you were up to."

Gina shifts her trombone to one hand and pulls out her own phone, shoving it under my nose and scrolling slowly past text after text after text.

KAT

Do you guys think Leo and Abby are into each other??

EVAN

Should we ask them?

GINA

No we should play it cool

The messages turn to a blur as Gina scrolls faster, until she stops on one from Evan, at five thirty-eight this morning.

EVAN

Red alert, Kat. Lemme know what you find out.

I blink at it. "Red alert?"

Evan grins like he's proud of himself. "Yeah, red alert. Get it? Red like *love,* like red hearts, and—"

"It's a dad joke, Evan," Gina says, with tired patience. "I told you."

Evan shoots her an injured look. "The point is, by the time the show was over yesterday, we thought you guys might like each other, but we weren't sure, so we all agreed we'd try to figure out what was going on once y'all got back. But then, obviously, it took you forever to get back. And then at the run-through, you said you were in love with Abby, so I texted Kat to let her know." He glances at Gina. "We thought we should find out if it was mutual."

"But Abby loves *Kat.*" I can't seem to let this go. It was the whole point of yesterday. "Abby's going to do a big, epic love scene or something, like in a movie . . ."

Gina rubs her eyes. "Yeah, you've said that, like, a hundred times."

"I'm just saying that it doesn't make any sense."

"Who cares!" Evan waves his arms. "Life doesn't make sense! Go with it!"

My head starts to hurt again. "Well . . . now what do I do?"

"Seriously?" Gina says. "You're asking us?"

"Who else would I ask?"

"Maybe yourself?" Evan looks almost annoyed. "Look, I love you, man, but sometimes you aren't the sharpest snare in the drumline."

Gina grimaces. "Evan, what does that even mean?"

"I know you've had a *time,*" Evan says, ignoring her. "So I get why you're like this."

I glower at him. "Okay, first of all, fuck you—"

"Leo." Evan glowers back at me. "My man. My dear, obtuse friend.

I know you've gotten used to people being assholes and thinking you're weird and don't need to be treated with respect—"

"Are you trying to make me feel *worse*?"

"—but sometimes it's like you're so prepared to get fucked over that you just do it yourself, before anybody else can. Honestly, I was kind of glad when you had that huge fight with your parents on Monday, because you'd been waiting to explode for ages."

Gina nods seriously.

"Well, I *told* you," I say. "My mom called, and that's getting patched up, so—"

"Yeah, that's fantastic, but I'm saying sometimes you need to go for it. *You.* Stop waiting for someone else to come to their senses first. Seriously, if you keep waiting for the world to say, *Okay, cool, you get to be happy now* . . . I mean, you're never gonna be happy. The world is *shit*. There's racism and climate change and homophobia and pandemics and—"

"Evan." Gina pats his arm. "Reel it in, man."

Evan takes a deep breath. "Just . . . maybe once in a while, make your own joy, Leo. Do the thing you want to do, and fuck what anybody else thinks."

I have never heard Evan talk like this. This intensely. Except maybe a few months back, when he got into an argument with Samantha Weller about which marching band arrangements have the best sousaphone parts.

"Um." I force my brain to work. "What would I even say to Abby?"

"How about the truth?" Gina says.

"That I didn't really expect anybody to ever fall in love with me because I'm trans?"

She rolls her eyes. "No."

Right. *Enough, Leo.* "That I love her, even though it's fucking terrifying to admit, because we've known each other for, like, twelve hours?"

Evan looks thoughtful. "I mean, twelve hours together is basically like twelve separate dates, which would normally be stretched over . . . what, like, three months? So it's fine."

Gina glances at him suspiciously. "You make a scarily good argument for someone who basically dates a tuba."

I let my breath out. Slow and shaky. "Okay. Fine. I'm ready. Give me your phone, Ev."

Evan holds it up out of my reach. "Heck no."

"What?" I swipe a hand through the air, but he's way too tall and the sousaphone is in the way. "What's wrong with you? You *just* said—"

"Kat said their band is behind us," he says stonily. "So if you go that way"—he points back the way we came—"you'll probably run into her eventually."

"You have got to be kidding."

He just grins innocently. "Big, epic scene, Leo. You better hurry up, because this time I don't think we'll be able to cover for you for very long."

I can't decide if I want to hug him or punch him. And I don't have time to decide. Any minute now, the buses will show up somewhere in this chaos of balloons and floats and people, and we'll load our stuff onto them and head off to lunch.

And the chaperones will absolutely be taking attendance once we're on the buses. So, if I'm going to do anything, I better hurry.

I pull off my shako and thrust it at Evan. "Watch my stuff," I say.

And then I turn, and I start to run.

TWENTY-FIVE

ABBY

FOR SOMETHING WE spent so long preparing for, the moment in front of Macy's goes by so fast.

Our formations are perfect. Our rhythm is tight. The crowd is cheering and it's everything I dreamed it would be . . .

And then it's over. More than a year of practice, fundraising, planning . . . and now it's over. We're turning away from the cameras and marching off the big green rectangle. I'm breathless and my adrenaline is crashing, and I'm realizing—*oh, god*—I still have to get up for band practice on Monday morning . . .

I mean, of course I do. It's not like everything just stops after this show.

But also, weirdly, I almost expected it to. This was it. This day was going to be *everything*. This trip was going to be everything. My magical moment in New York, with Kat, and now . . .

Now what?

I should have texted Leo the second I left the bathroom at breakfast this morning. Or as we were getting all our gear off the bus and heading to our spot in the parade route. Or while we were waiting behind our school banner and ahead of a huge Lego float.

But I didn't. I couldn't figure out what to text. *Sorry I screamed at you, I actually love you, too bad we're leaving New York*?

It all felt too big for a text message like that.

But now the parade is over, and we're falling out of formation, milling around in the street. The chaperones are distracted by a rene-gade group, led by Jared Nguyen, that's trying to sneak away to watch the rest of the parade from a vantage point on the sidewalk.

I pull out my phone. I'll text Leo now. That's better than nothing. He has to be around here somewhere, and maybe there's a chance I could find him.

And I have to find him.

ME

Hey, we just finished. Are you still here?

"Abby!" Kat careens into me, wrapping an arm tightly around me, her flute clenched in her other hand. "We did it! We did it!"

I hug her back, but her excitement feels distant. I can't seem to match it, no matter how hard I try.

She pulls away. "What's the matter?"

"I texted Leo. But he's not writing back."

Kat looks at my phone. "Give him a minute."

"Yeah." I know she's right. Maybe he's farther back in the parade, and he's still marching. Maybe he's distracted by loading up their bus. Or maybe he's on the phone with his family.

I hope everything turned out okay with his family.

I wait. One minute. Two minutes. Five minutes.

"Anything?" Kat asks.

I shake my head. Try to shrug. "It's fine."

It's not.

Kat watches me, chewing her lip. And then she digs in the pocket of her bibbers and pulls out her phone. "Abs, I should have asked first, and I'm sorry I didn't, but . . ." She's scrolling through her messages, too quickly for me to read them. "I was texting with Evan and this other girl Gina yesterday, because we were wondering what was up with you guys . . ."

What?

"Anyway, Evan texted me at, like, five thirty this morning, because . . . um . . ." She stops scrolling on her phone and holds it against her chest instead, looking at me nervously. "He said Leo likes you."

I stare at her. My brain freezes. All that comes out of my mouth is "You texted Evan?"

Kat winces. "I know, I should have asked you first . . ."

But I called Leo an asshole. I ruined everything.

"Abby?" Kat says.

I fumble with the chin strap of my shako and hold out my clarinet. "Can you . . . can you take this stuff?"

Kat catches my shako and somehow manages to hold my clarinet in the same hand as her flute. "Abby, what are you doing?"

"Leo's not answering his phone."

"Yeah . . ."

"I need to . . . I really need to find him."

Kat looks at me, and for a second, I think she might argue. But she doesn't. She lets her breath out and says, "Evan thinks they're farther ahead of us; it sounds like they finished earlier than we did." She jerks her head. "Go. You got cover from Jared anyway."

Which is true. The Jared-led rebellion seems to be growing, and the chaperones are clearly out of their depth, trying to round everybody back up.

"Thanks," I say to Kat.

She grins. "Tell him I said hi."

I turn, bouncing off Morgan, who's holding up her phone to film the rebellion, and slip through the barrier to the sidewalk. Nobody pays me any attention. I pull up Leo's number on my phone. Maybe if I try calling him . . .

But my call goes straight to voicemail.

If Leo's band was ahead of us, then I need to head for the front of the parade. Or what *was* the front, before everything dissolved into chaos.

God, maybe Leo's not even here anymore. Maybe his band is already on the bus, or already back at the hotel.

Or already leaving New York.

I start to run, dodging around people bundled up in coats and hats, people dressed up like elves, a group of dancers dressed up like candy canes, even a bunch of clowns wearing very large shoes and red noses.

"Excuse me! Sorry!" My heart pounds straight into my head. The cold air aches in my ears. I braided my hair to keep it out of my way for the parade, but it's coming loose now, curls blowing into my face.

The crowd just keeps going. More people in costumes. More people wrangling the ropes attached to the enormous, unwieldy balloons flying overhead, so massive they send building-sized shadows across the street. More people in vests with walkie-talkies. More people clambering down from floats shaped like gingerbread houses.

This is a mess. I'm never going to find Leo. There must be thousands of people here. And I don't have time to go much farther, or I'll never have time to get back. Not before someone notices.

"Abby!"

It takes a second for me to see him. Not just because of the crowd, but because I almost don't recognize him in his black-and-gold band uniform. The only giveaway is his hair—his messy dark hair that's still, *still,* sticking straight up on one side.

Leo is running straight toward me.

I'm suddenly weightless. I wave. I jump up and down while running at the same time, because I want to make sure he sees me, and knows I saw him, and *why am I so short.*

I catch glimpses of him as I weave through the crowd. People are taking pictures all around me—I must be ruining so many pictures. But I don't care. I'm smiling so hard it feels like my face will crack. I have to blink to keep my eyes clear and I don't know if it's the cold or because my heart is trying to burst out of my chest.

I dodge around a bunch of kids dressed up as dinosaurs (what float were they on?) and suddenly Leo is right there. We both skid to a stop, barely avoiding slamming into each other.

And I say, breathlessly, "I love you."

He smiles. A real smile. Bigger than any smile he's given me before. "I love you, too."

I reach up, grab the lapels of his band uniform, tug him down, and kiss him.

He kisses me back, his arms wrapping around me, and I feel like I could stay in this moment forever. Who cares what anybody around us thinks? Right now, we're back in our own liminal space—between *before* and *what happens next.*

There will be a Next. And kissing him, I suddenly feel ready for it. For going home, for coming out to my parents, for going back to school as a queer girl, whatever that might mean.

I don't know who pulls away first. Maybe we both do, at the same time, leaving the liminal space behind. Moving, together, into what happens next.

"I'm so sorry I yelled at you," I say.

"I'm sorry I threw a book at you," he says.

"I really like the book, though." My voice trembles. "Thanks for getting it for me. I met the author!"

"What author?"

"The author who wrote *Clara Jane*!"

He blinks. "Seriously?"

"Yeah! It was . . ." Wait. No. This isn't what I want to use my time for. "I'll tell you about it later. I have to go in a minute—"

"Me, too—"

"I want there to be a later," I say. "If you do. I mean—"

His face is full of relief. "I really do," he says.

"There's this summer band camp in Ohio. Next summer. It's near Cincinnati—"

"Ohio Summer Marching Institute." He grins. "Yeah. Evan and Gina have been talking about it for months—"

"I'm going to go. Next summer. I think I have a pretty good shot at getting in—"

"Maybe we can all go. You, me, Evan, Gina, Kat—"

"Well, that camp is four weeks." My heart rises in my chest, hopeful. "And after that—"

"Evan wants to visit the University of Iowa," Leo says. His words tumble over each other; I've never heard him talk so fast. "He's thinking about applying. I could visit, too, and we could drive to Missouri on our way or something—it's not far, right?"

Depends on how you define *far,* but I don't want to think about that now. "I want to visit colleges on the East Coast, too. Not just New York."

"North Carolina's kind of on the East Coast," Leo says. And he sounds hopeful, too.

Wait. North Carolina . . . "What happened with your family? Are you okay?"

He squeezes my hands and smiles. "Yeah. My parents are going to tell everyone."

My heart leaps so high I feel light-headed. "What? When?"

"I don't know." He actually laughs, shaking his head. "This morning? I guess? My phone's totally dead, so I don't know what happened."

"Do you want to use my phone?" But I don't want to let go of his hands. "You could text them or call them or—"

"No, it's fine." He lets his breath out slowly. "I'm actually really fine."

My throat tightens. "I mean, that's amazing—"

"I'll talk to my parents later, and then I'll tell you everything." He leans down and rests his forehead against mine. "I promise."

"Right. Yeah, we can FaceTime." His face swims in front of my eyes. I don't want to say it. I want my own time loop, so I can live today over and over again. "I have to go."

He pulls away, just a little. "Me, too."

I blink to clear my eyes, because I don't want this memory to be a blur. I want to see him perfectly—the freckles across his nose, the beautiful flecks of green in his eyes, the gap between his front teeth—before I have to settle for the grainier version on a phone screen. "I love you, Leo."

He smiles. Not so big this time. A small one, just for me. "I love you, Abby."

He kisses me, and I kiss him, closing my eyes to burn every detail of this moment into my mind, so I can keep it, to come back to, to visit, whenever I need to.

The kiss ends, and I open my eyes. There's so much more I want to tell Leo, so much more I want to ask him, but it'll all have to wait.

For right now, I'm out of time.

I squeeze Leo's hands. He squeezes mine back. And then we both let go.

And I turn and run.

LEO

I watch Abby disappear into the crowd on the sidewalk, which doesn't take long, since she's so short. For a while, I can see her, bobbing in between people. Her purple-and-white uniform. Her loose braid bouncing down her back.

And then she's gone.

So I turn around, and I start to run, too.

I'm gasping for breath by the time I reach Evan and Gina, who luckily haven't moved at all since I left them. Our whole band is still milling around. One of the chaperones walks past, muttering something into his phone about *buses held up in this damn traffic.*

"Well?" Gina says. "What happened?"

I bend over, hands braced against my knees, trying to get my breath back.

"Leo!" Evan shouts.

I straighten up, clutching at a stitch in my side. "I found her."

"And?"

"And it was epic. A big scene. Stop being nosy."

Gina whoops and Evan grabs me in a giant bear hug, which is incredibly uncomfortable, because he's still wearing his sousaphone. "Leon Brewer!" he bellows. "I am so happy for you!"

"Put me down!" I wriggle out of his grasp and rub my face. Pretty sure my cheek has an imprint of tuba tubes on it.

"Come on." Gina whacks my arm and jerks her chin. "We're moving."

The buses must have made it through the traffic, because the chaperones are rounding everybody up, and Ms. Rinaldi is tweeting on her whistle to get our attention. I pick up my shako and my snare harness as the band amoeba drifts down the street. At the end of the block, I can make out the hulking shape of a big black bus.

But I hang back, just for a moment, and look up at the skyscrapers. At the strip of blue sky between them. I breathe in the cold air and listen to the hum of the city around me.

It's what Abby would do.

I wonder if I'll run into her, at the hotel. I guess it's possible.

But then again, we're pretty tightly scheduled for the rest of the day. Lunch. Loading up. Taking naps. And then one last dinner out in Times Square—and honestly, I owe Evan and Gina some time, too.

Maybe there will be a moment, somewhere, for all of us to meet. Me, and Abby, and Evan, and Gina, and Kat. And if there isn't . . .

Well, there's texting. And FaceTime. Tomorrow, on the bus ride home, for as long as my crap phone can handle it. The day after, in Springfield. The week after. The month after.

I shoulder my snare harness, and I follow Evan and Gina.

There's time to figure out what comes next.

And that's enough.

ACKNOWLEDGMENTS

You'd think that after writing one book, the second would be easier.

That is a lie. Second books—or second *published* books, because this is most definitely not my second book—are hard.

To Patricia Nelson, who spent literal hours on the phone with me, brainstorming and talking through plot holes and sticking points: *Thank you*. You continue to be the best agent ever.

To Sylvan Creekmore, who acquired this book off a three-sentence pitch: Thank you for believing it would eventually be more than three sentences, and then, when it was, setting it off on the right path.

To Sarah Grill, who took on two-thirds of the editing journey and five-thirds of my anxiety about it: Thank you for every time you said, in the kindest way possible, "It's not quite there yet." You are an incredible editor.

Thank you to the production team of Eric Meyer, Melanie Sanders, Nicola Ferguson, and Lena Shekhter for wrangling my words into such a beautiful book. Thank you to Kerri Resnick for designing an epic fairy tale of a cover, and to Myriam Strasbourg for bringing it to life with warmth and magic. Thank you to my wonderful publicist, Meghan Harrington, and my amazing marketing team of Rivka Holler and Brant Janeway, plus everyone on the sales and library teams for spreading the word and helping to get this book into the hands of readers. I'm grateful for the support of the whole Wednesday Books team.

I was never cool enough to be in marching band, so a big thank-you to Erik Rose and Robyn Gerry-Rose for answering countless questions while I was drafting and then reading an early version to catch things like snare harness snafus. I'm also hugely grateful to the Greendale High School Marching Band for filming their experience traveling to Macy's so a fellow (former) Wisconsinite could learn from it, and to band director Tom Reifenberg for generously answering my questions. I have taken a few liberties for the sake of storytelling (most high school bands spend several days sightseeing in NYC and also practice while they're there; I've compressed the timeline), but I've done my best to be as accurate to the real experience as I can. (Yes, there really is a run-through for the cameras at 3 A.M. the night before the parade.)

Accuracy was also my (general) goal in the portrayal of New York City, and I need to give a special shout-out to my copy editor, Sam Dauer, for so much tireless fact-checking. Any remaining inaccuracies are either my own mistakes, or slight liberties taken in the name of romance vibes.

Thank you so much to every author who so kindly offered advance praise for this book. Thank you to the members of my writing community who have listened, advised, commiserated, and celebrated with me: Dahlia Adler, Jennie Bates, Deanna Day, Claire Forrest, Jen Ferguson, Caroline Huntoon, and Nicole Maggi.

To Laura: Thanks for believing in me and supporting me through another one.

And finally, the most heartfelt thank-you to all my readers: those who read *Always the Almost* and followed me here, and those who found this book first. I appreciate you all so much.